The One That Got Away

CLINT HOFER

PAGE PUBLISHING, INC.
New York, NY

First originally published by Page Publishing, Inc. 2019

ISBN 978-1-64424-888-1 (Paperback)
ISBN 978-1-64424-889-8 (Digital)

Printed in the United States of America

This book is for Gilda Tayuba.

Chapter One

It was Saturday, June 5th. The Great Flood of 1993 was less than a month away. The people of South St. Louis were oblivious to the approaching danger.

Dinty Smith was busy tending bar at his tavern on Lavender Street. His place was called the Stag Club and was located in the Lavender Hill neighborhood of South St. Louis. The neighborhood took its name from Lavender Hill, an enormous limestone bluff that rose three hundred feet above the Mississippi River.

A mauve mansion stood at the very top of the bluff. Constructed of purple Long Mead sandstone from Colorado, the Federal-style mansion belonged to Mrs. William Grosse, the infamous Lavender Lady.

The Stag Club was directly across Lavender Street from the Grosse Mansion. Dinty Smith and the Lavender Lady were good friends. The building that housed the Stag Club had been built in 1895 by the Grosse Brewing Company. Once the largest brewery in St. Louis and ranked among the top ten in the nation, Grosse didn't survive Prohibition. The huge brewing plant, which resembled a walled medieval city, was right next door to the Grosse Mansion. Beer hadn't been brewed there in nearly seventy-five years. A local developer owned the property and planned to turn the old brewing compound into a carnival complex of shops, restaurants, and theaters. Those plans had been put on hold, however. The neighborhood was depressed and could not sustain any further economic growth.

A shoe company had once used the old brewery as a warehouse, but they had moved out over five years ago. The buildings had been vacant ever since. Padlocked. Abandoned. Overgrown with weeds. Rats were the only inhabitants.

Less than a mile up the river, white smoke rose in clouds above the Anheuser-Busch Brewery that left the Grosse family and so many other competitors in similar straits of abandonment. The Anheuser-Busch facility in St. Louis was the world's largest brewery. Atop one of the buildings, the word BUDWEISER was spelled out in blazing red neon letters a story tall.

Although faded, the word BURGERMEISTER could still be seen on the smokestack of the old Grosse Brewery. Burgermeister had been Grosse's premium beer. It was the largest-selling beer in the country from 1895 to 1900.

Dinty Smith had lived in the Lavender Hill neighborhood his entire life. His father had worked for Grosse Brewing as a bottler. When the brewery folded in 1920 because of Prohibition, Dinty's father became an independent trucker. That was the same line of work that Dinty followed until his retirement in 1979. He then opened the Stag Club, fulfilling his lifelong dream to own a tavern. Dinty chose the name Stag Club because the establishment had originally been called the Leaping Stag Inn. Grosse Brewing had owned numerous taverns in the St. Louis area in order to increase beer sales. The Leaping Stag Inn had been their finest saloon, patterned after an authentic English pub. During Prohibition, the Leaping Stag Inn became a bakery shop. Dinty used to go there as a boy to buy bread for his mother. He would hear stories from the baker about the building's past grandeur. The Leaping Stag Inn had been a rendezvous spot for prominent businessmen, actors, boxers, and assorted sporting men and those who wanted to catch a glimpse of such celebrities.

Dinty realized he could never restore the Leaping Stag Inn to its former glory, but he wanted to try. He purchased the building in 1979 from Gus Zimmerman, whose father had established the Zimmerman Bakery during Prohibition. Gus had to retire because of ill health and had no male heir to continue the family business.

Dinty, who had been living in a nearby apartment, moved all his belongings to the second floor of his new tavern. He had never married and didn't need a large residence.

People were usually surprised and often disappointed when they entered the Stag Club for the first time. The name Stag Club was misleading. People expected to find a strip joint or a place that showed pornographic films. The fact that the Stag Club was in a run-down neighborhood helped reinforce the idea that it was a porno parlor. In point of fact, no girl had ever jumped out of a cake at the Stag Club. The patrons didn't sit around gaping at porno flicks. The Stag Club was simply a friendly corner tavern where neighborhood people came to relax and unwind after a hard day's work.

The clientele consisted mainly of blue-collar types who had moved to St. Louis from rural areas in order to find work. Most of Dinty's customers held minimum wage jobs and came to his place because of the low prices. Since Dinty provided the entertainment himself, he could afford to charge less for drinks and food. The kind of people that came to the Stag Club liked to listen and dance to country music. The Stag Club was one of the few country-western piano bars in the St. Louis area. Dinty performed nightly at the piano, singing country songs for his appreciative audience. As a boy, Dinty had studied piano and sung in the church choir. That was the extent of his musical training. However, he had practiced singing for years behind the wheel of his truck. Traveling down the highway, he would turn his radio to a country station and sing along. He knew how to put over a song. Dinty modeled himself after Floyd Cramer and Jerry Lee Lewis.

It was almost 3:00 p.m. on this rainy Saturday, June 5, 1993. Dinty had been watching Cardinal baseball on the TV behind the bar. During a periodic news update, he learned Conway Twitty had died earlier that day in Springfield, Missouri. Conway had collapsed on his tour bus after performing in Branson, Missouri. He had been rushed to Cox South Hospital in Springfield, where he died.

A faint frown line pulled Dinty's arching brows together. This was a sad day. Conway was his favorite country singer.

Dinty didn't notice the exquisite woman who had just entered the Stag Club, until he heard whistles from some of the male patrons. He glanced up and gave her a long, admiring look. Women this classy didn't come in the Stag Club very often. Dinty watched her approach the bar, her slender but shapely figure stylishly dressed in blue jeans and a bright yellow blouse. Even from a distance, the perfection of her profile was evident, as was the lustrous quality of her long raven-black hair. When she reached the bar, Dinty stared openly at her attractive features—the delicate uptilted nose, the bow-shaped mouth, and the lovely olive-green eyes.

"How you doing?" he asked in a husky voice, trying to seem younger and more vigorous than he really was. He had put on a Cardinal baseball cap to hide his gray hair.

"I feel shitty," she said, putting her purse on the bar. "Oh so shitty."

"What can I get for you?"

"I'll have Daniel's on the rocks."

"You mean Jack Daniel's?"

"I don't want anything with a man's name on it."

Dinty knew how to handle this difficult woman. He sensed there was warmth behind that cool facade.

"What's a nice girl like you doing in a place like this?" he asked in a lighthearted manner.

"I'm not that nice," she snapped. "I'm pregnant, and my boyfriend just dumped me."

"I'm sorry to hear that," Dinty said. "Care to talk about it?"

"I went to the doctor this morning and learned I was pregnant. When I told my boyfriend the good news, he left skid marks getting away from me. I've been in a daze ever since."

"With all the taverns in this city, how did you happen to walk into my place?"

"I'm Terri Zimmerman. I used to live on the second floor of this building with my parents. My dad ran the Zimmerman Bakery. This is where I spent the happiest years of my life. I thought it would cheer me up to come back here."

"Jeez," Dinty said. "So you're Gus Zimmerman's daughter. I bought this building from him back in 1979. I heard he died."

"He died in 1980 of diabetes. He was just fifty-nine years old. I was his only child."

"It's nice to see you, Terri. By the way, my name is Dinty. You know, like on the can of beef stew."

"You're name is Dinty Moore?"

"No. Dinty Smith."

"Glad to know you, Dinty. I was away at college when my dad sold this place. I don't think I ever met you."

"I remember meeting your mother. She was a very beautiful woman."

"Yes, she was. It was rough sledding for Mom and me after Dad died. We didn't have any money. I dropped out of college and took a job as a waitress. Mom wanted to remarry but couldn't find anyone who was interested. She was always carrying a torch for some guy or other. And now the torch has been passed to the next generation. I'm extremely unlucky when it comes to men. Do you think it could be my breath?"

"A man would have to be crazy not to want you," Dinty said.

"Thank you," Terri replied. "I think men feel threatened by beautiful women. Men would rather have an eight than a ten. Tenish women are perceived as being extravagant and hard to please. Men want no part of such high-maintenance women. Personally, I've always been content to live within my means. If a man truly loved me, I wouldn't care how much money he had."

"I'll mix you one of my famous margaritas," Dinty said, trying to calm this distraught woman who was pouring out her soul. "It'll clear your head and make you feel like a million bucks."

"Make it extra strength," Terri said. "I need a stiff drink. I don't know what I'm going to do. My baby is due in eight months, and I'd like to be married by then. The only problem is I don't know any available men."

"How about me?" Dinty asked, as he poured a jigger of tequila into a cocktail glass. "I'm an eligible bachelor."

"Unfortunately, you're also eligible for Medicare."

"If only I were fifty years younger."

Dinty added two jiggers of Cointreau and a jigger of lemon juice to the glass. He stirred the contents and then put in some chipped ice. After salting the rim of the glass, he served the margarita to Terri.

She pulled her wallet from her purse and paid Dinty.

"Why don't you get an abortion?" he asked, after Terri had taken a sip of her drink.

The crystal tumbler nearly fell out of Terri's hand. She began choking on the salt she had swallowed. With some effort, she raised the tumbler to her lips and took a long gulp of margarita.

"An abortion is out of the question." She coughed, after washing most of the salt down her throat. "I'm Catholic. And besides, I'm over thirty. My biological clock is running down. This is my last chance to have a baby."

"You'll have to excuse me for a second," Dinty said. "It's almost time for my favorite show. I have to switch stations." Dinty needed respite from this dolorous woman. During his years as a bartender, he had listened to many mournful tales of romantic rejection. However, he had never met anyone quite like this young woman.

As Dinty walked up to the television, a burly man at the bar started yelling in an angry voice. "Hey, old-timer," the man cried to Dinty. "Get away from that TV." The man was built like a football player with broad shoulders and a barrel chest. His big face was beefy, with the flesh beginning to puff under small, piglike eyes.

"Yeah," the man's skinnier partner said. "Touch that dial and die."

Dinty had never seen these two men before. They had probably come in the Stag Club thinking it was a strip joint or porno parlor. They were engrossed in the Cardinal baseball game. The Cardinals had runners at second and third with Todd Zeile at the plate.

"Why do you want to watch these bums?" Dinty asked rhetorically. "The Cardinals are a bunch of cellar dwellers. Give me the Cardinals of yesteryear. Hornsby, Dean, Musial. Those were ballplayers. Today's players just can't cut it. And when you stop to think of the money these bozos are making." Dinty pointed to the Cardinal cap on his head. "Take a good look at this St. Louis insignia," he said. "I'll swear it looks just like a dollar sign."

The two men paid no attention. Dinty paused for a second and then said, "Drinks are on the house if you let me switch to Channel 2."

"Great idea," the beefy man said. "I'm tired of watching the Cardinals lose all the time."

"Right," the thinner man said. "Who wants to see them blow another one? They haven't won a game since Memorial Day."

Dinty was able to change channels just in time. There on the screen was Barbara Grogan, hostess of a weekly television program about the sport of fishing. It was called *The Happy Hooker Show.* Ms. Grogan was a plain-looking woman with short-cropped blond hair. She was wearing blue jeans and a baggy sweater that concealed her extremely flat chest. Fishing pole in hand, she was sitting in a Ranger bass boat. Suddenly, she had a bite and began reeling in a large fish. The announcer's drawling voice could be heard over the loud theme music. "It's *The Happy Hooker Show* starring Barbara Grogan," the hayseed announcer said with an Ozark Mountain accent. "Today's special guest is country music legend Conway Twitty. This show originally aired on July 9, 1988. We are showing it again because Conway Twitty died this morning at the age of fifty-nine. He will be greatly missed by everyone. And now here's America's favorite sporting woman. The old Happy Hooker herself, Barbara Grogan."

"This is funnier than shit," Terri said to Dinty. "I take it you're an avid fisherman?"

"I love fishing," Dinty said. "It's my favorite sport." He motioned for Terri to keep quiet.

Conway and Barbara were cruising across Lake Taneycomo in a bass boat. Conway Twitty records were playing in the background. *Southern Comfort. Slow Hand. I'd Just Love to Lay You Down.*

"We're here at Lake Taneycomo near Branson, Missouri," Barbara said. "My special guest is Conway Twitty, who is currently appearing at the Jim Stafford Theater in Branson. Welcome to the show, Conway."

"Hello, darlin'…Nice to see you…It's been a long time." Conway was repeating the lyrics of one of his most famous songs.

"Will you knock it off," Barbara said. "We've never even met before."

"You're just as lovely as you used to be."

"Well, you got that part right," Barbara quipped.

Terri waited until the program had been on a few minutes before she resumed talking.

"Conway Twitty died at the age of fifty-nine, just like my father," she said. "That's too young."

"There will never be another country singer like Conway Twitty," Dinty said. "I saw him perform in Branson last year. He was great."

"What do you know about Barbara Grogan?" Terri asked.

"She grew up on a ranch in California. She talks about her girlhood all the time. The ranch was located in the Santa Cruz Mountains just south of San Francisco. She did a fishing show in California for a while. Then she was given the opportunity to do her show for a national audience. The show was originally called *Fishing with Barbara Grogan*. The name was changed in order to improve ratings. *The Happy Hooker Show* is produced here in St. Louis and is seen throughout America. Barbara lives in Little Egypt, about a hundred miles southeast of St. Louis. She comes here regularly on business."

"Little Egypt? What's that?"

"Southern Illinois has always been known as Little Egypt," Dinty replied.

"For a second there I thought you were talking about that famous belly dancer."

"Barbara has a large house on the Lake of Egypt near Marion in Southern Illinois. That's beautiful country down there. Lots of lakes and forests. I go fishing there quite often. It's not crowded or commercialized like the Ozarks."

Dinty's gaze returned to the television, where Barbara and Conway were singing a duet. "Please release me, let me go," they sang, as Barbara threw back a trophy bass. She always released every fish she caught in order to placate environmental groups who didn't like to see wildlife killed on television.

Conway had also caught a lunker bass. As he returned it to the water, he and Barbara sang the Fabian hit *Turn Me Loose*.

Conway was wearing a Tennessee Vols cap, which looked tiny on top of his enormous hairpiece. He had grown up on the banks of the Mississippi River and had done a lot of fishing when he was a boy. Friars Point, Mississippi, was his hometown. His father was the captain of a river barge.

"Do you have any fishing tips for my viewers?" Barbara asked Conway.

"When it comes to casting," he replied, "you need a slow hand."

"Thanks for that bit of wisdom," Barbara said. "And now I have a word for all you little fisher kids out there. All you little fisher boys and all you little fisher girls. Get hooked on fishing, not drugs. When I was a little girl, I used to go fishing all the time. I'd spend all day sitting on this hard wooden fishing pier. Talk about pier pressure. By the end of the day, my butt was as sore as hell. My poor butt was calloused and full of splinters. Now that's real pier pressure. And believe me, that's the only kind of pier pressure any of you little guys should ever know about. Get hooked on fishing, not drugs. That's my message for you today."

A cartoon drawing had appeared on the screen as Barbara was talking. A little girl, supposedly Barbara as a child, was sitting on a hard wooden fishing pier. There was a fishing pole in her right hand. Her left hand was rubbing an extremely sore butt. She was grimacing in pain. The artist had drawn X marks around her butt to indicate physical discomfort.

"Remember," Barbara said, "ignore pier pressure. Get hooked on fishing, not drugs."

Terri had never seen *The Happy Hooker Show* before, and she reacted with uncontrollable laughter. The show brought back memories of her girlhood, when she would go fishing with her parents at Montauk State Park near Salem, Missouri.

"You know what my greatest dream in life is?" Dinty said. "I'd like to meet Barbara Grogan. I'd like for her to come walking in here some Saturday afternoon at three o'clock, just in time for *The Happy Hooker Show*. We'd watch her show together and exchange fishing stories. I'd mix her one of my famous margaritas and cook her up one of my nationally known brain sandwiches. I could teach her a lot about fishing, and there's probably a few things she could teach me."

"Why don't you go to the television station if you want to meet her?" Terri asked.

"I tried that once," Dinty acknowledged. "Her show is produced at KTVI, Channel 2. The guard wouldn't let me see her. I waited in the parking lot for a while, but she never came out. I stood by the trailer she travels in when she films her show. The words *Happy Hooker* are on the side of the trailer in big letters. Needless to say, she always creates a great deal of excitement when she travels across the highways of America."

"Does the Happy Hooker have any men in her life?" Terri prodded gently.

"She's not married," Dinty responded. "And she never talks about any boyfriends. I don't think there's anyone. She's certainly not the most attractive woman on earth."

"I guess men aren't interested in marrying a hooker." Terri laughed.

Dinty leaned closer to the television set, his lips parted in concentration. A commercial for Drusky Outboard Motors had just come on. "I'm here at my favorite fishing hole," Barbara said, holding up a string of fish as she leaned forward in her boat. She then demonstrated how a Drusky Outboard worked. She explained one by one the benefits of owning a Drusky. Wearing a two-piece navy-blue swimsuit, she flashed the camera a sassy cover girl look. "A Drusky Outboard is the most versatile motor you can buy," she said, maneuvering her boat across a body of murky water that turned out to be the inside of a toilet bowl. The ad people had used special effects to make Barbara appear tiny.

Remembering the Ty-D-Bol commercials of a few years back, Terri erupted into such paroxysms of laughter that she knocked her drink over. Luckily, the glass was almost empty.

"How can you watch this fishing shit?" the beefy man yelled.

"I like it," Dinty retorted.

Another commercial came on in which Barbara wore the same two-piece navy-blue swimsuit. This time she was sitting inside a tent that had been filled with ten thousand hungry mosquitoes and biting flies. Although she had sprayed herself thoroughly with Amazon-brand bug repellent, she was still being eaten alive. With great difficulty, she pretended the product was protecting her. "They're not biting me," she said with a grimace, raising a can of Amazon for everyone to see.

"She's not fooling anyone," Terri chided. "Those bugs are making a buffet out of Barbara."

"Speaking of food," Dinty said. "How would you like one of my famous brain sandwiches?"

"Where do you get your brains?"

"My assistant Igor goes out and finds them."

"Okay. I'll try one. I've heard that brain sandwiches are a South St. Louis tradition."

"You're right," Dinty confirmed. "*Good Morning America* once did a story on my brain sandwiches."

In a corner of the Stag Club was a small grill upon which a few brain burgers were sputtering. Dinty's barmaid, a chubby Australian girl named Sydney, was watching after them.

"I ought to franchise my operation," Dinty said. "I can see it now. McBrain. Brainees. Taco Brain."

Sydney Melbourne, that was her stage name, had come to the United States from Australia in order to pursue a singing career. She had fallen on hard times and had been forced to take a job at the Stag Club. At Dinty's signal, she scooped a brain onto a bun. The IQ Burger, Dinty's name for it, looked strangely like an actual human cerebellum. Dipped in batter, it had the lumpy, convoluted, walnut-like shape of the cerebral cortex.

"I've got the best goddamned waitress in St. Louis working for me," Dinty said, as Sydney approached with the IQ Burger. She gracefully pivoted as she set the plate down on the bar.

Terri swiveled on her stool and faced Sydney. The Australian girl was strangely built. She was short and round, with a big outback. She was an Aussie with a big auss. Callipygian, Terri thought, remembering the novel *White Palace*, which was about a waitress living in St. Louis. Callipygian meant big-assed. The waitress in *White Palace* had been Callipygian.

Dinty introduced the two girls.

"Nice to meet you, Cindy," Terri said, deliberately mispronouncing the name. She did not like this Aussie. Terri had discovered over the years that big-assed women were usually bitches.

"It's Sydney," the Callipygian girl said haughtily, with a singsongy Australian twang. She scowled at Terri and then swaggered away.

Terri examined the brain sandwich that had been placed in front of her. She sniffed at it the way a dog sniffs at food. "This won't give me the shits, will it?" she asked. The bun was very soft, and when she pulled it away, bits of batter stuck to the bread. She felt a little queasy when she saw the actual brain matter, which was a putrid gray color. It looked like tofu.

"I use only 100 percent pure calf brain," Dinty said, watching Terri take a bite. "How do you like it?"

"It tastes like…chicken," Terri concluded, deciding to be tactful.

"It's an acquired taste," Dinty said. "You want some fries with that?"

"No, thank you," Terri mumbled. The brain sandwich was tough, and she was having trouble chewing. When Dinty turned to look at the television, she spat out a wad of stringy, unchewable brain and put it in her purse.

The commercial break had ended, and *The Happy Hooker Show* was back on.

"And now here once again is the First Lady of Fishing, Barbara Grogan," the rustic announcer said with a down-home diphthong.

Although their singing was scaring away the fish, Conway and Barbara didn't care. Earlier they had sung *Release Me*, and now they were doing *Louisiana Woman, Mississippi Man*. Both songs had been hits for the twosome of Conway Twitty and Loretta Lynn. "Hey, Louisiana Woman, Mississippi Man. We get together every time we can. The Mississippi River can't keep us apart, there's too much love in this Mississippi heart, too much love in this Louisiana heart. When she waves from the bank, don't you know I know, it's goodbye fishing line, see you a while ago. With a Louisiana woman waitin' on the other side, the Mississippi River don't look so wide. I'm going to jump in the river and here I go. Too bad alligator you swim too slow.

Well, that Mississippi River, Lord, it's one mile wide, and I'm going to get me to the other side."

Barbara was moving her fishing rod back and forth as she sang, her wrist and hand making small, swift movements, as though she were using the rod to conduct the Mormon Tabernacle Choir. Her deep alto voice was drowning out Conway's rich baritone.

"I like this song," Dinty said, tapping on the bar with his long, bony fingers. "It's one of the best songs there is about the Mississippi River. Most people ignore the Mississippi and take it for granted. I have a feeling all that is going to change in the next few weeks."

"What do you mean?" Terri asked.

"I think we're going to have a major flood," Dinty announced in a voice loud enough for everyone at the bar to hear. "All the signs point to it."

"The worst of the spring flooding is supposed to be over with," Terri said, referring to an article in the morning paper. She noticed someone had left a copy of the *Post-Dispatch* on the bar. Picking up the paper, she showed Dinty the story. The headline read, GRAFTON MOPS UP, REOPENS AFTER FLOOD. There was a photograph of a woman standing in her debris-filled yard. Her dog was sitting on a pile of rusted junk. The headline above the photo stated, YARDS EMERGE FROM FLOODWATER.

"When you've lived in St. Louis as long as I have," Dinty said, "you'll know stories like that can't be trusted. Mother Nature is a mean mother. There's been a lot of rain up north in Minnesota, Wisconsin, and Iowa. All that precipitation means high water down here in Missouri. The ground is already saturated from the spring flood. When this next tide of rainwater comes down the Mississippi, look out."

"If you feel that way, why don't you build an ark?" Terri kidded.

"They laughed at Noah too," Dinty said defensively. "I'm just glad I live here on top of Lavender Hill. This is the safest spot in the St. Louis area. When the flood comes, I'll be sitting high and dry."

"I live out in Crestwood," Terri said. "That's over ten miles from the Mississippi. I guess I'll be safe."

"Don't be too sure," Dinty warned. "Crestwood has several small creeks that could flood and cause a lot of problems."

"I think you're shitting me," Terri scoffed. "Anyway, I don't have to worry. I live in an apartment. If a flood comes, I'll let my landlord deal with the problem."

Dinty gave an ambivalent shrug. "How long have you lived in Crestwood?"

"Three years. I sell cosmetics at the Famous-Barr store in Crestwood Plaza."

"What line do you represent?"

"Estée Lauder," Terri replied, after taking a bite from the frontal lobe of her brain sandwich. "Did anyone ever tell you that an IQ Burger looks and tastes a lot like tofu?"

Dinty dismissed this question with a wave of his hand. "I want to hear more about your job at Famous-Barr."

"I'm a cosmetologist," Terri murmured. "A beauty advisor. I sell perfume and do makeovers. I can transform the most homely girl into a ravishing, gorgeous, luscious creature."

"What could you do with Barbara Grogan?" Dinty asked, pointing at the television.

"I could turn her into the Farrah Fawcett of Fishing. The Charlie's Angel of Angling."

"That would be quite a task."

"I can work miracles." Terri snickered.

It was now time for Barbara to say adios to her audience. She throttled down until the bass boat came to a complete stop. She pushed her sunglasses higher up onto her large nose and waited for the cameraman, who was in another boat, to give her the signal. Adjusting the wireless microphone which hung around her neck, she formed her thick lips into a fish-like pout and began speaking. "That about wraps it up for this time." She grunted, her voice low and throaty. No matter how hard she tried, she had never been able to get rid of a voice that was as flat as her figure. Whoever heard her knew she couldn't have come from anywhere but the land of the big sky and the wide open spaces. "Make sure to join me next week when I'll be fishing for Dolly Varden trout with, you guessed it, Dolly Parton."

People who do their own television shows usually say something ritualistic at the end of a program, a remark that might have some bearing on people's lives. Barbara was no exception. She always closed her show by saying, "Until next time, this is the old Happy Hooker wishing you good luck with your fishing and reminding you that you don't have to be outdoors to be an outdoorsman. So long, everybody. Tight lines!"

Barbara waited until Conway Twitty made a few closing remarks. Then she steered a course for home, the bass boat blasting through the water like a hydroplane, with only a foot and a half of boat touching the surface.

Barbara's theme song played for about a minute as the credits rolled by, and then a commercial came on. Dinty went over to the television and switched the baseball game back on. Ordinarily, he would have watched ABC's *Wide World of Sports*, which always followed *The Happy Hooker Show*. However, he figured the beefy man would start harping if the channel wasn't changed.

"Well, how did you like *The Happy Hooker Show*?" Dinty asked Terri.

"I think it's great," she said. "It's the funniest thing I've ever seen. I'll watch it every week from now on."

"Dolly Parton appears on the show at least three times each year. She and Barbara are good friends. Dolly did a lot of fishing when she was a girl growing up in Tennessee. That's true of a lot of country singers. Most of them are fishing enthusiasts, or fishing aficionados, as I like to call them."

"Are most of the guests on the show country singers?" Terri asked, impressed with Dinty's vocabulary. Only an avid reader of Hemingway would use the word *aficionado*, she thought.

"Barbara has on a wide variety of guests," Dinty answered. "About half are country singers. There are some professional athletes, some actors, and some television personalities. Many of the guests are just ordinary guys who happen to be good fishermen."

Terri was glad she had paid a visit to this little rainy-afternoon bar. She detected an undercurrent of closeness between herself and Dinty. She gazed around the Stag Club, trying to analyze her feelings.

She'd anticipated a momentous reaction upon seeing her girlhood home again. Instead, she simply wanted to forget the past and get on with her life.

The Stag Club seemed very clean, unlike most taverns. The smooth wooden floor looked as shiny as when the Zimmerman Bakery had been located here. A second glance revealed heel prints and scuff marks where large crowds had danced to the plaintive strains of Dinty's piano.

Dinty's concert grand piano was the centerpiece of the Stag Club, much the way a casket is the centerpiece at a funeral. A massive expanse of dark mahogany, the piano stood on a raised platform next to the fireplace.

The fireplace had been there from the very beginning, when the establishment was called the Leaping Stag Inn. It was one of those cavernous, Citizen Kane fireplaces, big enough to stand in.

A huge stag head, with fuzzy antlers, hung like a sentinel above the fireplace. Dinty had purchased the mangy, flea-bitten beast for five dollars at a garage sale.

In the past year, Terri had persistently dreamed of being a small child again in this building. Invariably, she would awaken with a pervading sense of loss. Now, bits and pieces of memory began to intrude upon her like flotsam and jetsam.

She could still picture her father, ghostlike with flour, baking bread here. She could still smell the aroma of the glutinous loaves as they cooled on a wire rack. She had not forgotten the location of each glass-fronted display case and still remembered what each case held. There were strudels, cannoli, cream puffs, lady fingers, bagels, cookies, cakes, pies, and many more kindred pastries. It was Terri's job to wait on the customers. The service counter had been located to the right of the main entrance, approximately where Dinty's pool table now was.

Two overweight young men were playing rotation pool on the green-topped table. They had a bet on the game and were lost in concentration. Terri heard only the click of the balls and an occasional low-voiced exclamation.

Suddenly, a memory came floating back to her. She recalled an elderly lady who used to come in the bakery quite often to buy fresh bread. The woman was a strange old bird who dressed entirely in purple. She was known as the Lavender Lady.

The impression must have gone deep, deep into the girlish mind, for fifteen years later, Terri still retained a sort of storybook mental picture of this purple-haired, purple-clothed matron who would come in the bakery laughing and bright-eyed and fill the room with the miasma of her lavender-scented perfume.

"Hey, Dinty," Terri called softly, "does Mrs. Grosse still live across the street in that decaying mansion?"

The Lavender Lady's full name was Anna Louise Grosse, née Picker. Her husband had been William Grosse, president of the Grosse Brewing Company. Most of her fortune had dried up in the early 1920s, after Prohibition forced the Grosse Brewery out of business. Her husband had committed suicide in the family mansion on January 16, 1920, the very day that Prohibition became law.

"She's still there," Dinty replied, with a smirk on his face. "She's ninety-three years old now and needs someone with her constantly. Her grandson has that job. He serves as her nurse, housekeeper, and groundskeeper."

"Grandson?" Terri inquired innocently, her interest aroused.

"Yes. He's been living with her for several years. He's a writer and is working on a book about the Grosse family. That's why he wanted to be close to her. She supplies him with all sorts of information."

"You know, I think I remember playing with him when we were kids."

"They should be in here later this afternoon," Dinty said. "Neither one likes to cook, and they come over here all the time for dinner."

"Mrs. Grosse has always been a mystery to me," Terri articulated. "She's like that Ms. Havisham in *Great Expectations*. An eccentric old lady living next door to a deserted brewery. Could you tell me more about her? You must know her pretty well."

Dinty opened a long neck bottle of Busch Bavarian Beer and took a swift swig. After wiping his mouth with the back of his hand, he let out a tremendous belch. He then smacked his lips, cleared his throat, and proceeded to tell Terri the story of the Lavender Lady.

Chapter Two

Born in 1900, Anna Louise Picker, the daughter of Austrian immigrants, lived with her parents on a large farm in Calhoun County, Illinois. Located just north of St. Louis, Calhoun County is a narrow peninsula between the Illinois River and the Mississippi. The primary crop of Calhoun County has always been apples, and that was exactly what the Pickers grew on their two-thousand-acre spread. They were known far and wide as the Apple Pickers. Their land extended for miles alongside the Mississippi River. Anna, like one of the Hesperides, looked after the plethora of apple trees that covered the property. She enjoyed working outdoors in the bountiful orchard, and the physical activity kept her in good shape. She was one of the most attractive girls in the entire area.

In 1913, a large St. Louis company, Mississippi Waterways Incorporated, announced it would build a fine new riverboat to be named the *Belle of Calhoun*. The boat would carry agricultural products, grown in Calhoun County, down the Mississippi to the St. Louis marketplace. The company then asked the people of Calhoun County to designate which young woman should receive the title Belle of Calhoun. An election was held, and the winner proved to be Anna Picker, who was just thirteen at that time.

Anna, who looked mature for her years, was given a great deal of publicity. The waterways company hired a famous artist to do an oil painting of her. When the Belle of Calhoun was launched, the painting was placed in the pilothouse. It remained there until the boat was retired from active service after an accident. The portrait was then donated to the Missouri Historical Society.

After she became the Belle of Calhoun, Anna attracted the attention of William Grosse, the virile, handsome, but mentally unstable scion of the Austrian American brewing family. He had fallen in love with her portrait, which had been reproduced in every St. Louis newspaper. Grosse was among the spectators on the St. Louis riverfront when Anna christened the *Belle of Calhoun*. With great ceremony, she broke a bottle of champagne against the boat's hull, as a brass band played *Anchors Aweigh*.

Afterward, Grosse introduced himself to Anna and her parents and accompanied them on the maiden voyage of the *Belle of Calhoun*. Thrilled to meet the wealthiest man in St. Louis, Anna spent the entire trip engaged in conversation with him. Her parents, who were having financial problems at the time, did not discourage this budding romance, even though their daughter was only thirteen.

Grosse, who was thirty-three, had never met a girl like Anna before. He was smitten with her. When the boat returned to St. Louis, he invited the three Pickers to have dinner with him at his restaurant, the Leaping Stag Inn. He wanted this to be a memorable evening, so he pulled out all the stops. He instructed his chef to whip up a lavish meal of Lobster Thermidor, Oysters Rockefeller, shrimp, caviar, Jerusalem artichokes, and Potatoes O'Brien. His employees fell all over themselves providing service. The Pickers were waited on like royalty.

Grosse, who had never double-dated with a girl's parents before, was a gracious host. During dinner, he told of how his Viennese grandfather had founded the Grosse Brewery in St. Louis just before the Civil War. Mr. Picker promptly announced that he and his wife were also from Vienna, which at that time was the capital of the Austro-Hungarian Empire.

Realizing Anna's ethnic background was similar to his own, Grosse began to hum a waltz tune reminiscent of Gay Vienna. Anna and he were meant for each other. She was his grande passion.

At the end of the evening, Anna, wearing the same purple velvet dress as in the portrait, put her silky arms around Grosse's neck. As she gave him a hug, he whispered that he liked her dress, that it matched the color of her eyes. There was something wonderful about Anna's large violet eyes, something that made Grosse forget the creamy smoothness of her cheeks and the elegant texture of her light-brown hair. All he could remember were those Svengali-like eyes that had hypnotized him and made him fall in love.

Before he met Anna, Grosse had a reputation as a playboy and bon vivant, but all that suddenly changed. He knew there would be only one woman in his life from now on.

The couple achieved some degree of notoriety during their courtship. The newspapers had a field day. Anna became known as the Lavender Lady because of her fondness for that color in her apparel. Apparently in imitation of Empress Alexandra of Russia, she surrounded herself with none but lavender appointments. Grosse bought her all kinds of expensive purple pleasantries. She created a sensation wherever she went—stores, hotel lobbies, on the street. Passersby would gape at her as though she were a figment, or perhaps pigment, of the imagination.

In winter, she traveled about in a lavender great coat edged with ermine, and on her head she wore an ermine-tipped lavender toque. In summer, she donned her regal lavender frock and large hat with a lavender veil that covered her face.

After the couple became engaged in 1914, Grosse began construction of a magnificent purple palace next to the family brewery. He named the estate Lavender Hill in Anna's honor. Soon the entire area became known as Lavender Hill.

The marriage of William Grosse and Anna Picker occurred on Valentine's Day 1916, just two weeks after Anna's sixteenth birthday. It was the biggest wedding St. Louis had ever seen. More than seven hundred people attended, including politicians, businessmen, millionaires, professional baseball players, and relatives from Milwaukee who were also in the brewing business. The service was held at St. Boniface Catholic Church, a Southside landmark across the street from the Grosse Brewery, and next door to the Leaping Stag Inn, where the reception was held.

Anna designed her wedding dress and entire trousseau by herself. The gown, purple satin with grapelike beads embroidered in soft viny patterns, was long and flowing, and she carried a bouquet of African violets. Her bridesmaids wore purple chiffon instead of pink.

Two small girls, with flower baskets, ambled down the aisle strewing spikes of French lavender instead of the more traditional rose petals.

The ceremony was performed by the archbishop of St. Louis, who wore gold-embroidered violet robes that swept far behind him. To please her Catholic husband, Anna, an agnostic, had studied and adopted his religion. The couple planned to have many children to continue the Grosse line. However, this was not meant to be. They had only one child, a daughter who was born on June 21, 1918.

Anna looked beautiful in her purple wedding gown. The bridal veil cascaded around her face like lavender mist. She wore an elegant tiara that was encrusted with large amethysts. Her father had to fight back tears as they walked solemnly down the aisle to the strains of Lohengrin, and children in the audience pointed at the bride.

Grosse grinned as he watched her approach, and he felt warm all over. This was the moment they had waited for. It had finally come. It was done. And as she smiled at him through her lavender veil, he knew he had done the right thing. She looked lovely. And in moments, she would be his wife. For always.

As soon as the wedding ceremony was over, everyone rushed next door to the Leaping Stag Inn for the reception. This gala party would prove to be the biggest beer blowout in St. Louis history. Guests passed quickly through the reception line into the beer line. Bottles of Grosse beer were cooling in an enormous ice-filled tank. Ten bartenders, hired especially for the occasion, were opening bottles of beer with precision speed. A German band played beer-drinking music to get people in the mood.

Grosse, who looked like a baldish Buffalo Bill, raised a glass of beer to toast his new bride. He told his assembled guests that Anna had come into his life at just the right time, just when he was ready to settle down and start a family. He poured Anna a glass of Burgermeister and smiled knowingly. She lifted the frothy amber brew to her parched lips and drank. Then, she toasted her husband, proclaiming what a terrific guy he was and what a wonderful father he would be to their children.

The best man at the wedding was the groom's cousin Frederick Schlitz, of the famous Milwaukee brewing family. Acting as master of ceremonies, Schlitz formally congratulated the happy couple and expressed his sincere hope that their first child would be masculine. Then, he hoisted a glass of Grosse Bohemian Beer and saluted the bride and groom.

Forgetting her bridal dignity, Anna allowed herself to become quite drunk. During the traditional first dance with her husband, she behaved in a seductive fashion that shocked the entire wedding party. Transformed by her drunkenness and eager virginity, she almost consummated the marriage right there on the dance floor, as all the guests were watching. This gave rise to speculation that she was not a virgin. After all, her wedding gown was a color other than white.

There were many unmarried women present at the wedding who were jealous of Anna. They couldn't understand why Grosse, the most eligible bachelor in town, had chosen this nymphet. Anna was nothing more than a St. Louis Lolita, a sixteen-year-old girl who arouses an older man's passion.

All through the evening, men waited in line to dance with Anna, grabbing her arm to become her next partner. She still considered herself the belle of the county, the cutest little trick in shoe leather. She loved being the center of attention, and she flirted with each man in a teasing, joking way. This did not upset Grosse for he wanted his wife to be popular. It was good for business.

Grosse was very tolerant of his new bride. He was aware of her limitations, of her little crudities, but what if she did make a few mistakes in etiquette, a few mistakes in taste, occasionally. She was wonderfully sweet-tempered, always amiable, still very much a child.

Grosse thought that he could make her over, rub down the rough edges once he had her alone to himself. Of course, she was different from the spoiled debutantes he used to date. But he required somebody different.

In many respects, the wedding reception was Anna's coming-out party, her formal introduction into St. Louis society. For the most part, she was well received. The notoriety she generated endeared her to the guests.

Frederick Schlitz took a special liking to Anna and wondered why she had wrapped the vines of her affection around such a rickety arbor as Grosse. Four years later, after Grosse's suicide, Schlitz made an attempt to court Anna but had no success.

The reception lasted until dawn. At some point during the evening, the beer supply ran out. Upon making this discovery, Grosse flew across the street to the brewery, where he instructed several night-shift workers to haul kegs of beer over to the Leaping Stag Inn.

There was enough food at the reception to feed an army. The guests were preparing to chow down, as Grosse helped the bartenders tap the kegs, and Anna stood smiling beside him. The tables laden with food seemed to stretch on forever, lobsters and crabs, steaks and chops, mostaccioli and ravioli, vegetables and salads, and a huge white wedding cake shaped like the steamboat *Belle of Calhoun*.

Finally, it was time for Grosse and his bride to bid farewell to their beer-guzzling guests. Anna went upstairs to change and took off the purple gown she'd never wear again. She looked at it sadly for a moment, thinking of her endless hours of work and her attention to detail. She had spent nearly a month just on the frills, the added adornments: hundreds of purple grape-like beads embroidered in soft viny patterns. Now, she would have to put the gown away, to save for her own daughters to wear. She had on a white silk suit with a lavender trim when she came downstairs and a purple hat from Paris.

The happy couple then left on their honeymoon. Their destination, Hawaii, was kept a secret to protect them from reporters. Grosse's private railroad car was docilely waiting for them on the siding at Union Station, ready to be picked up by the Missouri Pacific's crack Sunshine Special that hurtled across the continent to California. After thirty-six hours in the gritty luxury of their private railroad car, the bride and groom reached San Francisco, where they boarded a cruise ship to Hawaii. They stayed at the Royal Hawaiian Hotel on Waikiki Beach, and the days drifted by like moments as they lay on the beach and went back to their room several times a day to make love.

After their honeymoon, the couple took up residence in their recently completed mansion on Lavender Street next to the family brewery. Anna and William loved each other very much, and their first two years of marriage were extremely happy. They entertained the rich and famous in their lavish home and also traveled extensively.

However, by the time their daughter was born in June of 1918, things were no longer quite so rosy.

America's entry into World War I had brought increasing anti-German and anti-Austrian sentiment, which hurt the Grosse Brewery. Also, there was the looming threat of Prohibition. The brewery failed to show a profit for the first time in sixty years. Grosse began neglecting his business and family, spending more and more time away from home with his idle companions.

In 1899, Grosse and seven of his wealthy cronies founded the Edgewater Hunting and Fishing Club. They were known as the Edgewater Eight. They would gather every week in the hospitality room at the Grosse Brewery. Situated above the Mississippi River, the brewery was the ideal place for them to meet. A stone stairway led down the bluff to a private dock where they kept a large boat. They had purchased an island about forty miles downstream, and they would take the boat there for fishing and duck hunting. They had also stocked the island with various exotic animals, like boar and bison, which they systematically hunted down and slaughtered. One time, they even hunted a toothless lion, which they had purchased from a circus that was going out of business.

On cold winter evenings, the eight club members would gather around the fireplace in the hospitality room and swap adventure stories while drinking lots of Grosse beer.

It was on one such night, in 1920, that the club met for the last time. It was January 15, 1920. Prohibition was to become law the next day. The men had gathered to drink beer legally one last time. They wanted to consume as much as possible before midnight, when the Volstead Act took effect. They had invited women of questionable virtue to help them deplete Grosse's stockpile of beer.

At some point during the evening, it began to snow precipitously. It was the heaviest snowfall in years.

Anna, who was next door in the family mansion, could hear the shouts of the drunken revelers when they came outside to frolic in the snow. The noise woke up her little daughter, who began crying.

Anna had been worried about her husband for some time now. He had become increasingly despondent over his failing business. The Grosse Brewery was on the verge of bankruptcy. She worried that he would take his own life. Anna had good reason to fear for her own safety as well. Her husband was preoccupied with the idea of double suicide. An avid student of Austrian history, he spoke frequently about the tragedy at Mayerling, a hunting lodge outside Vienna where the bodies of Crown Prince Rudolf and Marie Vetsera were found in January of 1889.

Typical of a person suffering from a depressive condition, Grosse had talked to Anna about making a suicide pact.

In the wee hours of January 16, 1920, Anna was awakened by Grosse pounding on her door. He had come home drunk from the party and was in a vile mood. When she did not answer his knock, he forced his way into the room. Without provocation, he tore the pajamas from her body. His eyes glaring, he grasped her by the throat and dragged her downstairs to his study, where he had just lit a roaring fire. Picking up the fireplace poker, he began to inflict on her several severe and violent blows before throwing her down on a couch. Anna was powerless and attempted to scream, but Grosse placed his fingers in her mouth and tried to choke her. She was now in a position to do anything he wanted.

He sat down next to her on the sofa and convinced the terrified girl that it would be beautiful and wonderful for them to die in each other's arms. Grosse proposed an unholy communion. He kissed Anna and handed her a tulip glass filled to the brim with poisoned wine. He had poured a similar drink for himself. They touched glasses in a gesture of farewell. After drinking, they smashed the glasses in the fireplace. Grosse snuggled against Anna's naked body. She wrapped her arms around him. Together, on the sofa, the ill-fated lovers waited for death to overtake them.

Grosse died almost immediately because his body was already loaded with alcohol. However, Anna, who had second thoughts about dying, was able to retch and vomit until most of the poison passed from her system. She staggered to the front door and cried for help. A passing policeman heard her, and she was rushed to Barnes Hospital, where her stomach was pumped.

Anna spent three weeks in the hospital. She was unable to attend her husband's funeral.

At 2:00 p.m. on July 26, 1920, the once magnificent Grosse Brewery was relegated to the auction block. Anna received only eight cents on the dollar for the brewing plant and adjacent buildings. She had lost everything except her home. Much of the money she received from the auction went to pay her husband's creditors. She was in serious financial trouble. However, she had one ace in the hole. A hole in the ground, so to speak. Underneath the brewery and family mansion was a vast network of caves.

The main reason St. Louis became a brewing capital, in the mid-1800s, was because of these caves. The caverns offered a place where beer could be stored and aged at temperatures that stayed below fifty degrees year-round.

Anna's plan was simple. She would open a speakeasy in the cavern beneath her home. She went into partnership with several of her husband's friends who knew the brewing business. Secretly, they moved beer-making equipment down into the cave. They also made arrangements with bootleggers to have prime Canadian whiskey delivered via the Mississippi.

Since there was minimal law enforcement on the river, this was the safest way to transport illegal hootch. Shipments of booze were dropped off at the private dock that had once been used by the Edgewater Hunting and Fishing Club. There was a secret entrance to the cave down by the river. The dock was on Anna's property. So was the stone stairway leading down to the river. Anna's partners in the speakeasy business had all been members of the Edgewater Club, which disbanded shortly after Grosse's death. Their boat, still tied up at the private dock, was used in some of the rum-running operations.

Anna recognized the folly of Prohibition and the unenforceability of the Volstead Act. Her establishment, which she named the Catacombs Cabaret, soon became the most successful speakeasy in St. Louis. No other blind pig in the city could compete with the talent of its star entertainers, the beauty of its chorus girls, or the virtuosity of its orchestra, which alternated jazz with operatic medleys. At the flick of a switch, hydraulic lifts raised the dance floor on which bobbed-haired flappers with low-waisted skirts and their tuxedoed escorts gyrated to whatever the current fad dictated—one-step, two-step, Boston, turkey trot, fox trot, Charleston, Big Apple, Ballin-the-Jack, grizzly bear, bunny hug, Castle Walk, the Black Bottom—to the beat of *Tiger Rag*, *Ja-da*, *Pretty Baby*, *Dardanella*, *Goody Goody*.

The festivities, which seldom got up full steam before midnight, sometimes went on past dawn. Accessible women, on Anna's payroll, freely mingled with the male patrons. There was illegal gambling in the back of the cave behind solid steel doors.

Only the most fashionable people came to the Catacombs Cabaret, and the nightly throng was a miscellany of sporting figures, big businessmen, collegians, judges, politicians, journalists, gangsters, the rich, the chic, the famous and infamous, the tourists.

Rogers Hornsby, one of Anna's many boyfriends, was a frequent visitor to the underground cabaret. Babe Ruth would stop by whenever the Yankees came to St. Louis to play the Browns. St. Louis author Fannie Hurst was a welcome guest. Fanny, who wrote such tearjerkers as *Back Street* and *Imitation of Life*, was a good friend of Anna's. St. Louis mayor Victor J. Miller was a valued customer of Anna's. Abe Bernstein, the head of Detroit's Purple Gang, would drop by whenever he was in St. Louis on business.

Anna bought most of her illegal hard liquor from the Purple Gang, a group of Detroit Jews who distributed Canadian whiskey throughout the Midwest. This got her into trouble with Egan's Rats, a gang of St. Louis bootleggers. The Rats tried to extort protection money from her after she refused to buy their inferior products.

Anna, who was no shrinking violet, became the Queen of the Roaring Twenties in St. Louis. Dressed in a feathery purple outfit, she would flit from table to table, gesticulating grandly, charming the men and amusing the women, ordering champagne and cigars on the house. She had always wanted to be a singer, and now she had her chance. She became the star attraction, enchanting the customers every night with a repertoire of 1920s songs like *Poor Butterfly*,

Melancholy Baby, It Had to Be You, Ain't We Got Fun, Mississippi Mud, River Stay Away From My Door, Yes…We Have No Bananas.

Yes, Anna came of age in the 1920s. She seemed to symbolize the tragic waste and corruption of this decadent decade. She became something of a folk hero in St. Louis, where Prohibition was especially hated. As far as the public was concerned, the Prohibition agent, not Anna, was the criminal. Anna had made violating the law a public sport. Her establishment was never raided by the authorities, because she had all the cops and politicians in her hip pocket.

In the Roaring Twenties, an era of opulence and extravagance, Anna spent money as lavishly as she made it. Once again, she was able to indulge in luxuriant living. She had a wardrobe that Joan Crawford would have envied. Her income from the Catacombs Cabaret was substantial. In addition, she had set up a bootleg brewing operation in the cave and was selling beer to other speakeasies.

Anna was making so much money that she rehired several of her former servants—her maid, butler, and chauffeur. Also, a nanny was chosen to look after Anna's little daughter. Anna's daughter attended Wedgeworth Academy, the most exclusive private grade school in St. Louis.

Life was good. Too good.

The stock market crash of October 1929 hurt Anna badly. She had invested heavily in stocks and lost over a hundred thousand dollars. At first, the Catacombs Cabaret appeared able to weather the Great Depression, but then the coup de grace was administered. Prohibition was repealed in December of 1933, and Anna's speakeasy went out of business.

Almost broke, she was in desperate need of a job. Using what influence she had, she pulled a few strings and was hired as the society editor of the *St. Louis Globe-Democrat*.

Anna had never studied journalism, but this didn't matter. E. Lansing Ray, the publisher of the *Globe-Democrat*, was one of her bosom friends. He had been a regular at the Catacombs Cabaret.

Once a socialite herself, Anna became an arbiter of the St. Louis Upper Crust. She controlled absolutely the amount of ink that would be expended on any social event by the city's second-leading newspaper. Her snips and jibes and bitchiness sold papers. She was irreverently called the Czarina, partially because she dressed in purple like Russia's Alexandra the Grape and also because her influence was malevolent and destructive like Alexandra's.

Anna developed a notably florid prose style full of elaborate embellishments, swirls, and flourishes. She resurrected long-dead words and never used an everyday term if an archaic one would do. She also invented words. St. Louisans were amused by her deep-purple prose and soon began collecting favorite Anna-isms.

Her personal vendettas became famous and made good copy. She especially hated the Busch family, whom she blamed for much of her misfortune. She was jealous that Anheuser-Busch had survived Prohibition. Her favorite method of revenge upon someone who had offended her was the fashion attack (she was a fine one to talk about fashion). She would write, "Mrs. Busch appeared in her customary brown," or "Ms. Busch wore the green toilet [Anna's word for dress] in which she always looks so well," or "Mrs. Anheuser appeared in the blue dress which has graced several previous occasions."

One of the first stories that Anna covered was the suicide of August A. Busch, Senior, in February of 1934. He was extremely ill and shot himself in the Busch family mansion. Two weeks later, Alice Busch, his widow, appeared at an indoor horse show where her son, Gussie, was one of the star performers. The widow was all in black, but Anna spitefully reported that the lady appeared in her box "in a gorgeous red toilet."

The Busch family found it pitiful that St. Louis would tolerate Anna's terrorist tactics and brought one libel suit after another against the *Globe-Democrat*. Whenever she was threatened with legal action, Anna turned all dewy-eyed and apologetic. But there were never any retractions.

Anna's goal was to make the most distinguished people look undistinguished. To this purpose, she invented many clever stunt parties at which members of St. Louis society were knocked off their pedestals, and since she had much more character and intelligence than most of her victims, she succeeded in making them appear wonderfully foolish.

One of her favorite kinds of party was the pet hate party, in which habitues of St. Louis society came dressed as the person or type of person they admired the least. Also, there was the scavenger hunt, a party game that Anna had learned in England. Anna presided over the first scavenger hunt staged in St. Louis in the fall of 1934. Hundreds of couples came to the Chase Park Plaza Hotel to pay an admission charge of one hundred dollars for the benefit of Children's Hospital. Then, they were sent out by a starter's gun to race around the city, securing a list of odds and ends which Anna had taxed her brain for a week to devise. The lists included one of Dizzy Dean's shoes, an Anheuser-Busch Clydesdale, a spittoon, a No Parking sign, and a chimp from the St. Louis Zoo. When the laughing contestants straggled in, towing Clydesdales, monkeys, parking signs, and stray bits of clothing, Anna distributed prizes, and the party continued in the ballroom until dawn.

Prominent St. Louis families consulted Anna before planning anything. If it was a wedding, Anna would not only set the date but would also select the orchestra, the caterer, the florist, and the site of the reception. If a family did not accept her advice, she simply refused to report that particular wedding in the *Globe-Democrat*. Anna also decided who could be a debutante and who could not and arranged the winter's schedule of coming-out parties. To a hopeful mother, Anna might say, shaking her head sadly, "No, I don't think your daughter is ready to come out this year," or "I don't think Agnes would be happy as a debutante. The crowd this year is so different from hers."

As Anna grew older, her eccentricities increased. She began to think of herself as a great lady, a grand dame out of the Belle Époque, a wealthy dowager out of the Gilded Age, a powerful matriarch from the Mauve Decade of the 1880s.

One day in 1955, soon after the *Globe-Democrat* was sold to the Newhouse Chain, Anna walked out of her newspaper office at lunchtime and never came back. She was discovered, it was said, to be suffering from mental illness. Her convoluted prose style had become harder and harder to follow and her temper tantrums more frequent. Aside from planning parties, attending them, and writing about them, she had seemed to have no life whatsoever, but now the woman who had enjoyed twenty-one years of glory and unchallenged power retired from the public eye into a deep and total seclusion at her Lavender Hill home.

Chapter Three

After he finished his narrative tale about the Lavender Lady, Dinty took a long sip of beer. He swallowed, looked thoughtful, and then smiled like a child who had just recited a Christmas poem. Had he done all right? As a raconteur, Dinty was at his charming best that day. He had captured the essence of Anna Grosse. He had delved into her character, revealing the subtle nuances that distinguished her from other women. His agile mind had darted from scenario to scenario with the flashing movement of a barracuda. Terri was enthralled by his Lavender Lady story, which had been phrased with a dry, impish humor.

"I may have improved the truth in a few places," Dinty said. "I sometimes blend fact and fiction to add more excitement to a story. But over 90 percent is true."

Terri did not doubt the accuracy of Dinty's story. Anna Grosse had been the apotheosis of the American woman.

"She was quite a gal," Terri said, studying Dinty with affectionate amusement. It was impossible not to admire him.

"Do you have any questions?" the reptilian old man asked, thrusting his neck forward like a tortoise.

"Yes, Dinty. Can you tell me more about her later life?"

"Anna was a recluse for many years, and no one knew anything about her. It wasn't until 1971 that she began reemerging in public. That's the year we met. There's something I forgot to tell you. She and I are an item. We're a couple."

"You mean you're her fancy man? Isn't she a little old for you?"

"We get along famously. We used to have a very active social life. We'd go to dances and movies. Now she's too old for that sort of thing. But she does come over here practically every day for dinner."

"Do you still go out on a date once in a great while?"

"Yes. I will be escorting her to the christening of the new river-boat casino on June twenty-third."

"I've been reading about that. I've forgotten the name of the boat."

"It's the *Belle of Calhoun*, the same boat that Anna made famous eighty years ago. They resurrected it from the dead and spent twenty-eight million dollars to refurbish it. The *Belle of Calhoun* sat in drydock for fifty-seven years, until Gateway Gaming bought it and turned it into a casino. They were looking for a boat with lots of open space, and the *Belle of Calhoun* fit that bill since it was originally designed to haul agricultural products."

"Where's the boat moored?"

"Over in Cahokia, Illinois, directly across the river from here. Gateway Gaming bought the entire shipyard where the *Belle of Calhoun* was in drydock. Cahokia Shipbuilding and Steel Company went out of business last year, and the property was for sale. That's the same company that built the *Belle of Calhoun* back in 1913. They were a subsidiary of Mississippi Waterways Incorporated. During the Civil War, James Eads owned that property and built some of his ironclad gunboats there."

"Are they going to honor Anna on June twenty-third?" Terri asked, raising a quizzical right eyebrow.

"They want her to christen the *Belle of Calhoun* with a bottle of champagne just like she did in 1913."

"Do you think Anna can take all that excitement?" Terri asked mindfully.

Dinty nodded his head yes. Anna still loved the limelight even though she was old and in poor health. She had been hoping to make a comeback into high society. This was her chance. Once again she would be the acknowledged social leader of St. Louis, with her quick repartee, her amusing stories, her theatrical flair. When Gateway Gaming had approached her with their generous offer, she had accepted immediately. She would be paid handsomely. They wanted to use her old portrait in all their promotions. In addition, Anna would make public appearances to promote the new floating casino.

She had been practically penniless before this offer came along. Now she would be in the chips once again. Throughout her life, Anna had known lean years and plush years. Her financial condition, like the Mississippi River, had ebbed and flowed alarmingly. She was fond of having money. "Money," as she used to write in her society column, "is always chic." Anna had known both kinds of wealth. She had possessed both old money and new, depending on whether it was inherited or earned. "Old money kept its frock coat on," Anna used to say on her society column. "New money was still in shirtsleeves."

At Terri's insistence, Dinty continued his lengthy colloquy about the Lavender Lady. Eventually, Terri turned and peered at Dinty, her stare melding with his.

"Have you ever figured out why Anna wears purple all the time?" she asked with a hint of challenge.

"It's just her way of stating who she is," Dinty replied. "She's just being herself."

"How does Anna feel about having her name associated with a gambling boat?"

"She has no moral qualms against gambling. She likes to gamble. She and I used to make regular visits to Las Vegas."

"I take it you're a gambler?"

"I like to gamble. I like to drink. I like women. Lots of them! These things constitute my way of life."

"Have you been up to the Alton Belle?"

"I go there regularly. But once the *Belle of Calhoun* opens, I will change over."

"By next year, they'll have riverboat gambling here in Missouri. Are you looking forward to that?"

"Yes. But they're supposed to have a five-hundred-dollar loss limit. I'll probably still go across the river to the *Belle of Calhoun*."

Engrossed in conversation, Terri completely lost track of the time. She had originally planned to go next door to St. Boniface for five o'clock Mass. St. Boniface was her girlhood church. She had attended their grade school. Father O'Meara, the priest who had administered first communion to her twenty-five years ago, was still there.

Terri heard the bells of St. Boniface sonorously toll the five o'clock hour. She would have to leave now if she wanted to make the church service. Then, she remembered that this was June 5, the Feast Day of St. Boniface. The church would be packed. There would be special activities going on. Father O'Meara would be too busy after Mass to hear her confession.

Presently, Terri decided to remain at the Stag Club. She was having a good time and wanted to stick around in case the Lavender Lady showed up. Besides, bartenders were even better than priests when it came to hearing confessions.

She smiled worshipfully at Dinty. He was a great guy. Told terrific stories. Loved talking about the old days, and she loved listening to him. He was a real person. That's what she liked. And he reminded her a little of her grandfather. Maybe that's what they had going, a sort of grandfather-granddaughter thing.

"I want you to know that I don't sleep around," Terri said, lighting a cigarette with a disposable. "I really thought the guy loved me."

"What is the man's name?" Dinty asked softly. He was used to playing father confessor. It was part of his job. Bartenders were supposed to be the keepers of secrets and the possessors of clandestine knowledge.

"The man who got me pregnant is named Steve Davis. He's a Crestwood policeman. A worthless, no-good bastard. I hope some burglar shoots him."

"How did you meet?"

"How? I was working at Famous-Barr, spraying perfume, you know."

Dinty knew. The store or the perfume company put these good-looking, well-dressed women out on the floor at the end of the aisles with a silver-plated tray loaded with perfume samples or sometimes just a bottle. They'd spray anyone who let them in an attempt to steer someone over to the perfume counter.

"Well, I'm working there, and he comes in, you know. The perfume section is always the first thing you see when you enter a department store. Somehow, we started talking about sports and about the Cardinals, you know. And we just hit it off."

As usual, whenever Terri confessed her sins, a sense of Catholic guilt overwhelmed her. She found it painful and difficult to talk about her disastrous love affair. Tearfully, Terri confided her inner-most secrets to Dinty. She explained how Steve Davis had seduced her after a night of drinking in her apartment, how he had promised to marry her, how he had lied about not having other women in his life.

Dinty was very understanding. "Come over to the piano," he said in a raspy voice, a voice that had been burned by a lifetime of liquor and cigarettes. "I'll play something to cheer you up."

They took their drinks with them and walked over to the piano. "Scoot over!" Terri yelled at Dinty, as they both slid onto the piano bench.

Dinty needed to limber up for that evening's performance. Without asking what Terri wanted to hear, he proceeded to belt out a heart-shredding ballad called *Bartender's Blues*, which had been made famous by George Jones. Dinty was a singer who could boom from the depths of baritone into keening tenor. His singing style could best be described as countrypolitan, a blend of country and city.

Terri couldn't explain it, but she actually did feel better after hearing Dinty's song. Country music was the music of pain, she thought to herself. Dinty had gotten to her with his alternating tack of furious delivery, high, lonesome ache, and lowbrow taste.

Dinty bummed a cigarette from Terri. "Do you have any requests?" he asked.

"Play Misty for me," Terri said, lighting Dinty's cigarette.

Gazing at the beautiful girl sitting next to him on the piano bench, Dinty felt like a seventyish Svengali trying to entrance a much younger Trilby. He took a long, extended drag on his cigarette and then placed it in an ashtray on top of the piano. Without fanfare, he launched into the great Erroll Garner classic Misty. Garner's style was easy to duplicate, with striding rhythmic chords from the left hand underpinning the melodious right-hand tremolo. Dinty lived for the piano, and it sprang to life at his gentlest touch. In his hands, which had a personality of their own, the keyboard whispered, sighed, sang, shouted, pealed.

"You play almost as good as John Tesh," Terri said, her leg jiggling at three times the beat. Her knee accidentally brushed Dinty's knee.

Distracted by this physical contact, Dinty hit a discordant note. The sweet scent of Terri's perfume and the sideways view of her shapely breast were nearly disabling.

"You're a real beautiful woman," Dinty said. "It's almost kind of an honor sitting next to you."

Terri laughed softly. It then occurred to her that what had further bolstered the kinship she felt for Dinty during these first few hours of their friendship had been their common passion for music.

"I also know how to play the piano," she stated, limbering her fingers with a few scales. "Let's do a four-handed version of Chopsticks."

Dinty didn't respond, and Terri saw that he was looking toward the doorway. She followed his gaze and noticed that a handsome, well-built young man and a plumpish, purplish old lady had just entered. Dinty explained that this was Anna Grosse and her grandson, Glen Wunsch.

Anna was the kind of person who couldn't just walk into a room. She had to make a grand entrance. She was possessed with a sense of personal theater. As she and her grandson walked arm in arm down the short stairway that led into the Stag Club, she was a princess descending the staircase of the palace, the Merry Widow descending the staircase of the embassy, Scarlett O'Hara descending the staircase at Tara.

Anna was wearing a purple pantsuit with matching pumps, and she carried a purple purse. She had on tons of amethyst jewelry—earrings, rings, bracelets, necklaces—which cast a purplish luster. Even the purple vein throbbing in her forehead was a fashion statement. Her white hair had been dyed purple. Her fingernails had been painted purple. Her face was covered with purplish powder, and she had on purple lipstick and purple eye shadow.

Watching Anna's "purp" walk, Terri had thoughts of juicy, sugar-laden bunches of Concord grapes with translucent purple skin.

She could almost taste the imaginary grapes as she rolled her tongue over her lips.

Dinty began playing the same song he always performed whenever Anna entered his club:

"The sun is sinking low behind the hill. I loved you long ago, I love you still. When the deep purple falls..."

Upon hearing the music which she considered to be her theme song, Anna broke free from her grandson's grasp. Extending her arms lithely, she descended the stairs like a Las Vegas showgirl, testing her poise while executing the showgirl's trademark lilting sidestep: spine erect, hips forward, palms down, legs bent softly at the knees, toes slightly pointed.

"She looks like one of those dancing raisins on TV," Terri observed after Anna finally made it to the bottom of the stairs.

Dinty was just finishing up his rendition of the Mitch Parish hit Deep Purple:

"And as long as my heart will beat, lover we'll always meet, here in my deep purple dream."

Dinty enjoyed performing hits like *Deep Purple* from the Great American Songbook. He made the tune sound more countryish by playing in an unconventional meter.

"Boy, is she fat," Terri said coolly.

"She's as big as the *Titanic*," Dinty allowed.

"Yeah...and look at the size of those icebergs," Terri exclaimed, gazing at Anna's abundant breasts.

"Now you know what they mean by the term Purple Mountain Majesties," Dinty disclosed, giving a snort of laughter.

Anna and Glen waved to Dinty as they moved hurriedly to their usual table, which was kept reserved for them at all times. Glen held Anna's chair for her as she sat down. She heaved her enormous bosoms, and they seemed to flop on the table.

"That's the same spot where Anna sat when she had her wedding reception here in 1916," Dinty told Terri.

"You mean back when this place was called the Leaping Stag Inn?"

"Right. They used to call it the Stagger Inn for short."

"Wasn't it Emily Dickinson who wrote, 'A wounded stag leaps highest, I've heard the Hunter tell, 'Tis but The Ecstasy of death, And then the Brake is still?'"

"That sounds like something she would write," Dinty said.

Sydney Melbourne approached Anna and Glen to take their orders. Before Glen could sit down, Sydney had her arms around him and was giving him a kiss.

"That's what I call friendly service," Terri remarked to Dinty.

"They're involved with one another," Dinty said. "They've been dating for several months."

Sydney scribbled the drink orders down in her notepad and then asked about the main course.

"Brains…fresh brains," Glen said in a guttural voice, mimicking the zombies in the *Living Dead* movies.

Glen accompanied Sydney to help her make the brain sandwiches.

Terri and Dinty left the piano and walked over to Anna's table. Terri felt awestruck in Anna's presence. There she was, live and in purple, Anna Grosse, Die Grosse Anna. The Last of the Belles. Terri seemed to remember reading a short story called *The Last of the Belles* when she was in college. It was by F. Scott Fitzgerald. The title character had been named Ailie Calhoun. What a coincidence. Of course, that story was about a Southern belle, a steel magnolia from Georgia. Anna was really not a Southern belle, since Calhoun County is in Illinois.

Anna flashed Terri an excited smile. "I remember you," she said confidently. She had a surprisingly deep voice for such an old person. "You're Terri Zimmerman, that sweet little girl who used to wait on me in this building when there was a bakery shop here."

Terri lowered her slender frame into a chair and then leaned across the table to speak to Anna. "I'm so glad you remember me. Dinty was just telling me all about you."

"What's a nice girl like you doing with a bum like this?" Anna inquired.

"I'm not that nice," Terri reaffirmed.

"Don't get any ideas," Anna said in a jovial way. "Dinty is spoken for. He's my man."

Terri broke into laughter

"Don't worry," Dinty said with a chuckle. "I'm seventy-eight and she's thirty-three."

Terri was laughing so hard that she didn't hear what Dinty said. Otherwise, she would have wondered how he knew her age. He had seen her driver's license when she was reaching into her wallet to pay him.

"We just met for the first time today," Dinty continued. "She came back to visit her old haunts. She asked me to tell her the story of the famous Lavender Lady."

Suddenly, Terri was overtaken by an uncontrollable urge to tease Anna. "Lavender Lady," she muttered, nudging Dinty who had just sat down beside her. "Sounds like a racehorse."

"What?" Anna asked, a hard expression on her face.

"Nothing," Terri said, winking at Dinty.

"It's no fun being the Lavender Lady anymore," Anna lamented. "Now when people hear you're called the Lavender Lady, they think it's some kind of gay thing. We've had gays move into the neighborhood just because of the name Lavender Hill."

"How's it going?" Dinty asked abruptly, trying to change the subject. "Are you okay?"

"I'm okay, I guess," Anna replied. "Some kids called me Barney the other day. They think I look like that purple dinosaur on TV."

"I guess that's better than being called a Purple Smurf," Terri said.

Anna remained silent in the face of Terri's sarcasm.

"Barney," Dinty annunciated. "That's a good name for you. That's what I'm going to call you from now on."

Terri and Dinty both laughed.

"What is it they used to call you years ago?" Terri asked with a sideways glance at Dinty. "The Belle of Amherst?"

Anna sighed heavily. She stared at Terri and frowned with purple, unplucked eyebrows. "That's Emily Dickinson," she said curtly, unamused, sensing that Terri was having some fun with her. "I was known as the Belle of Calhoun. In fact, I'm still known as the Belle of Calhoun."

Whenever Anna was teased, she became a little pretentious. It was her way of reacting to pain. "I'm a celebrity," she boasted. "That new gambling boat is named after me."

Terri nodded and felt somewhat embarrassed. Anna didn't deserve to be made fun of. Zinging the purple lady had given Terri a great deal of pleasure, but she wasn't sure why. Now, she was sorry she had behaved in such a manner.

Anna got up from the table and headed for the lav before Terri had a chance to apologize.

"Do you feel some sort of animosity towards Anna?" Dinty asked, after watching the old lady walk stiff-legged into the women's lavatory near their table.

"No," Terri said sheepishly, giving Dinty a closed-mouth Stepford smile.

Dinty and Terri leaned forward, their heads close together, and talked animatedly about Anna for several minutes.

Then they heard the toilet flush. The bathroom door flew open, and Anna came out.

By this time, Glen Wunsch had returned with a platter of food and drink, which he placed on the table. Lean and muscular, he was wearing an attractive green T-shirt with the sleeves cut off. His massive upper arms were covered with sweat. "Do not adjust your picture," he whispered into Terri's ear. "She actually is that color." Glen went over to help his grandmother who was having trouble walking.

"Hey, Barney," Dinty called out. "Be careful. Don't fall."

Anna did not care for this satiric nickname. After taking her grandson's arm, she sang a parody of the Barney theme, which is done to the same melody as *This Old Man*. "I hate you...you hate me," she warbled, pointing at Glen. "We're a dysfunctional family," she continued with a sweep of her right arm. "With a great big slug." She waved her fist in the air and then punched Glen in the jaw. "And a kick from me to you." She kicked Glen in the shins. "Won't you say you hate me too."

Grimacing, Glen extended his free arm in Terri's direction and made a backhanded fanning motion to indicate that his grandmother was a total whacko.

Terri laughed quietly and lip-synched her thoughts.

"That's a cute girl...who is she?" Glen asked his grandmother, as they slowly made their way back to the table.

"Terri Zimmerman," the hobbling old lady replied.

"That name sounds familiar."

"Her father was a baker."

"She's a nice piece of pastry."

"Yeah...fruit cake...She's a little peculiar, I think."

"Wasn't there a Zimmerman Bakery in this building years ago?"

"That's right. She used to live here with her parents. She's come back to renew old memories."

"You know...I think I remember playing with her when we were kids."

Anna's forward progress was impeded by foot pain. She came to a halt.

Dinty saw this and shook his head disapprovingly.

"She looks like she's on her last lap," Terri observed.

"I don't know about that," Dinty said. "I don't think she'll ever die." He paused for a few seconds and then added, "Old purple ladies never die...they just fade away." Dinty turned to Terri and cracked a smile. He failed to notice that Anna was moving again. He continued to speak about the Lavender Lady.

"Keep quiet," Terri cautioned a little too loudly, thinking Anna was out of earshot. "Here comes the purple people eater now."

"I heard that!" Anna barked, as she limped up to the table. "You got a problem with purple?"

"No," Terri said obsequiously, exchanging glances with Dinty. "I don't discriminate on the basis of color. No matter what that color might be."

Terri caught Anna's eye and smiled, but the old lady glowered at her.

"There's something you have to know about my grandmother," Glen interceded. "She's known as the Belly of Calhoun."

"That's Belle!" Anna huffed. "Anyway, she already knows that."

"It's good to see you again, Terri," Glen said, helping his grandmother sit down.

Terri couldn't get over how handsome Glen had become. He looked like a dashing young German officer in a World War II movie. His blue eyes, blond hair, powerful physique, and strong Teutonic features made him the prototype of Hitler's Aryan man. Terri would soon discover that this young man, who looked like a product of Nazi eugenics, was very proud of his Nordic background.

"It's nice to see you again too," Terri acknowledged. "Remember all the good times we had together as kids?"

"Of course I do," Glen rejoined, hugging Terri, and then sitting down next to her.

At this point, Sydney Melbourne arrived with the side dishes, french fries and coleslaw. She threw Terri a dirty look.

"Please bring me another brain sandwich, Cindy," Terri said, just to get rid of this jealous female.

It was now time for Terri and Glen to become reacquainted after so many years apart. They talked about how they had played together as kids. In the late 1960s and early 1970s, Glen and his parents had lived with Anna at the Lavender Hill estate. Terri would walk across the street to Lavender Hill, and the two children would spend the day together. They would walk along the shoreline of the river, playing hide-and-seek and hitching rides on barges. They would fish and swim in the river. Once, when it was very hot, they went skinny dipping. They would explore the abandoned Grosse Brewery and the caves underneath. They played wiffle ball in vacant lots and became masters of many sidewalk games.

Terri and Glen were interrupted by Dinty, who asked if they wanted anything more to drink.

"I just did a lot of exercise, and I'm really thirsty," Glen said in a parched voice. "Give me a Tommy Atkins mango tonic with a kiwi twist."

"You look like you could use some exercise," Dinty said. "You're a stout fella."

Dinty returned to the bar to fix the drink. He used the juice of freshly squeezed Tommy Atkins mangoes and then added two ounces of vodka and two ounces of tonic water.

"The old fart," Glen said after Dinty had gone. "He just called me fat. I ought to punch his lights out."

"You're wrong," Terri said consolingly. "He didn't call you fat. Old people speak a different language than we do. The term 'stout fella' is just an antiquated expression. What Dinty actually meant is that you're macho and strong…that you look like an athlete who needs to work out."

"I'll never understand old people." Glen sighed. "I think they're all senile. And speaking of senile. There's the Queen of Se-nile." He pointed at his grandmother.

At this moment, an attractive Asian girl burst into the Stag Club and waved excitedly to Terri, who waved back.

"Who's the Chinese chick?" Glen asked when he saw that Terri recognized the girl.

"She's from the Philippines," Terri answered. "She lives in the apartment next to mine. She knew I was coming here."

"Wow, she's hot!" Glen exclaimed. "I like foreign women."

Terri's best friend was a girl from the Philippines named Paz Militante. In 1987, Paz had come to the United States as a mail order bride. Her prospective husband, a St. Louisan, deserted her after several months, and she was left to fend for herself. Paz lived next door to Terri in an apartment building near Crestwood Plaza. Terri and Paz worked together behind the Estée Lauder counter at the Famous-Barr store in Crestwood Plaza. It was Terri who had obtained the Estée Lauder job for her neighbor Paz. The two girls were both very beautiful. They were the same age, had similar interests, and both were unlucky in love. Paz still spoke the Tagalog language and liked to tag along wherever Terri went. Terri had mentioned to Paz that she was coming to the Stag Club, and now Paz had also come. Paz was worried about Terri, who had acted depressed after being jilted. Paz was afraid that Terri might do something rash, like commit suicide.

"Here comes my shadow," Terri said to Glen as Paz approached.

"Mabuhay," Paz said in a clipped voice. "I am so concerned about you," she continued in pidgin English. She spoke fast and was hard to understand.

"Mabuhay to you too," Terri chortled. "You don't have to worry about me, Paz. I'm okay."

Paz was a light-skinned Filipina who was a member of the Igorot tribe of North Luzon in the Philippines. Terri liked to remind her that the Igorot village had been a prominent attraction at the 1904 St. Louis World's Fair. The Igorots gained notoriety at the fair because of their love of eating dog meat. The St. Louis neighborhood known as Dogtown received its name because stray dogs were captured there and given to the Igorots for food.

Terri liked to kid Paz about the primitive tribe of savage natives known as the Igorots.

"Have something to eat, Paz," Terri offered. "I think you'll like the brain sandwiches."

Paz only shrugged.

Terri introduced Glen to Paz with the disclaimer: "You better watch out for him. He has a thing for foreign women."

"Nice to meet you," Glen said, taking her hand, which he kissed and clung to.

"Likewise," Paz said before playfully disentangling herself. "I'd like to eat you," she told Glen. Terri explained to Glen that the comment was not sexual. Paz came from a tribe of headhunters in the Philippines.

Paz greeted Anna and Dinty and then said, "Paz is Spanish for peace and Militante is Spanish for militant, so you see, my name is a contradiction in terms. My name is an oxymoran."

You're a moran, Terri thought to herself.

"I can't help it that I have a split personality," Paz protested. "One half of me is calm and peaceful, and the other half is hostile and warlike. I'm just a simple, humble, poor girl from the Philippines."

Paz was so simple and humble that she made Dickens's Uriah Heep seem like an egomaniac.

"No one ever thinks that I'm from the Philippines," Paz continued. "They think I'm either Chinese or Japanese or Korean or

Vietnamese or Thai or Cambodian or Laotian or who knows what else. That's despite the fact that 11 percent of the Philippine population lives outside the country. That's the highest percentage of expatriates for any nation on earth."

Paz was very oriental-looking even though she had Spanish blood running though her veins. Many Filipinos were of Spanish descent because Spain had once ruled the Philippines.

Paz was slightly taller than the average Pinay. She was five feet, four inches. Her bouffant hairstyle made her seem even taller. Paz was proud of her shiny, slick raven-black hair. She often wore her hair straight and parted in the middle, but today she had just come from the beauty parlor. Terri made a favorable comment about her friend's new china doll hairstyle. Paz was wearing amber earrings that matched the color of her exquisite almond-shaped eyes. Her eyebrows were plucked as thin as two wires. The only flaws in her appearance were her hands, small brown monkey paws with bitten nails no manicurist's art could disguise.

"Nobody wants a penniless girl from the Philippines," Paz said despondently.

"That's not true," Terri said calmly. "St. Louis is a Filipino-friendly city. It all stems from the Philippine Exhibition, which was the largest and most popular attraction at the 1904 St. Louis World's Fair. The Filipinos had seventy thousand exhibits. The Philippine Islands were acquired from Spain in 1898 after the Spanish-American War. Americans were eager to learn about their new possession."

Paz did not seem impressed.

"Let me order you something to eat and drink, Imelda," Terri said to Paz. Terri often referred to Paz as Imelda Marcos, the famous first lady of the Philippines who was known for her undue extravagance.

"You know I hate it when you call me that," Paz said painfully. "You hurt me. I am nothing like Imelda Marcos. I'm just a poor, simple girl from the Philippines. I don't aspire to great wealth. You make it sound like all Filipinos are after money. I'm just a simple girl. I only own three dresses and only four pairs of shoes."

"Whatever you say, Imelda," Terri concluded.

"You don't like Filipinos?" Paz asked.

"That's not true at all," Terri replied. "God should have made everyone Filipino. If Adam and Eve had been Filipino, we'd all still be living in paradise." Terri was a Filipinophile and did not suffer from Filipinophobia.

"Why is that?" Paz asked skeptically.

Terri paused and then said in a matter-of-fact voice, "They would have eaten the snake and not the apple."

Paz did not find this amusing. "Nobody wants a plain-looking girl from the Philippines." She groaned.

"You're beautiful," Terri exclaimed. "You're drop-dead gorgeous."

It is a common trait among Filipinas to underestimate the extent of their beauty.

Paz began talking to Dinty, who had been stationed in the Philippines during World War II. Although she liked talking about herself, she eagerly listened to what Dinty had to say. This seemed to cheer her up. Dinty told Paz all about his wartime experiences as an Army paratrooper who had helped liberate the Philippines. He had been wounded in battle and still carried shrapnel in his body. He had fallen in love with a beautiful Filipino girl, but he had been wounded and shipped home before he had a chance to propose to her. She had been the great love of his life. She had looked exactly like Paz. When Dinty mentioned this remarkable resemblance, Paz said curtly, "We all look alike." When she saw that Dinty was hurt by her comment, Paz sought to make amends by asking, "Do you think you will ever go back to the Philippines?"

"I shall return!" Dinty proclaimed. "I knew Doug MacArthur. He was my commanding officer. It was me who suggested he buy all his corncob pipes from the Missouri Meerschaum Company in Washington, Missouri. I also knew Rod Serling, who was a paratrooper in the Philippines during World War II."

"You knew Rod Serling?" Paz exclaimed, very impressed. "I love the *Twilight Zone*."

After hearing Dinty tell Paz about his affair with a Filipina during World War II, Terri tried to picture Paz as the war bride of an American soldier stationed in the Philippines during World War II.

Then, Terri pictured Paz being raped by a Japanese soldier stationed in the Philippines during World War II. Dinty had extolled the superiority of Filipinas. Filipinas spoke English fluently, unlike women from other Asian countries. Filipinas were Christians, whereas women from other Asian nations were mainly Buddhists. Filipinas were leaner and more petite. And lastly, Filipinas were superior lovers for they had hot Spanish blood coursing through their veins.

Glen had been listening to the conversation and stated it was a common misconception that Douglas MacArthur had said "I shall return!"

Glen had a smile on his face. "This is what he actually said." Glen mimicked Arnold Schwarzenegger and slowly declared...... "I'll be back!"

Sydney Melbourne came over to see what Paz wanted to order, and Terri introduced the two girls.

"Nice to meet you, Paz," Sydney said, bowing, making a long, ninety-degree bend at the waist.

"I'm not Japanese," Paz said irritably. "You don't have to bow to me. I'm from the Philippines."

"I'm Sydney Melbourne from Australia. Many Orientals live in Australia."

"Are you from Sydney?" Paz asked.

"No," Sydney replied.

"Melbourne?"

"No."

"Where are you from, then?"

"Perth," Sydney said, pronouncing the name very slowly.

Dinty overheard this conversation and recited a poem: "There was a young lady from Perth, who dreaded the thought of childbirth. As her waist-line got tighter, she said she'd get lighter, hoping it was just natural girth!"

"I'm not pregnant," Sydney exclaimed.

"I'll have another brain sandwich," Terri said. "What will you have, Paz?"

"I'll also have a brain sandwich," Paz said. "And a Bud Right." Orientals pronounce the letter *L* as though it were the letter *R*.

ABC's *Wide World of Sports*, the program that always followed *The Happy Hooker Show*, had been preempted for the running of the Belmont Stakes. Terri and Paz walked over to the bar to watch the TV because there was a woman jockey riding in the Belmont. The two girls were followed by Brent and Wade, two Stag Club regulars who spent their time playing pool until some fresh female talent came in.

"I'm gonna get me some Asian ass," Wade said, referring to Paz.

"Okay," Brent agreed. "You take the Oriental. I'll take the Occidental." The two guys were dressed shabbily in blue jeans and white T-shirts. Brent was wearing a cap that advertised farm equipment, and Wade was wearing a cap that advertised chewing tobacco. Brent took a swig from a bottle of Budweiser. Wade stuffed a wad of chewing tobacco into his mouth, the same brand that was advertised on his cap. Both guys were overweight, and their faces were puffy. Brent and Wade swaggered over to the bar. They had the poise of good old boys.

Brent sat next to Terri and placed his bottle of Budweiser on the bar. He moved his barstool a little closer to Terri. Wade sat next to Brent. A commercial for exercise equipment was on TV, and a physically fit man was demonstrating how to get rock-hard abs.

"How are your abs?" Wade asked Brent.

Brent leaned back and patted his large beer belly. "I've got Anheuser-Busch abs," he replied. "I've got six-pack abs…from drinking too many six-packs of Anheuser-Busch products."

Brent engaged Terri in conversation, and Wade moved over to sit next to Paz. "What the puck," the girl from the Philippines said as Wade brushed against her.

"You're hot, baby," Wade said salaciously. "You look like a Bangkok bar girl."

"I'm from the Philippines, not Thailand," Paz said, pursing her lips together, trying to hold back her anger.

"We're a couple of good old boys from Illinois," Brent told Terri, who was puffing away at a cigarette. Smoke was encircling her head like a wreath.

Terri looked at Brent and then edged her barstool away from him. "I don't think you're good old boys," she said suddenly. "I think you're bad young men."

"We're volunteer firemen," Brent said brashly. "We saw smoke and came over to investigate."

Terri quickly put out her cigarette. "I don't like firemen," she said. "A bunch of fat guys who sit around and do nothing all day. And they keep demanding more and more money for sitting around and doing nothing all day. And on top of all of that, they act like we're supposed to treat them like heroes for sitting around and doing nothing all day."

"Can I buy you a drink, honey?" Brent asked. "What are you drinking?"

"What good are firemen anyway?" Terri continued. "What good does it do to keep half a building from burning down? The owner will just have to pay a fortune to have the rest of the building torn down. It would be cheaper to let the fire consume the whole building."

"We're not just firemen," Brent said haughtily. "We're also a pair of medics."

"It makes me want to puke when I hear about firemen putting their lives on the line to protect us," Terri added. "When a fireman dies in the line of duty, it's usually not from burns or smoke but from a heart attack...because he was out of shape...from sitting around and doing nothing all day."

Brent slid his barstool up against Terri, and their knees touched.

"I am not interested in men who are only looking for casual sex," Terri hissed, backing away from Brent.

"I am not looking for casual sex," Brent said defiantly. "I'm looking for...formal sex."

Wade started to make a move on Paz. "Get lost!" she cried. "I don't like first responders!"

"We're not first responders," Wade admitted. "We're second responders. We go in when it's safe."

Dinty employed an off-duty St. Louis policeman named Mike Dolan as the Stag Club's bouncer. Mike was a burly man who learned how to become a bouncer by watching the 1989 movie *Roadhouse* starring Patrick Swayze. Mike followed the three simple rules of bouncing as laid out in the movie. Firstly, never underestimate your opponent. Expect the unexpected. Secondly, never start anything inside the bar. Take it outside. And thirdly, be nice.

Mike had just arrived, and he was temporarily working behind the bar until later, when he would check IDs at the door. Mike always tended bar until the Stag Club became crowded. Then he had to keep his eyes peeled for troublemakers, drunks, and underage drinkers. If he had to physically eject someone, he would do it, but he didn't like resorting to violence. He would seek to resolve a problem peacefully if he could.

"If you don't stop bothering these young ladies, I'm going to run you in," Mike told Brent and Wade, who were always looking for trouble. It was a nightly ritual for Mike to issue warnings to these two barroom Lotharios.

"We was only funnin', and there's nothing you can do about that," Wade grunted.

"You can't go to jail for what you're thinking," Brent said defensively.

"Yeah, or for that phweet-phew look in your eye," Wade added, flapping his fingers back and forth in a suggestive manner.

These two young men made Terri think of the swinish volunteer firemen in the movie *Ragtime* who wound up getting killed by Coalhouse Walker Jr.

Mike Dolan escorted the two sleazoid firemen back to the pool table.

Now it was time for Dinty's nightly show, and he sat down at the piano and said, "Friends, Romans, and country fans, lend me your ears." The audience applauded loudly, and there were whoops and hollers.

The crowd always loved Dinty's country music, which he played from the heart. Dinty looked toward Terri, who was still sitting with Paz at the bar. After adjusting the microphone, he began playing the Ray Price classic *For the Good Times*, which seemed to sum up all that poor Terri had just gone through with her no-account boyfriend.

"Don't look so sad, I know it's over," Dinty sang plaintively. Terri gave a thumbs-up signal. "But life goes on, and this old world will keep on turning." Terri raised her cigarette lighter and slowly waved the flame to show Dinty that she approved of the song he had chosen. "Let's just be glad we had some time to spend together. There's no need to watch the bridges that we're burning."

Couples began slow-dancing to the music. Glen moved onto the dance floor and motioned for Terri to join him. "Why don't you find someone to dance with," Terri suggested to Paz. Paz nodded as Terri dismounted from the barstool and walked over to be with Glen. A respectable-looking young man was drinking alone at the other end of the bar. Paz sashayed over to him and said with an exaggerated Filipina accent, "Hi, Joe…buy me a drink."

As she passed Dinty, Terri whispered in his ear, "I'm going to dance with Glen, and when the time is right, play something romantic to get us started."

On the dance floor, Glen took Terri in his arms and asked, "Do you know the Texas two-step?"

"No," Terri replied, "but I do know the Tennessee quick-step."

"What's that?"

"That's what you do when you've got diarrhea."

With great difficulty, Glen taught Terri the Texas two-step, which is a progressive dance that proceeds counter-clockwise around the floor. Terri and Glen quick-stepped around the perimeter of the dance floor, while the other couples were slow-dancing.

"Let's slow down the pace a little bit," Terri advised, hooking her left thumb around Glen's belt. She rested her head against his chest. She signaled to Dinty that now was the time for him to sing a romantic love song.

Dinty stopped what he was playing and made a seamless transition to *Blue Moon* by Rodgers and Hart, a selection from the *Great American Songbook*.

"Blue moon," Dinty wailed. "You saw me standing alone, without a dream in my heart, without a love of my own." Terri snuggled even closer to Glen. "Blue moon," Dinty continued in his sonorous baritone voice. "You knew just what I was there for. You heard me saying a prayer for someone I really could care for. And then there suddenly appeared before me. The only one my arms will ever hold. I heard somebody whisper 'Please adore me.' And when I looked the moon had turned to gold."

Terri was now dancing with her feet off the floor. She was standing on top of Glen's shoes as she whispered into his ear, "I think you're a Hunk."

"No way," Glen exclaimed. "My ancestors were Austrian, not Hungarian."

"No, no," Terri said quickly. "I mean you're extremely attractive."

"Blue moon," Dinty concluded. "Now I'm no longer alone. Without a dream in my heart. Without a love of my own."

Sydney Melbourne was becoming angrier by the minute as she watched Terri and Glen dance so intimately. Sydney also provided entertainment at the Stag Club. She filled in for Dinty when he needed to rest his voice. She had come to the United States to pursue a career as a country singer, and she loved singing country songs for the Stag Club audience. People in Australia had told Sydney to go to a place called Nashville, and she thought they meant Nashville, Illinois, which is just across the Mississippi River from St. Louis. At least, that's the story Sydney always told when asked how she ended up working at a dive honky-tonk in South St. Louis.

Sydney took the stage and the microphone. Dinty remained at his piano to provide accompaniment. Sydney had a bottle of Southern Comfort in her hand, and she took a drink. She was a big fan of Janis Joplin, who enjoyed quaffing Southern Comfort. "I just love my Southern Comfort," Sydney said. "It's made right here in St. Louis on the banks of the Mississippi River." Dinty played the lead-in to Sydney's opening number. "Well, I've got a man in Alabam," she sang. "And one or two in Louisian. And when I'm feeling bluer than a piece of turquoise. I go to the arms of those good old boys. And get that Southern Comfort. Whenever my soul aches. Southern Comfort. You make me feel so fine. So fine!"

"I didn't know this was karaoke night," Terri said to Glen as they tried to dance to Sydney's song.

"Sydney is part of the act," Glen remarked casually. "She works here as a singing waitress, although she prefers to be called a waitressing singer."

"She doesn't have the best of voices," Terri commented after listening to *Southern Comfort* for a few minutes. Sydney's throaty, growling rendition of *Southern Comfort* reminded Terri of Conway Twitty, who made the song famous.

Dinty's arrangements helped to disguise Sydney's limited vocal range. She had a smoky, world-weary singing voice, which she used to great effect when performing country songs.

"Well, I was born a coal miner's daughter," Sydney sang in her husky contralto voice reminiscent of Marlene Dietrich.

"That's how she got lung disease," Terri whispered to Glen. "She sings like a canary in a coal mine."

"In a cabin on a hill in Butcher Holler. We were poor, but we had love. That's the one thing that Daddy made sure of. He shoveled coal to make a poor man's dollar." Sydney moaned the rest of the song, wrapping up with the lines: "Well, a lot of things have changed since way back then. And it's so good to be back home again. Not much left but the floor. Nothing lives here anymore. Except the memories of a coal miner's daughter…Anthracite…Lignite…Bituminous… coal miner's daughter."

Sydney glared at Glen as she began another song: "I hate to see that evening sun go down. Hate to see that evening sun go down. 'Cause, my baby, he's gonna leave this town. Feelin' tomorrow like I feel today. If I'm feelin' tomorrow like I feel today. I'll pack my trunk and make my getaway. St. Louie woman with her diamond ring. Pulls my man around by her apron string. If it weren't for powder and her perfumed hair. The man I love wouldn't have gone nowhere, nowhere. I got the St. Louis blues, just as blue as I can be. 'Cause my man's got a heart like a rock cast in the sea. Or else he would not have gone so far from me."

"You think she's trying to tell me something?" Glen asked rhetorically.

"Why are people always singing the blues?" Anna muttered to herself as she ate dinner at her table. "Why don't they sing the purples instead?"

Paz was now dancing with the man she had hustled for a drink.

The Stag Club bustled with customers, and every table was occupied.

Sydney was now singing *Faded Love* made famous by the great Bob Wills. "I miss you, darling, more and more every day, as heaven would miss the stars above. With every heartbeat, I still think of you and remember our faded love."

"She's really letting me have it," Glen exclaimed, holding Terri closer to make Sydney even more jealous.

Next, Sydney did *There Goes My Everything* made famous by Jack Greene. "There goes my reason for living, there goes the one of my dreams, there goes my only possession, there goes my everything."

After Sydney was through wailing mournful ballads about lost love, Dinty sang *Wolverton Mountain*, which was the hit that launched Claude King's career in 1962. The song was based on a real character, Clifton Clowers, who lived on Wolverton Mountain in Arkansas. Dinty explained to his audience that the song was based on a true story.

"They say don't go on Wolverton Mountain if you're looking for a wife, 'cause Clifton Clowers has a pretty young daughter. He's mighty handy with a gun and a knife…"

Dinty finished the song with the words, "I don't care about Clifton Clowers. I'm gonna climb up on his mountain. I'm gonna take the girl I love."

Dinty paused to catch his breath. He took a quick swallow of beer.

"And now I'm going to do a little stand-up comedy," Dinty said, getting up from the piano bench. He grabbed the microphone and held it close to his lips.

"Just like in the last song about Wolverton Mountain in Arkansas, it was once a common practice for Southern men to go up into the mountains to find a wife. Back in 1902, there was a man named Homer Bull who lived in the Appalachian Mountains in central Virginia. Talking to a friend, Homer learned that on White Oak Mountain, the single women would congregate in caves and wait for men to come courting. Homer was told to stand outside the cave and give the love sound, the love signal, which is 'WOO-OOO, WOO-OOO, WOO-OOO, WOO-OOO,' and if he heard a similar response, then he would go in and introduce himself and that's it. So Homer climbs high atop White Oak Mountain. He finds a large cave and stands outside and gives the love signal: 'WOO-OOO, WOO-OOO, WOO-OOO, WOO-OOO,' and sure enough, a response comes back: 'WOO-OOO, WOO-OOO, WOO-OOO, WOO-OOO,' so he goes in…and he's knocked down by a train."

The audience responded with muffled laughter mixed with moans and groans.

"And that train just happened to be…the Old '97," Dinty shouted, sitting back down at his piano to begin the song *The Wreck of the Old '97*.

Anna hobbled onto the dance floor and asked to cut in and dance with Glen. Terri said it was okay and returned to her seat. As soon as Anna and Glen started dancing, Dinty stopped playing *The Wreck of the Old '97* and switched to *Here Comes the King*, which is the Budweiser theme song. He knew how much Anna hated Anheuser-Busch. He did this to irritate her.

> Here comes the King, here comes the big Number
> One!
> Budweiser beer, the king is second to none.
> Just say Budweiser, you've said it all.
> Here comes the King of Beers, so lift your glass,
> let's hear the call.
> Budweiser Beer's the one that's leading the rest,
> And beechwood aging makes it beer at its best.
> One taste'll tell you so loud and clear.
> There's only one Budweiser beer!
> There's only one Budweiser beer!
> When you say Bud there's nothing left you can say.

When you say Bud, the King is right on his way!
The King is coming, let's hear the call,
When you say Bud you've said it all!

Anna shook her fist playfully at Dinty.

Terri had forgotten about the brain sandwich she ordered, and when she returned to the table, Sydney brought the sandwich over.

"This is your brain," Sydney said hostilely, extending the plate toward Terri. "This is your brain after I get through with it," she continued, tearing up the sandwich and throwing the pieces on the floor. "Any questions?"

"What did you do that for?" Terri lamented. "A brain is a terrible thing to waste."

Terri lunged forward, wrapping her arms around Sydney's large torso. The two girls fell backward on top of a table.

"Catfight," Dinty muttered to himself. Dinty remained behind his large piano, which served as a buffer between him and rowdy patrons. One time, a disgruntled customer had fired a pistol at Dinty, and the bullet lodged in the piano. The bullet hole was still visible. There were dents in the piano from beer bottles thrown by drunken country music fans who didn't like Dinty's singing. Dinty continued to perform while the two girls fought.

Sydney had a pointed head like a gorilla. She head-butted Terri. Sydney weighed at least thirty pounds more than Terri. Sydney picked up a bottle and was going to strike Terri when Paz knocked the bottle away.

This was a classic catfight between a dark-haired girl and a light-haired girl. Terri had black hair, and Sydney was a blonde. There was something titillating and sensual about two girls fighting each other. The crowd roared and howled in the smoky, dimly lit honky-tonk.

Sydney fought dirty and kicked Terri in the stomach. The two girls began to wrestle each other like on the television series *GLOW*, the Gorgeous Ladies of Wrestling.

"I've never had two women fight over me before," Glen murmured to his grandmother.

"You're a lousy singer!" Terri yelled, punching Sydney in the face. Blood spouted from Sydney's nose.

The two young women resorted to scratching, slapping, hair-pulling, and clothes-shredding.

In addition to grabbing and clawing each other, they also traded numerous verbal insults.

This skirmish made the Marlene Dietrich-Una Merkel catfight in *Destry Rides Again* look like table tennis.

Sydney applied a chokehold to Terri, who could not escape. Using a stranglehold was a dirty way to fight. Terri could not break free from the headlock. Suddenly, Paz came over and hit Sydney on top of the head with a chair. Terri broke free and jumped to her feet. Sydney was not hurt by the chair, which shattered in many pieces. Enraged, she had no regard now for the rules of the game. Her anger was hard and hot, and every instinct urged her to punish Terri. Sydney was an experienced fighter, whereas Terri had no experience at all. Sydney twisted Terri's arm and threw her to the floor. Terri tried to get up, but Sydney was upon her. Sydney's every movement was easy, swift, and certain. She would not give in until her rage was satisfied. She fought wildly. The two girls rolled the length of the room. Terri struggled bravely but ineffectually. Finally, Sydney pinned Terri down and kneeled upon her. Terri couldn't move. She was red-faced and weary, while Sydney seemed hardly to have exerted herself.

Dinty continued to perform during all this mayhem, sort of like Nero playing the fiddle while Rome burned. "Oh yes, I'm going to hire a wino to decorate our home," he sang. "So you'll feel more at ease here, and you won't need to roam. We'll take out the dining room table, we'll put a bar along that wall, and a neon sign will point the way to our bathroom down the hall."

Next he did *Behind Closed Doors*, closing with the line, "Oh no one knows what goes on behind closed doors…well, they have some idea of what's going on…behind closed doors."

Finally, Dinty realized that Terri was no match for this gorilla girl, and he wisely stopped the fight. He signaled for Mike Dolan to separate the two girls. Sydney punched Mike Dolan after he helped

Terri to her feet. Terri brushed herself off and smoothed her hair. She was glad the catfight was over.

Glen suggested that it would be a good idea for Terri to leave the Stag Club and come over to his grandmother's house. Terri said goodbye to Dinty and Paz.

Chapter Four

Anna, Glen, and Terri left the Stag Club and headed toward the Grosse mansion across the street.

"Look out!" Terri cried as Anna was nearly run down by a young Caucasian couple jogging down the sidewalk. The couple, dressed in skimpy exercise clothes, paid no attention and continued on their way.

Terri shook her head. "Those people are in good shape physically...but bad shape mentally."

The Grosse mansion was located next to the Altenheim nursing home. Some old people were walking slowly down the sidewalk. They were residents of the Altenheim. They were roaming like zombies, appearing lost and disoriented.

"What are they doing?" Terri shouted, voicing her alarm, as the elderly people lumbered and trudged into the street.

"They're walking for exercise," Glen said calmly and matter-of-factly.

"That looks like *Night of the Living Dead*," Terri exclaimed, watching the sunken-eyed old people risk death trying to cross the street. The senior citizens ignored the passing cars. Terri heard honking and the screeching of brakes.

"Yes," Glen agreed. "*The Walking Dead*."

Terri and Glen helped Anna cross the street. When they reached the other side, Anna paused to catch her breath.

"What's the matter?" Terri asked, continuing to hold Anna's hand, afraid she might fall.

"I always take time to stop and smell the roses," Anna said, sniffing some red roses that were growing on her property.

As Terri approached the house, she recalled the lyrics of an old song: "Her home is on the south side, high upon a ridge, just a half a mile from the Mississippi bridge." But then she remembered the song was about Memphis and not St. Louis. As Terri looked at the old, decaying mansion and then at the deserted brewery building, she thought of the novel *Great Expectations* by Charles Dickens. "You could drink without hurt all the strong beer that's brewed there now, boy." That was a comment Estella had made to Pip as they passed the deserted brewery next to Satis House, where Ms. Havisham lived. Anna was Ms. Havisham, Terri thought. Hope she doesn't put on the rotting purple wedding gown and torn lavender veil. Then Terri pictured Pip in a torn undershirt, kneeling on the sidewalk, shouting, "Estellaaahhh! Estellaaahhh!"

Upon entering the house, Terri looked around at the decor in the main parlor. This was the Purple Parlor. Everything was purple. The walls were painted purple. The drapes, carpets, chairs, and sofas were all purple. "I don't think I'm in Kansas anymore," Terri said in shock.

"No, you're in Missouri," Glen stated.

"Look at all this purple. What did you do…hire a wino to decorate your home?"

On the wall of the parlor were some framed advertising posters from the glory days of the Grosse Brewery. There was one for Burgermeister Beer, featuring the jovial Burgermeister holding a tankard of the frothy amber brew. The bearded Burgermeister was very fat and had on a regal sky-blue tunic surcoat with three embroidered heraldic golden crowns. A small sword was tucked into his wide leather belt. He was wearing medieval boots that reached to his knees. There was a glove on his left hand, but he had removed the glove from his right hand so he could grasp the tankard of beer, which he was bringing to his lips. A Teutonic cape, attached at his neck, hung alongside him and in back of him. On his head was a King Henry the Eighth hat with a gold-tone tapestry finish on the brim. The happy-go-lucky Burgermeister embodied the good life, *der gemutlichkeit*, which was what Grosse beer was all about.

In another advertising poster was Bertha the Beer Girl. For many years, she had been the poster girl for Grosse beer. She looked like a typical German farm girl with blue eyes and blond hair. Her hair was braided into pigtails. She was a heavy, buxom, plain-looking girl with a big smile on her face. She was wearing a long flowing German Dirndl dress with a blue-striped apron and a white blouse. The dress extended all the way to the ground. She was standing outdoors in a garden. She was holding a bottle of Grosse Berliner Beer in her up-raised right hand. There was a pink rose in her left hand. Back in the late 1800s and early 1900s, the general feeling of bar patrons was "If she starts to look good to you, then you've had too much to drink."

"I'd like to introduce you to the original beer babe," Glen said to Terri, pointing at Bertha's poster.

Then Anna cut in, "As you can see, beer advertising was a little bit different back then. The women were all homely, chubby, and fully clothed. And the men were all out of shape, not a bit athletic, with big beer bellies."

A third poster showed Bertha and the Burgermeister together. Bertha was sitting in the Burgermeister's lap.

The advertising posters of Bertha and the Burgermeister helped sell a lot of Grosse beer, but the most successful advertising campaign involved the use of the painting *Custer's Last Battle* by Russell Winchester, the same man who had painted *All Quiet on the Western Frontier*, which depicted a vanquished Indian warrior on his downtrodden horse. The original oil painting *Custer's Last Battle* was hanging in Anna's parlor. The painting was the most valuable possession she owned. The Grosse Brewery had distributed lithographs of the painting throughout the United States. Back in the late 1800s and early 1900s, the painting could be found in taverns from New York City to Los Angeles. The images depicted in the painting were extremely graphic. The savages were beginning to cluster around Custer. The scene was one of carnage and destruction. Indian warriors were engaging in acts of unspeakable violence. The Indians were scalping and mutilating the bluecoats. Custer, in the center of the painting, had just been fatally shot by Rain in the Face. This was a cuter Custer than usual. He looked like Erroll Flynn. Custer, in the throes of death, was standing with both arms raised above him. His head was tilted backward. His eyes were raised to heaven. He appeared to be uttering some last words. The expression on his face was one of exquisite pain, as if he knew that glory was now his forever. Some of the men appeared to be cussing at Custer for leading them into this massacre. Only a handful of bluecoats were still alive as the Indians swarmed from all directions.

Anna stood in front of the painting and began telling Custer jokes.

"When General Custer saw the Indians coming, he held his ground and shouted firmly to his men, 'Retreat Hell…they're in back of us too.'"

Anna walked up to the painting and pointed at a redskin wearing a warbonnet and pointing a rifle at Custer. "This is Chief Rain in the Face. He was a real pain in the ass. He's the Indian who killed Custer." She pointed at another hostile Native American who had overpowered a member of the Seventh Cavalry. "This is Chief Kicking Bull…kicking some bluecoat butt." Anna's hand moved to another Indian warrior. "This is Chief Running Water, and these are his two sons, Hot and Cold. See these squaws over here mutilating the dead. This is the wife of Crazy Horse. Her name was Three Horse, because all she ever did was nag, nag, nag."

Anna paused while the others laughed at her jokes. Then she asked in a serious tone, "What did General Custer say after he was shot at the Little Big Horn?"

"I don't know," Terri said skeptically. "What?"

"I've fallen," Anna proclaimed, raising her arms like Custer in the painting. She tilted her head backward, like the fatally wounded Custer, and looked toward heaven. "And I can't get up!"

Terri tried to stifle her laughter.

"I'm an expert on Custer," Glen said. "I've been a Custer fan all my life. I've done extensive research, and I've read just about every Custer book there is."

"Okay, if you're so smart," Terri needled, "what was the name of General Custer's dog?"

"Blucher," Glen said in a superior tone. "Every time Custer would call his dog by name, all the horses would whinny and rear in the air."

"Why would he name his dog Blucher?" Terri asked.

"Blucher was the name of the Prussian field marshal who helped Wellington defeat Napoleon at the Battle of Waterloo. Custer was an ardent student of military history."

"That's very interesting," Terri said. "I heard that General Custer never touched liquor. Is that true?"

"Yes, that's true," Glen confirmed. "It's sort of ironic that the Grosse Brewery used Custer to help sell beer."

"I think the name Grosse must have hurt your sales," Terri said.

"Not really," Glen said. "The word *gross* didn't have any negative connotations back then. It was just a word like any other."

"Did they worry about drunk driving back then?"

"Not really," Glen said. "Back then, horses were the designated drivers, and as long as they stayed sober, you were okay."

"What were some of your advertising slogans back then?"

"Let's see," Glen said tentatively. "Oh yeah. You only go around once in life…so you have to reach for all the Grosse you can get.

"Go for the Grosseto," Terri snickered.

"When you're out of Grosse…you're really grossed out."

Glen began singing an advertising jingle: "When you say Grosse…you've said a lot of things nobody else can say. When you say Grosse…"

Back in the late 1800s and early 1900s, Grosse had been the largest-selling beer in America.

"For a while," Glen said, "Grosse far outsold all the Milwaukee beers, like Schlitz and Pabst and Miller. The problem became so bad that Milwaukee's economy went into a tailspin. There was widespread unemployment. So one of our advertising slogans was 'Grosse, the beer that made Milwaukee famish.'"

"Is that really true?" Terri asked.

"Yes," Glen said. "Back then, a bottle of beer only cost ten cents, so another one of our advertising slogans was 'If you've got the dime, we've got the beer.'"

Anna pointed to some paintings next to the Custer painting. "These are scenes of Austria," she said, "the country where I was born. My *heimat*…my homeland."

"She was born in the United States," Glen grumbled to Terri. "She's getting worse. She has old timer's disease."

"You mean…Alzheimer's disease," Terri corrected, emphasizing the first syllable of the word Alzheimer's.

"Yeah, right," Glen said. "ALL the lights are on, but nobody's HEIM."

Terri suddenly heard footsteps on the main staircase and realized someone else was in the house. "Is that the resident ghost I hear?" she asked.

"That's our caregiver, Harriet Winslow," Glen said. "I can no longer take care of Anna all by myself, so we hired someone to help out."

Terri and Glen walked to the foot of the stairs and greeted Harriet, who was a heavyset young woman who weighed over two hundred pounds. She was a homeless person until Glen hired her. She was very difficult and hard to get along with, but Glen did not want to fire her and send her back out on the street again.

Glen introduced the two girls. "Terri, this is Harriet Winslow, the health caregiver from hell. Give 'em health care, Harriet."

"Nice to meet you," Terri said tentatively.

Harriet grunted a response. She was a plain-looking and plain-speaking young woman. "You better watch out for him," Harriet began. "One time, he was either drunk or on drugs, and he came on to me."

"I don't remember anything like that happening," Glen said defensively.

"That's because you were either drunk or on drugs."

"Honey, if I came on to you, I must have been either drunk or on drugs."

Harriet was wearing blue scrubs, the uniform of a health care worker. She scoffed at Glen's comment.

"I don't know what she's worried about," Glen continued. "She weighs more than I do. If I would do something she doesn't like, she'd flatten me." Glen paused and then added, "It's been my experience that it's always the fattest, ugliest girls who are the first to yell sexual harassment. It's some kind of ego trip for them. Beautiful, attractive women like for men to notice them."

Harriet began to rant and rave in response to Glen's comments, and she appeared ready to strike Glen with her fist. There were two sides to Harriet. One minute she could be very nice and friendly. The next minute she could be very mean and hostile.

"I thinks she's bipolar," Glen remarked, listening to Harriet's tirade.

"Bipolar?" Harriet inquired. "What does that mean? I hope it's nothing sexual. If Santa Claus opened a workshop at the South Pole, that would make him...bipolar."

"It means you have a split personality," Glen said harshly. "Your emotions run the gamut from extreme euphoria to absolute despair."

Harriet did not wish to comment about her roller-coaster emotions. "Okay, Granny," she barked. "Let's go. It's time for your medicine." Harriet and Anna got on the elevator, which was an original feature of the house. They went up to Anna's second-floor bedroom, where she kept her medicine.

Glen showed Terri a room he was remodeling. He planned to restore the room to its former elegance. He had renovated several other rooms in the house. The room was a mess with sawdust and paint shavings all over the floor. There were numerous power tools, including a saw, lathe, sander, and drill. The smell of fresh paint was in the air. Empty tubes of caulk littered the floor. Terri was reminded of the PBS program *This Old House* and half-expected to see master carpenter Norm Abram come crawling out of the woodwork.

Glen and Terri passed through the kitchen, where Glen got a beer. Then, they walked down the hallway to the Grosse family trophy room.

Terri bumped into a suit of armor as she entered the trophy room. Here's my knight in shining armor, she thought. She gawked at all the animal heads.

Glen gave Terri a tour of his trophy room. "Did you shoot all these animals?" she asked.

"Some of them," Glen replied after taking a swig from the bottle of Grosse beer he had brought with him. "My father, grandfather, and great-grandfather all shot some. Members of the Grosse family are taught from an early age to love hunting, fishing, and the outdoors."

"Did you shoot this wild boar?" Terri asked, pointing to a life-size stuffed wild boar next to the fireplace.

"My great-grandfather killed that boar on an estate he owned in Austria. Boar hunting is very popular in Europe."

"I shot this boar," Glen said, indicating a boar head on the wall next to the gun cabinet. "It was at a game preserve in Texas."

Glen looked around at the multitude of stuffed animal heads and proclaimed, "The only thing missing is a trophy wife."

"How's this?" Terri asked, wrapping her arm around the neck of the wild boar head on the wall. She stared forward with a fixed expression on her face.

"Perfect," Glen exclaimed, framing her image with his hands. "That's the great thing about taxidermy, it goes with everything."

Terri sat down and examined all the objects in the trophy room. In addition to animal heads, there were also some Remington bronzes. She recognized *The Bronco Buster*, which depicted a cowboy on a bucking bronco, and *Coming Through the Rye*, which showed four cowboys on horseback wildly firing their pistols in the air. The Remington painting *A Dash for the Timber* was on the wall. Eight mounted cowboys, pursued by Indians, were galloping for the safety of a stand of trees. One cowboy was shot, and his friend was keeping him from falling out of the saddle. Several of the cowboys were firing back at the Indians.

There were animal heads from all over the world, from African antelope to American elk. Staring at each other from the four walls, and also at startled visitors, were buffaloes, moose, various types of deer and goats, bighorn sheep, and black wolves, just to name a few of the trophies. There was an antique gun case that held shotguns for quail hunting and thirty ought sixes for bigger game. On top of the gun cabinet were stuffed game birds. On a wall was a llama skin rug from Peru. The floor was covered with three big rugs made from the hides of buffaloes, and even the ceiling was covered with the skins of bears and bobcats.

In a corner were blowguns, spears, bows and arrows, and other elementary but sinister weapons of destruction. There was a stuffed fox that a member of the Grosse family had killed during a mounted fox hunt. A large fox-hunting horn was hanging next to the fireplace. Fox hunting was a sport for the wealthy. The Grosses were also avid anglers, and mounted game fish were displayed throughout the room. There was a huge swordfish named Oscar that Glen had caught off the coast of Acapulco. There was a life-size African lion in the game room, but this trophy had not been bagged in Africa by a member of the Grosse family. Grandfather Grosse had shot this lion in 1916 on an island in the Mississippi River. On the wall were framed newspaper stories of the hunting expedition Grandfather Grosse had made to the island, bringing along his own lion, which he had purchased from a circus that was going out of business. He released the lion on the island. The lion was given a "sporting chance" to get away before Grandfather Grosse and his hunting buddies went after it. They systematically tracked down the beast, and Grandfather Grosse killed it with one shot to the head.

This hunting expedition had received a great deal of criticism by animal rights activists. The lion, however, was not the prize trophy of Grandfather Grosse. His favorite kill was a gigantic polar bear he had bagged on a hunting trip to Churchill, Manitoba, the Polar Bear Capital of the World.

Terri examined the nine-foot-tall stuffed polar bear which hovered menacingly above her. She felt dwarfed by the nine-foot bear.

"This is a bipolar bear," Glen explained.

"A polar bear fell on me!" Terri shouted, pretending the bear was attacking her. "Ahhhhhh!" she cried in alarm.

"Check out the palmation on that buck!" Glen exclaimed, pointing to a large deer head with a rack of antlers that measured fifty inches across.

"This is a Medusa Buck with antlers that twist like snakes."

The Grosse Brewery had used hunting and fishing as advertising themes. There was a framed poster of a fisherman reeling in a large trout, and bottles of Grosse beer were chilling in the icy water of the trout stream. Bertha the Beer Girl was duck hunting in another advertising poster. Wearing her long flowing dress, she was sitting in a rowboat with a Golden Retriever and numerous decoy ducks. She held a shotgun in her left hand, and there was a bottle of Grosse beer in her right hand. "The Beer Hunter" was the caption. Guns and alcohol, always a winning combination.

There were some examples of trench art, World War I artillery shell casings that had been turned into lamps with expensive Tiffany lamp shades. Glen turned on a lamp and sat down in a chair. Next to the chair was an antique smoking stand that held Cuban cigars.

He rested his beer bottle on top of the smoking stand and selected a cigar. He lit the cigar and then picked up a book. "There's nothing I like better," he said, "than to settle back with a good read and a good smoke."

Terri spied a decanter of brandy and poured herself a drink. She also poured a drink for Glen. He put down his book and placed his cigar in a buffalo hoof ashtray from the Schwarz Taxidermy Studio in St. Louis. He took a sip of brandy followed by a beer chaser. Many of the animal heads in the room had been prepared by the Schwarz Studio, the oldest taxidermy business in the United States. Frank Schwarz founded his company in St. Louis in 1882.

Terri wandered into Glen's office, which adjoined the trophy room. On the rear wall, there was a portrait of Adolf Hitler next to a Nazi swastika flag. Terri looked around skeptically. Glen came rushing into the room. He seemed anxious. "You're not one of those neo-Nazis are you?" Terri asked Glen.

"Ja wohl," Glen replied, clicking his heels together and giving a Nazi salute. "Ich bin ein neo-Nazi."

Great, Terri thought to herself, *the boy next door who just happens to be a neo-Nazi. Norman Rockwell meets George Lincoln Rockwell.*

"Heil," Glen shouted out, giving another stiff-armed Nazi salute as he faced the portrait of Adolf Hitler.

"Who would have thought it," Terri said. "Neo-Nazis right under our noses."

"You're not going to report me, are you?" Glen asked.

"How could I report you? I think I'm falling in love with you. You big, beautiful, brown-shirted, jack-booted thug."

"Thanks," Glen replied, feeling relief.

"You big, beautiful, street brawling, beerhall-putsching thug."

Glen began to sing the *Horst Wessel Lied*. "The flag on high! The ranks tightly closed! The SA marches with quiet, steady step. Comrades shot by the Red Front and reactionaries march in spirit within our ranks. Clear the streets for the brown battalions. Clear the streets for the storm division! Millions are looking upon the swastika full of hope. The day of freedom and of bread dawns! For the last time, the call to arms is sounded! For the fight we all stand prepared! Adolf Hitler's banners fly over all the streets."

"What would you say to a policeman if he asks if you're a neo-Nazi?" Terri inquired.

"I would say...nicht schuldig!"

"What does your caregiver, Harriet Winslow, think about you being a neo-Nazi?" Terri noticed that Harriet had walked into the other room.

"She doesn't care," Glen said matter-of-factly. "I think she has right wing sympathies. She reminds me of Ilse Koch, the Bitch of Buchenwald."

Suddenly, Terri felt terrible. She contemplated what her marriage to Glen would be like. Her newborn baby would be raised as a neonatal neo-Nazi. She decided to wait before telling Glen that she was expecting a child.

Glen heard Harriet moving around in the adjacent trophy room. She liked looking at the animal heads. Glen indicated to Terri that he was going to have some fun. He picked up his beer bottle and walked to the doorway. When he had Harriet's attention, he drank from the bottle and then waved it in the air. "Hey, baby," he said, slurring his words as though drunk. "How about you and me getting nipple to nipple?"

Harriet made a throw-away gesture and then left the room.

"You and your neo-Nazi friends are against Jews and blacks?" Terri asked.

"Yes," Glen declared, "and we're also against foreigners."

"All foreigners?" Terri questioned.

"Just foreign men, not foreign women."

There were bookcases on both sides of the fireplace. Terri walked over to the bookcase on the left. She saw a copy of *The Turner Diaries* by Andrew Macdonald, which was the bible of the neo-Nazi movement. There were books about Nazi Germany. One shelf was devoted to hunting and fishing books.

Another shelf was given over to books that Anna liked to read. *The Purple Plain* by H. E. Bates. *The Purple Land* by W. H. Hudson. *The Color Purple* by Alice Walker. *A Purple Place for Dying* and the *Long Lavender Look*, both by John D. MacDonald. *Lavender and Old Lace* by Myrtle Reed. There was one book that didn't belong with all the other more exciting titles. On the middle shelf, on the far right side, was a thick volume of *The Economic Consequences of the Peace* by John Maynard Keynes. Terri thought about why such a dull book was mixed in with all the others. Curious, she pulled out the voluminous tome and dusted it off. She quickly paged through the book and replaced it on the shelf, discovering to her surprise there was a doorknob in back. The large book was concealing a hidden doorknob.

Terri was startled by Glen's presence behind her. "I see you like to read John Maynard Keynes," he said succinctly.

"What is this doorknob for?" Terri asked sheepishly.

"This is a Murphy bookcase door," Glen replied. It leads to the subterranean cave system beneath the house.

"I've always wanted to see a secret door," Terri said ebulliently.

"The bookcase door was placed here when Prohibition began in 1920. There was a speakeasy down in the cave. This is an original first edition of *The Economic Consequences of the Peace*, which came out in 1919. The book has been in this same spot all these years."

"That was smart using a dull book to hide the doorknob."

"The speakeasy was never raided by Federal Revenue agents."

Glen opened the squeaking bookcase door. A book fell to the floor, and Terri put it back on the shelf. Glen switched on a light, revealing a wooden stairway that led down into the subterranean cave.

"This is where I work out," he said. "I follow a twelve-step program to keep in shape." He motioned for Terri to follow him. "Every day, I walk up and down these twelve steps for an hour. It's great exercise!"

Cautiously, Terri made her way down the rickety wooden stairs. There was no hand rail to hold.

"Welcome to my man cave!" Glen proclaimed when they had reached the bottom of the stairs. He hit a switch to illuminate the cave.

Terri looked around at the cave system, which extended for miles underneath South St. Louis. The cave was honeycombed with secret passageways, and there was a subterranean lake.

"What's the difference between a stalagmite and stalactite?" she asked.

"A stalagmite rises from the floor of a cave," Glen responded. "A stalactite hangs like an icicle from the roof of a cave."

Glen gave Terri a tour of the microbrewery he had set up in the cave. He used the original copper brew kettle of the Grosse Brewery. The kettle dated back to the 1850s, when the Grosse Brewery first opened for business in St. Louis. The Missouri History Museum wanted the kettle for a special display about St. Louis breweries, but Glen still needed it to brew beer.

Terri looked inside the large kettle at a foaming batch of beer. "So this is where you make your illegal hootch." She laughed. "I half expect to see a dead body in here, like in a horror movie," she said, thinking of the 1953 movie *House of Wax*, where Vincent Price falls into a vat of molten wax.

Terri heard the sound of water dripping from the stalactites hanging above. She heard the flutter of wings as a bat dive-bombed past her head. Her foot suddenly caught on a rock, and with a loud shriek, she fell to the floor, her hands landing on slippery limestone worn away by years of water rushing through the cave. She scraped her face on a stalagmite. There was blood alongside her nose.

"Are you okay?" Glen asked, giving her a handkerchief to wipe away the blood.

"I'm fine," Terri replied, removing the blood from her nose.

Glen hired homeless people to help him out in the brewery. The indigent people lived in a tent city next to the river. There was a cave entrance alongside the river near the makeshift shanty town. That was the same secret entrance used by the Underground Railroad before the Civil War. Concealed by shrubs and bushes, the entrance was also used by rum runners during Prohibition. A homeless man had come in through the secret passageway to check on the beer that was brewing in the copper kettle.

"Jesus saves!" he mumbled, giving Terri a curious look. He had a slovenly appearance. He was dressed in tattered clothes. He appeared to be mentally ill.

"No, he doesn't," Terri retorted. "He has a beard."

"I said 'Jesus saves,' not *shaves*," the homeless man responded.

"What is it like being a bum?" she asked.

"Please!" the man exclaimed. "I prefer the term *transient*."

The homeless man stirred the malt-and-hops mixture in the kettle, and then Glen told him he could leave.

There were several cylindrical-conical fermentation tanks where the wort-and-yeast mixture was aging.

Terri reached into an open bin containing green Cascade pellet hops from the Cascade Mountains of Oregon. Cascade hops are the most widely used hops by craft breweries in the United States. Terri picked up one of the dark-green elongated hop cones and placed it in her mouth. The hops had a pleasant aroma and tasted like citrus fruit.

"Don't eat that," Glen said. "You don't want to turn into a hop head."

There were rows and rows of strong wooden barrels where Glen aged his beer. The barrels consisted of wooden staves held together with iron hoops.

Terri and Glen made their way deeper into the bowels of the earth. They were now underneath the river's bed, and water fell in drops from above.

Terri thought of the short story *The Cask of Amontillado* by Edgar Allan Poe.

"Here's some of the finished product," Glen said, indicating a rack of beer bottles on the wall of the cave.

"How many bottles are up there?" Terri asked.

"Oh…about ninety-nine," Glen replied. "Take one down."

Terri laughed as she reached for a bottle of Grosse Berliner Beer. Glen took out his Swiss Army knife and opened the bottle for her.

The temperature in the cave was a constant forty-five degrees, and the beer was nice and cold. Terri took a trial sip of the frothy urine-colored beer.

"Tastes like…Schlitz," she announced after the beer had trickled down her throat.

Glen explained that the Schlitz family of Milwaukee and the Grosse family had been very close. Friedrich Schlitz wanted to marry Anna. He was her husband's cousin.

Glen printed all the beer labels himself. On each label, the name Grosse was spelled with an Eszett, which is a common German symbol, shaped like a cotter pin, that indicates a Double S. In the German language, an Eszett is also called a Scharfes S.

Glen needed another beer. He took down a bottle of oatmeal stout and dusted it off. "This is one of my newest beers," he said. "Grosse Breakfast Beer. It's made with oatmeal." Glen decided it was too late in the day to have a breakfast beer, so he placed the bottle back on the rack and made a new selection. "This is my latest creation," he proclaimed, showing Terri a bottle without any label. "This is my new light beer. I haven't come up with a name for it yet. It has half the carbs of Bud Light. Only ninety-nine calories."

"How do you make light beer?" Terri asked.

"I just add water to regular beer. That's all I do."

"I'm going to help you come up with the perfect name for your light beer," Terri said enthusiastically. "How about Burgermeister Light?"

"No way," Glen said. "That big fat tub of lard can't represent a light beer."

"This beer is really Grosse," Terri said after taking a few more sips of Berliner. "Are you sure the name Grosse didn't hurt your sales?"

"No," Glen reiterated. "The word *gross* didn't have any negative connotations back then. It was just a word like any other."

"How did you learn how to make beer?" Terri inquired.

"I majored in beer when I went to college," Glen said seriously.

"Most students major in beer when they go to college," Terri informed Glen.

"No, I mean I actually studied how to make beer when I went to college. I'm a graduate of the Siebel Institute of Technology in Chicago, where I became a master brewer. I took the World Brewing Academy's Master Brewer course, which is a twenty-week program designed and presented by the Siebel Institute and Doemens Academy in Munich, Germany. As the final step of my training, I studied how to make beer in Munich, the beer capital of the world."

Glen dusted off an enormous book that contained many Grosse family beer recipes. "I am remaining true to the Grosse family tradition," Glen said, "faithfully brewing beer just like it was done in the old days. I am recreating the same delicious Grosse beer that St. Louisans enjoyed one hundred years ago."

"That little old beer maker you," Terri observed. She was thinking of the famous advertising campaign for Italian-Swiss Colony Wine about the little old winemaker. Terri was Italian Swiss. Her mother was of Italian extraction, and her father was of Swiss descent. Terri liked to joke that one half of her was calm and peaceful, and the other half was fiery and hot-blooded.

"The Grosse Brewery was bigger than Anheuser-Busch at the turn of the century," Glen said sadly. "If it weren't for a quirk of fate, it would have been me with the big bucks and the Clydesdales and the bull terriers."

Glen pointed out where the Catacombs Cabaret had been located during Prohibition. There was a rotting wooden stage, where Anna had performed for her patrons.

A plaster of Paris formation, with a painting, had been constructed as a backdrop for the stage. The painting was of the Grossglockner, the largest mountain in Austria. The snow-covered mountain was surrounded by evergreen forests, and there was a lake down below. The word *gross* means "big" in the German language.

The word *glockner* means "bell" in German. The Big Bell Mountain has the shape of a large bell. Terri looked up at the roof of the cave and saw rusting spotlights directed at the stage. The spotlights still worked and were part of the cave's electrical system. The old wooden bandstand was off to the side.

Glen took Terri in his arms, and they swayed across the dance floor of the Catacombs Cabaret. Terri felt like a flapper in the Roaring Twenties. Now, all she needed was a short skirt, bobbed hair, a long string of pearls, a cloche hat, a feathered boa, and a headband with a feather. Glen sang a tune popular in the 1920s. "You're the cream in my coffee, you're the salt in my stew," he began.

"Is it Dinty Moore Stew?" Terri asked rhetorically. She pictured Anna entertaining here in the Roaring Twenties. Anna epitomized the glitz, glamor, and promise of the post–World War I era.

There had been an illegal casino behind solid steel doors in the back of the cave. Terri and Glen passed through the steel doors to check out the site of the cave casino. Terri tried to imagine all the high rollers who had gambled here in this secluded spot. Babe Ruth was probably here, gambling, drinking, and womanizing.

"Thanks for showing me your microwave brewery!" Terri said, taking another look at Glen's extensive brewing operation as she followed him out of the cave.

"Microbrewery, not microwave brewery," Glen corrected.

The two young people then left the cavern.

Glen wanted to show Terri his houseboat before darkness arrived. Terri and Glen made their way down the precipitous path to the boat dock. The stone stairway veered sharply to the left through dense undergrowth. They passed close to the Altenheim nursing home. Some elderly residents were sitting out on a terrace.

"This place is called the Altenheim," Glen told Terri. "That's German for old folks home."

"Welcome to Club Med!" a senior citizen called out to them.

"The Med stands for medicine!" another oldster yelled.

"Those people are a little weird," Glen hinted to Terri.

"What did you say the name of this place is? The Alzenheim?"

The two young people continued down the slippery path, holding on to small trees to keep from falling. They found it necessary to remove wild grape vines that covered the trail. The vines were everywhere, completely enveloping bushes and small trees. Also known as the riverbank grape, the wild grape vines produced bunches of delicious purple grapes. Terri and Glen helped themselves to the grapes.

Terri thought of Isaiah chapter 5 about a vineyard on a fruitful hill that brought forth wild grapes.

"There's the House of the Good Shepherd," Glen said, indicating an old mansion that once belonged to a well-known riverboat captain named Isaiah Byars. Isaiah was the neighbor of the Grosse family for many years. He died in 1935 and left his property to a group of Catholic nuns, who established the House of the Good Shepherd.

"What's the House of the Good Shepherd?" Terri questioned, munching on a handful of grapes.

"It's sort of a halfway house…for girls…who went all the way," Glen responded, picking some grapes off a vine. "It's a home for unwed mothers. A maternity home." He dangled the cluster of grapes above his mouth and nibbled on them.

Both the Altenheim and the House of the Good Shepherd were interested in buying Anna's property to expand their operations.

Terri noticed some pregnant women milling about on the lawn over at the House of the Good Shepherd.

There were over three hundred steps leading down the side of the limestone bluff. These were the Osage Steps, so named because an Osage Indian Mound was located here. The Grosse Mansion was built on top of an Indian burial mound, but no ghosts of Indian warriors had haunted the house yet.

"This spot is called Lover's Leap," Glen said, referring to an outcropping of rock hundreds of feet above the river. "A jilted Indian girl committed suicide here many years ago."

Terri walked out on the rock overhang and pretended she was going to fling herself to her death.

"Don't do it, baby!" Glen yelled. "You're young. You have your whole life ahead of you."

They continued their trek down Lavender Hill, eventually reaching the bottom. Terri saw the homeless camp which was located near Glen's houseboat. There were tents, mattresses, and hypodermic needles. Various articles of clothing were scattered about. She walked over to a smoldering campfire and talked to a haggard-looking woman who was drinking a Grosse beer. The homeless woman worked in Glen's microbrewery, helping her husband, who was the man Terri had talked to in the cave. He was standing nearby.

"This is my first beer of the day," the homeless woman told Terri, raising the bottle, her words badly slurred. Her name was Sherry. She had been assaulted by her husband a few weeks earlier, and her face was still showing the signs. So was her right arm, a softball sized knot at the elbow, the entire limb reddish-black. A walker was in front of her so she could steady herself after several drinks. Her husband's name was Zack. He did not like his wife talking to strangers. Terri started to back away.

"I haven't eaten in three days," Sherry told Terri.

"I admire your willpower," Terri said.

"I haven't eaten because I don't have the money for food," Sherry lamented.

Glen allowed the homeless people to come aboard his houseboat to use the head. They were grateful for the chance to clean up. Glen was careful not to leave anything valuable aboard his boat. He tried to help the homeless people by giving them employment in his microbrewery, and he also provided food for them.

Terri contemplated why people became homeless. Although it seemed hard to believe, some people were homeless by choice. They were too proud to accept help. *That is very sad,* Terri thought. The tent communities were a refuge for homeless people who didn't want to be constrained by the rules of formal shelters.

Sherry and Zack had been living in their van in a Walmart parking lot until they lost their van in a traffic accident. Walmart's policy of allowing overnight stays in their parking lots was intended to boost sales, but had the tangential effect of creating a subculture around its locations.

Terri studied this dark underbelly of American life. This place was like a small Hooverville, she thought. In 1930, St. Louis had the largest Hooverville in America, consisting of four distinct sectors that were racially integrated. The Hooverville was located along the riverfront and depended on private funding from wealthy St. Louisans. There was a mayor who was elected by the residents. There were churches and other social institutions. The Hooverville remained a viable community until 1936, when the federal Works Progress Administration demolished the shanties in the name of civic progress.

This homeless encampment was called Hopeville, and there was a large sign that said WELCOME TO HOPEVILLE. The camp was on Glen's property, so no government officials could come and run off the people or tear down the small wooden shacks that had been constructed. In Hopeville, there were five wooden shanties and twenty tents. Terri learned that Zack was the mayor of Hopeville, so he and his wife lived in one of the wooden shacks.

An extension cord stretched from Glen's houseboat to the homeless camp so the residents could have some electricity.

Built in 1988, Glen's houseboat was a fifty-foot Gibson with a fiberglass hull. The boat was named *My Way* because Glen loved that Frank Sinatra song written by Paul Anka. Glen took good care of his boat, which was designed for freshwater travel. The boat had a 270-horsepower inboard MerCruiser engine. There was a marine radio, a depth sounder, a vapor detector, a fire extinguisher, a heater, and an air conditioner. A Westerbeke Generator provided the power. There was a convection oven, a stove, a microwave, and a full-size refrigerator. The sink had a foot pump. The head had a rain locker. That's nautical talk meaning the bathroom had a shower stall. There was a composting toilet.

Glen gave Terri a tour of his houseboat. She was impressed by all the galley cupboard space. She also liked the large pantry and large closet. She thought the drapes looked a little faded and needed to be replaced. When she married Glen, this would also be her houseboat.

Chapter Five

Glen and Terri climbed back up the Osage Steps and found Anna sitting out on the terrace in her favorite spot underneath a mulberry tree. It was twilight time. Anna loved this time of day. Everything was so…purple. Looking eastward across the river, Anna was inspired by the purple-colored clouds that marked the end of day. The sky was a majestic shade of lavender.

"She walks in beauty like the night…Lord Byron," Glen told Terri as they approached Anna, who was lost in contemplation.

The *Belle of Calhoun* floating casino was moored directly across the river from the Grosse mansion. There were two large billboards on the shore alongside the boat. Your Ship Has Just Come In, one of the billboards said. The message on the other billboard was The Luck Boat, Exciting and New, Come Aboard, We're Expecting You! The lights of the floating casino had just been turned on. There was only a skeleton crew on the boat, preparing for the grand opening on June 23.

"That boat was named after me," Anna remarked, staring at her old portrait, which had been reproduced in gigantic fashion on the billboards. The young and beautiful Anna was looking back at the old and withered Anna. On the billboards, Anna was described as Lady Luck, Dame Fortune, and Lady Bountiful. There were also pictures of the boat with the message, The Belle of Calhoun, It's the Ultimate Floating Crap Game.

Glen noticed lights on the casino dock where he would moor his houseboat on June 23. He would take Anna, Dinty, and Terri across the river. It was a great shortcut.

Anna stretched out her arms toward the dark river in a curious way. "They're building a hotel over there for the casino patrons," she said, "but it won't be completed for several more months."

"I never thought there would be gambling in the St. Louis area," Glen said, "but now they've turned the Mississippi Valley into Glitter Gulch."

Anna had lit some citronella candles to ward off mosquitoes. After darkness fell, she began singing *Midnight, The Stars, and You*, which was one of the numbers she had performed in the Catacombs Cabaret in the 1920s.

> Midnight with the stars and you
> Midnight and a rendezvous
> Your eyes held a message tender
> Saying "I surrender all my love to you"
> Midnight brought us sweet romance
> I know all my whole life through
> I'll be remembering you
> Whatever else I do
> Midnight with the stars and you

Terri tried to remember where she had heard this song before, and then it came to her. This was the creepy and haunting tune played at the end of the 1980 movie *The Shining*, starring Jack Nicholson. *That has to be one of the greatest endings in movie history,* Terri thought. Al Bowlly, accompanied by the Ray Noble Orchestra, sang in an eerie, hollow voice as the camera zoomed in on a framed photograph of Jack Nicholson at a Fourth of July Ball in 1921. An authentic photograph from the 1920s was used with Jack Nicholson's head superimposed on one of the men in front. The producer didn't want to hire a lot of extras and have them dress up in period costumes. There was one slight error. The photo appears to have been taken at a New Year's Eve party for a man was blowing a New Year's horn. Also, the people were dressed in formal clothes, more appropriate for New Year's Eve than the Fourth of July. Ray Noble was an

English orchestra leader. Al Bowlly died in 1941 when his flat was hit by a German bomb during the Blitz on London.

There must be a lot of ghosts around this house, Terri thought. The ghosts of Osage warriors who were buried here in the Indian Mound. The ghosts of flappers and bootleggers who had come to parties here in the Roaring Twenties. Perhaps even the ghost of William Grosse, who had committed suicide here in 1920. The Grosse mansion was located on the site of an Indian burial ground, just like the Overlook Hotel in *The Shining.* Maybe the blood of Indian warriors would come pouring out through the elevator doors.

"The stars are ageless, aren't they?" Anna said after finishing her song.

"The stars are in alignment tonight," Glen added. "That's a good sign."

Terri took a stroll around the terrace, while Glen and Anna had a private conversation.

"A girl like that is only after one thing," Anna informed her grandson.

"Yeah...my body," Glen replied.

"No, no," Anna said caustically, punching Glen. "I mean money. I hope you told her we don't have any. She probably thinks we're loaded."

"We're talking about getting married," Glen said.

"That was quick." Anna gasped.

"We've known each other all our lives," Glen explained.

Terri tried to picture the Gatsbyesque parties that had taken place here in the Roaring Twenties. She imagined elegant men and women sipping champagne beneath the stars while a full-piece orchestra played romantic Jazz music. "You can't repeat the past," Nick Carraway told Gatsby. To which Gatsby replied, "Why of course you can!" Terri thought it was possible to repeat the past. She remembered being here on this terrace when she was a little girl, visiting Glen and his family. That was in the 1960s. Everything looked about the same. Nothing much had changed. The ornamental fountain in the middle of the terrace was still spouting water as faithfully as in the 1920s. Terri imagined flappers jumping into the fountain like in *The Great Gatsby*. She and Glen had gone swimming in the fountain when they were children. Suddenly, like Zelda Fitzgerald jumping into New York City's Union Square fountain, Terri raced forward and leaped fully clothed into the fountain.

Glen and his grandmother were alarmed. They offered assistance to Terri, but she decided to remain in the cool water.

"What did you do that for?" Glen asked after first proffering his hand.

"I'm hot and wanted to cool off," Terri remarked, eluding Glen's grasp. She splashed around in the water and then dove beneath the surface to see if there were any coins at the bottom of the fountain. She stayed underwater for close to a minute. After resurfacing, she asked Glen if he remembered swimming with her in the fountain when they were children.

Eventually, Terri emerged from the fountain, and Glen gave her a towel to dry off.

"You'll need some dry clothes," Anna said. "I'll let you wear some of mine. I think my current clothes would be too large for you, so we'll go up in the attic and find some clothes I wore when I was your age."

Anna led Terri back into the house and up the grand staircase. As she climbed the stairs, Terri studied the portraits of Grosse family members that hung on the wall. She asked Anna to identify the various people. Terri thought she noticed a resemblance between Glen and his great-great-grandfather Grosse, who had come to the United States from Austria in 1840, a penniless young man with all his worldly possessions inside a large wooden steamer trunk. Anna now kept some of her old clothes in the trunk, which was stored in the attic. Anna and Terri climbed a second flight of stairs to the attic, which was used only as storage space. The cluttered attic, like something out of a horror movie, gave Terri the creeps. Anna and Terri walked across the creaking floorboards to the far corner of the attic, where the trunk sat underneath a window. The trunk was large enough to hold a corpse. The old lady and the young girl dragged the trunk away from the wall. Anna produced an antique iron key and opened the lock. She slowly lifted the lid, and the aroma of lavender sachets wafted up from inside the trunk. There were many articles of clothing inside the antique trunk. Anna's purple wedding gown was lying on top. The gown was trimmed with yards of lavender lace.

Lavender and old lace, Terri thought to herself. *Well, at least that's better than arsenic and old lace.*

"I designed this gown myself," Anna boasted, carefully removing her wedding dress from the trunk. The stiff satin dress swished and crackled as it unfolded. The dress was quite long and trailed on the floor. Terri swallowed hard to keep from laughing. It was one of the most beautiful dresses she had ever seen and also one of the strangest. The gown was bunched up with hundreds of grapelike beads embroidered in soft viny patterns.

"Would you like to try on the dress?" Anna asked. "You'll get to wear it when you marry Glen. His mother wore it when she was married. I think we should continue the family tradition."

Terri agreed and sought some privacy to change clothes. *I can see it now as I walk down the aisle,* she thought. *Here comes the Fruit of the Loom girl.* She took off her wet clothes and hung them up to dry. Painstakingly, Terri slipped into the wedding gown, which fit her perfectly. It was as though the dress had been made for her. The dress wouldn't need any alterations for her marriage to Glen. Terri admired herself in a beveled glass cheval mirror that was being stored in the attic. Anna was pleased that the wedding gown fit Terri. Rooting around in the trunk, Anna brought out her lavender veil, which was still in good condition. Terri put on the dark veil and viewed herself in the mirror. Now, she knew how Jimi Hendrix must have felt looking at life through a Purple Haze. "Is this veil for a wedding or a funeral?" Terri asked Anna.

Digging deeper into the trunk, Anna pulled out some of her clothes from the 1920s. These clothes would fit Terri. The 1920s was the decade in which fashion entered the modern era. It was the decade in which women first abandoned the more restricting fashions of past years and began to wear more comfortable clothes, like short skirts and trousers.

Anna selected some blouses and several pairs of slacks for Terri to look at. "Choose any color you like…as long as it's purple," Anna said, paraphrasing Henry Ford.

Terri selected a blouse and a pair of slacks and smoothed out the creases. She took one last look at herself in the mirror and then took off the iconic purple wedding gown. After changing clothes, she handed the wedding dress to Anna, who carefully folded it and placed it back in the trunk.

"Do you see many ghosts up here?" Terri asked Anna.

"There are ghosts up here," Anna replied seriously. "There are ghosts all over the house. We've had psychic investigators come here to do research. Every Halloween, Jim Gray from KMOX Radio arranges to broadcast a séance to contact the spirit of my husband, who committed suicide in the Purple Parlor. Thankfully, I survived our suicide pact, or else they would also be trying to contact my spirit. Jim Gray brings in a multitude of paranormal researchers, mediums, witches, folklorists, parapsychologists, and other assorted oddballs who search for supernatural phenomenon. They all gather in the Purple Parlor."

Anna and Terri returned to the first floor of the house. "I tried on your grandmother's wedding gown," Terri told Glen. "It fits perfectly."

"Why didn't you let me see?" Glen admonished.

"It's bad luck for the groom to see the bride in her wedding dress before the wedding day." Terri laughed.

"I think we should have a séance," Anna said. "I would like to contact the spirit of my husband. I'm a medium."

You look more like a large, Terri felt like saying.

"I'm a trained spiritualist," Anna continued. "The first step in conducting a séance is to put out a food and drink offering for the spirit that we're trying to contact. Since it's my husband, we'll put out a glass of Burgermeister, which was his favorite beer along with a basket of croissants, his favorite food."

"Can I have a croissant?" Terri asked. "I love French pastry."

"Excuse me," Glen said, "but croissants were invented by the Austrians, not the French. That's why my grandfather loved croissants so much. It was the Austrian archduchess Marie Antoinette who introduced croissants to the French people. 'Let them eat croissants,' she said."

Glen paused for a second to review his knowledge of Austrian history and then stated, "A Viennese baker invented the croissant in 1683 to celebrate the victory of the Austrians over the Ottoman Turks in the Battle of Vienna. The croissant is shaped like the crescent moon on the Turkish flag. Through the years, the Turks made numerous attempts to enslave the Austrians and take over their country."

Anna, Terri, and Glen went into the kitchen to get the food and drink for the séance.

"Let's have some frosty refreshment first," Anna suggested. "I'm going to make Purple Cow Smoothies for us. That'll taste really good on this hot day."

Anna took a bottle of Welch's Purple Grape Juice from her refrigerator and poured some into a blender. "Take the time to taste the Welch's," she sang, after sipping from the bottle. "Take the time to roll it round. Savor all that Concord flavor. Let it trickle slowly down." Next, she added vanilla ice cream, ice cubes, and milk to the blender. This was a special Ninja blender with special Ninja blades for really tearing things apart. Anna used the fastest setting and soon had a perfect purple cow smoothie concoction.

Glen recited the famous poem by Gelett Burgess: "I never saw a Purple Cow, I never hope to see one; But I can tell you, anyhow, I'd rather see than be one."

"I'd rather have a purple cow smoothie," Anna said.

After they finished their purple cow smoothies, Terri and Glen went into the Purple Parlor and sat down at a round table in front of the fireplace. This was the exact spot where William Grosse had committed suicide in 1920 and where Anna had come close to dying.

Anna brought in three candles, which she placed on the table. Glen borrowed Terri's lighter and lit the candles. Next, Anna set a bottle of Burgermeister and a glass on the table. Glen opened the bottle with his Swiss Army knife and poured some beer into the glass. Anna laid the basket of croissants on the table, and Terri reached for one of the delicious, buttery, flaky, Viennoiserie pastries. Glen slapped her wrist to indicate the croissants were only for the spirit of the dearly departed. Anna turned off the lights and sat down at the table.

The candles threw waving shadows on the walls. "Let us make a circle by holding hands," Anna intoned.

"This is fun," Terri said, clasping Glen's hand. Hands were clasped all around the table.

Anna gazed straight ahead, concentrating, clearing her mind of everything. She appeared to be going into a trance as she spoke in a sonorous voice: "We are trying to contact the spirit of my husband, William Grosse, who committed suicide in this room on January 16, 1920." The candlelight accentuated the contours of her cheekbones and eye sockets.

At that moment, a thunderstorm began, and there was rain, lightning, and thunder. *How appropriate,* Terri thought.

"I'm going to ask him a test question about beer," Anna said. "To see if his spirit is here among us."

"He could probably use an ice-cold beer where he's at," Glen quipped.

Anna kicked Glen under the table to indicate her displeasure. "Is there beer in heaven?" she continued. "Knock three times on the ceiling if the answer is yes." She paused for a second and then sang: "Twice on the pipes if the answer is no."

Terri laughed, remembering the hit song by Tony Orando and Dawn that was at the top of the charts in January of 1971.

Everyone heard some distinct tapping noises, probably caused by the storm raging outside and not the ghost of Grandfather Grosse.

Anna had placed a framed photo of her deceased husband on the table. There was also a tambourine like the kind used by mediums in Victorian séances to create the illusion that the deceased was there in the room. Through the medium's trickery, the tambourine would float around the room. Anna had a vintage Salvation Army tambourine that had once been used by Salvation Army workers on street corners to save souls. A destitute man, staying at a Salvation Army shelter, had sold the tambourine to Anna for ten dollars. A tambourine is a drum when it is struck and a rattle when it is shaken. Terri picked up the tambourine and made noise with it.

"Don't break the circle," Anna commanded, feeling Terri's hand slip away.

"I'll just take a second," Terri said, shaking the tambourine alongside her head like Valerie of Josie and the Pussy Cats. The tambourine had red, white, and blue streamers attached to it. In the center of the tambourine was the Salvation Army Crest, which has a crown and the words *Blood and Fire* and the letter *S* wrapped around a cross and a pair of crossed swords. The name Miriam was printed on the wooden frame, referring to Miriam in the Bible who played the tambourine. Terri broke into song. "Hey! Mr. Tambourine Man, play a song for me. I'm not sleepy and there is no place I'm going to. Hey! Mr. Tambourine Man, play a song for me. In the jingle jangle morning I'll come following you."

Terri put down the tambourine and grabbed Anna's hand so the circle was once again unbroken.

"Bob Dylan's real last name is Zimmerman, just like mine," Terri exclaimed. "Maybe we are related. He wrote the words and music for *Mr. Tambourine Man*, and he was also the first to record the song in 1965."

"Quiet!" Anna shouted. "My husband is speaking to me. I can hear his voice. He answered my question. He said that in heaven, there is no beer. That's why people drink it here. I'm glad he cleared that up for me."

Anna explained to Terri and Glen that two of the greatest icons of the 1920s had both been in that very room.

"Who were they?" Terri asked eagerly.

"Babe Ruth and Harry Houdini," Anna quickly replied.

Terri was astonished. "Wow! You knew Babe Ruth?"

"Yes," Anna happily admitted. "He was a womanizer. He had a thing for me. He was here numerous times. He came to St. Louis when the Yankees played the Browns. In 1922, the Browns finished just one game behind the Yankees in the race for the American League pennant. The Yankees played the Cardinals in the World Series in 1926 and 1928."

"I never knew Babe Ruth was your boyfriend," Glen cut in.

Anna nodded. "The Babe used to say he only had one superstition. He always made sure to touch all the bases whenever he hit a home run."

"That's pretty good." Terri chuckled. "He also had some other clever sayings, like, 'It's déjà vu all over again,' 'The place is so crowded nobody goes there anymore,' 'When you come to a fork in the road, take it.'"

"That was St. Louis native Yogi Berra, not Babe Ruth," Glen clarified. "When I was a teenager, I played baseball for the same athletic club as Yogi Berra and Joe Garagiola."

"I think we should have a séance to contact the spirit of Babe Ruth," Anna proposed.

"In that case, we'll need a food offering of hotdogs, cigars, and twelve-year-old Scotch," Glen recommended.

"I'll get some hotdogs," Anna said. "We already have beer on the table. Babe Ruth loved hotdogs and beer."

Anna went into the kitchen and brought back a plate of hot dogs, which she placed on the table. The croissants were used as hotdog buns.

Anna, Terri, and Glen huddled around the table. The Boston Red Sox had traded Babe Ruth to the Yankees on January 5, 1920. That's when the Curse of the Bambino began for the Boston Red Sox. William Grosse had committed suicide on January 16, 1920. Anna pointed this out to Terri and Glen. Babe Ruth was the Sultan of Swat. William Grosse was the Sultan of Suds.

"Babe Ruth once gorged himself on so many hotdogs that he passed out and had to be rushed to the hospital," Anna said. "He could eat more, drink more, smoke more, swear more, and enjoy himself more than any of his contemporaries."

"Let's have a hotdog-eating contest like Babe Ruth used to do," Terri coaxed, reaching for a hotdog encased in a croissant. Once again, Glen slapped her wrist to indicate the croissant dogs were only for the Babe.

"Babe Ruth died of throat cancer on August 16, 1948," Anna said. "Do you remember what other famous person also died on August 16?"

"The King," Terri replied. "The King of Rock-and-Roll. Elvis Presley."

"Exactly right."

"If we're going to contact the spirit of Elvis, we'll need a plate of peanut butter and banana sandwiches," Glen remarked. "The Sultan of Swat and the King of Rock-and-Roll both died on August 16. I wonder what's so special about that day."

"In memory of Elvis, I always eat a peanut butter and banana sandwich on August 16," Terri informed the others. "Now, I will have to add a hotdog to my sandwich in memory of Babe Ruth."

"Since legends never die, we should be able to contact Elvis and the Babe," Anna said. "They were both pop culture icons who were larger than life. Both men came from humble beginnings south of the Mason-Dixon Line. Babe Ruth was born in Baltimore, which is just a stone's throw south of the Mason-Dixon Line. Elvis was born in Tupelo, Mississippi, in the Deep South. Both men were womanizers who were known for their wild behavior and excesses. Both had weight issues. Elvis was a good athlete, and the Babe was an accomplished musician."

"I can feel the hair standing on the back of my neck," Terri murmured. "This is spooky."

"They say Jimmy Piersall, of the Boston Red Sox, used to talk to the ghost of Babe Ruth in the outfield at Yankee Stadium," Anna said.

"I believe ghosts and spirits exist in the human mind," Glen speculated. "We all have a sixth sense beyond the regular five senses of sight, hearing, taste, smell, and touch. But we are looking for proof that communication from beyond the grave is possible and that there is such a thing as clairvoyance."

Suddenly, there was a loud noise as though a cannonball had just struck the roof of the house.

"That must be the ghosts," Terri said.

"I think that was thunder," Glen conjectured. He wanted to make an additional comment, but there was another clap of thunder right above the house, after which the lightning flashed continuously, bolt after jagged bolt accompanied by a tumult so deafening it seemed the roof must give way at any moment. The lightning lit up the dark room even through the drawn curtains. The thunder rolled and rumbled and reverberated, shaking the house to its foundation. There was a great gush of wind, a spatter of raindrops against the windows, and then the roar of a tremendous downpour. Speech was impossible for many minutes, until gradually the lightning and thunder died away, and the wind dropped until there was no sound but the rush of steady, drenching rain.

"Are you sure the ghosts aren't making all that racket?" Terri asked when it became possible to speak again.

Glen nodded. "That storm is so bad," he said. "I think you should spend the night here. You don't want to venture out in this monsoon. Remember when we were kids, we wanted to spend the night together in a tent here in the backyard but our parents wouldn't let us?"

"Yes," Terri recollected. "I remember helping you set up the tent. I think I should stay here tonight. My car will be safe. The lot at the Stag Club was full, so I parked right here on Lavender Street in front of your house. After all these years, we can finally spend the night together."

The night passed by very slowly. Terri, Glen, and Anna remained at the table to try and contact spirits but didn't have much luck. There were no ghostly apparitions or spiritual manifestations. Glen did his Elvis Presley impersonation, pretending he was the ghost of Elvis. However, there was no visitation from the ghost of the real Elvis.

Terri and Glen engaged in some hugging and kissing after Anna went to bed.

In the morning, everyone gathered in the kitchen for a breakfast of croissants and coffee.

After breakfast, Terri said goodbye to Glen, but first they made a date to meet at Forest Park on Sunday, June 13.

Chapter Six

On Saturday, June 12, Barbara Grogan gave a fishing clinic at Crestwood Plaza in South St. Louis County. Terri and Paz worked at the Famous-Barr store at the west end of the plaza. Barbara conducted her fishing clinic at the east end of the mall in a large enclosed courtyard between Dillard's and Sears. Many people showed up to get some fishing tips and to see Barbara Grogan in person.

Dressed in western garb, Barbara gave a tutorial on bass fishing. She explained to her audience that without the proper techniques, it really didn't matter what kind of lure you were using. Barbara demonstrated the proper handling of jigs, spinners, and crank baits.

There were several hundred people in the audience. Most of the spectators looked like rural folks who had traveled to Crestwood Plaza from the surrounding countryside. There were still plenty of hicks living just thirty miles south of the St. Louis suburb of Crestwood. Crestwood Plaza is located alongside the old Route 66, the Mother Road, and country people reached the plaza by driving up Interstate 44, which is the new name of Route 66.

After Barbara concluded her bass-fishing tutorial, she fielded questions from the audience. Responding to an elderly man's query, she explained how to tell the difference between a large-mouth bass and a small-mouth bass. "A large-mouth bass has a bigger mouth than a small-mouth bass." The audience roared with laughter.

Another man asked why Barbara had sought out a career in fishing, to which she replied, "I've always felt that if you give a man a fish, you've fed him for a day, but if you teach a man to fish, you've fed him for a lifetime." The audience again roared with laughter.

"People think that fishermen just sit around on their butts all day," Barbara lambasted. "But believe me, fishing is hard work." She then put in a plug for Jack's Sporting Goods Store, which was located nearby in the mall. Jack's had paid Barbara a great deal of money to make this personal appearance. Some employees from the sporting goods store were handing out advertising circulars that featured fishing merchandise. Attractive male and female models, wearing the latest fishing fashions, walked across the stage as Barbara described the clothing in detail. She also mentioned that these fishing outfits were available at Jack's Sporting Goods.

After the question-and-answer session, the people waited in line to meet Barbara Grogan and get her autograph. Copies of her new book, *The Mayfly Madam*, were for sale. People purchased the book before getting in line, and then Barbara autographed the title page.

In the audience was a seven-year-old girl who wanted to meet Barbara Grogan very badly. The little girl, whose name was Earline, idolized Barbara and wanted to be like her. Earline's parents had succumbed to their daughter's pleading, and the family made the long trip to Crestwood Plaza. The family came from a small town out in the sticks. They were pastoral people who looked and acted like they came from a small town out in the sticks. As she waited in line to meet Barbara Grogan, Earline rested firmly against her father's muscular body. He looked exactly like the country singer Eddie Arnold. His face was weather-beaten from numerous days spent fishing on the rivers and lakes of Missouri. Earline's mother was a rotund woman who looked like she enjoyed country cooking. She ran a comb through Earline's hair to make her daughter more presentable when meeting Barbara. Unfortunately, the family had ended up at the back of the long line, and Barbara left early before meeting everyone. Many people in the audience were disappointed, especially those who had purchased books. Refunds were offered for unsigned books. Earline's father had purchased a copy of *The Mayfly Madam* but didn't ask for his money back. The book was going to be one of his wife's birthday presents. Earline was almost in tears, and her parents consoled her with a group hug.

Standing near the Estée Lauder counter at the Famous-Barr store in Crestwood Plaza, Terri was spraying perfume on women who were walking by. She was using an atomizer. Resembling a vaudeville comedian with a seltzer bottle, Terri followed several women before spraying them in the face. The women did not appreciate these "free samples" and were annoyed by Terri's antics. One of the women coughed and brushed away the cloying perfume. Another woman used profanity. Occasionally, however, Terri was able to win over a customer with this highly original sales approach. "I always feel like Harpo Marx whenever I do this," she told a middle-aged lady who seemed interested in making a purchase.

When she was through spraying unsuspecting customers, Terri returned to her usual position behind the Estée Lauder cosmetics counter, which overflowed with new products, overshadowed by photographs of beautiful young women with flawless, glowing skin.

"I have a chemical dependency on Estée Lauder perfume," she said, spraying some of the product on herself.

"Me too," said Paz, who was busy taking inventory.

"This perfume is great," Terri continued. "If I want to attract a man, I spray some on myself. If I want to repel a man, I spray some in his eyes. It works just like a pepper spray."

"Thanks," Paz said. "I can use that as part of my sales approach." Paz rolled her eyes and puckered her lips. "Which perfume are you referring to?"

"White Linen Parfum Spray," Terri answered. "I love that name. It conjures up images of a bygone era." Terri sang the first verse of a popular old song:

"As I walked out in the streets of Laredo, as I walked out in Laredo one day, I spied a young cowboy, all wrapped in white linen, wrapped up in white linen and cold as the clay."

Terri took a whiff of White Linen perfume and savored the fresh, clean, outdoorsy scent, a mixture of bulgarian rose, jasmine, muguet, violet, orris, vetiver, moss, and amber.

"I'm going to wrap myself up in White Linen, a perfume for all seasons," she said, dousing herself with her favorite product.

The counter manager was gone, and Terri and Paz were in charge for the moment. The two salesgirls wore white lab coats to project a clean image. They looked like medical technicians.

A semiattractive woman came up to the counter and started browsing. Surveying the stock of scents before her, the lady looked like a small child in a candy store. Over a hundred perfume bottles were scattered on top of the glass display cases. The bottles were round, square, elliptical, teardrop-shaped, and pear-shaped. There were Lalique crystal flacons and apothecary bottles with glass stoppers.

Terri watched the woman peruse the merchandise. "I'm sorry. I won't be able to help you. You're so beautiful you don't need any of our products." This was Terri's standard opening line when greeting a customer.

"Bless you," the woman said, raising her right hand and flicking her wrist the way a priest does when granting absolution.

"This is just a small sampling of our merchandise," Terri said. "Help yourself. Browse all you want."

The woman opened bottles greedily, sniffed, and dabbed fragrances up and down both her arms and also in the hollows of her elbows. After about fifteen minutes, she said casually, "I'll take this one,"

"An excellent choice, madam," Terri said, ringing up the sale.

When it came to waiting on customers, Paz liked to snub unattractive women and women who didn't look like they could afford to spend much, sort of like in the movie *Pretty Woman*, where Julia Roberts gets snubbed at the fashionable Rodeo Drive boutique. But Terri treated all the women with a great deal of respect. She treated homely women as if they were goddesses and fat women as if they were pencil thin.

A lady approached the counter and began to speak, but Paz gave her the cold shoulder, probably thinking that this woman looked like a rodeo type, not a Rodeo Drive type. The lady was dressed in blue jeans held in place by a belt with a boots and saddle buckle in solid brass. She had on a red plaid shirt, and on her head was a cowboy hat with a fishing lure attached to it. Barbara Grogan had come to the Estée Lauder counter to make a purchase. Terri did not recognize Barbara at first and said, "I'm sorry, I won't be able to help you. You're so beautiful you don't need any of our products."

"Well, you got that part right," Barbara said in her throaty western voice.

"Oh my god," Terri cried, after recognizing that unmistakable ranch-style parlance. "You're the Happy Hooker!"

Paz had chosen to wait on an elegantly dressed woman who looked like she was worth a million dollars. This woman reacted in horror when she heard the words "Happy Hooker," and she scowled at Barbara and then spoke to Paz in a hostile tone of voice, saying something about shopping at another store from now on. Paz only laughed.

"Ssh, you want to keep it down," Barbara said to Terri.

"If you're looking for Lady Stetson perfume, we don't sell it here," Terri told Barbara.

"I want to purchase White Linen perfume," Barbara said.

A cow girl wrapped up in White Linen, Terri thought to herself. "What brings you to Crestwood Plaza?"

"I was conducting a fishing clinic at the other end of the mall. After I finished, I signed a lot of autographs. I'm afraid I made some people unhappy because I didn't have time to meet everyone."

"I know an elderly man whose greatest dream in life is to meet you," Terri said to Barbara.

"Really," Barbara said. "What's his name?"

"Dinty Smith. He runs a tavern called the Stag Club in the Lavender Hill neighborhood."

"I always enjoy meeting my adoring public," Barbara said. "Maybe I can arrange to see him. I won't be coming back to the St. Louis area until July third. Give me his address."

Barbara wrote down the address.

"If you don't mind my saying, I wouldn't think an outdoor woman like you needs much perfume."

"Oh, I don't buy it to wear," Barbara exclaimed. "I use it when I go fishing. I spray it on bait. Boy, does this stuff help attract fish!"

"Thanks," Terri said. "I can use that as part of my sales approach. What a novel idea. Estée Lauder White Linen perfume used as a stink bait."

After finishing with the elegant lady who had refused to buy anything, Paz came over to talk to Terri.

"Who's this?" Barbara asked Terri.

"This is my faithful Filipino sidekick," Terri said. "Her name is Paz Militante."

"Don't I know you from somewhere?" Paz asked.

"She does a television program about fishing," Terri said.

"So that's where I've seen you," Paz said.

"You like to fish?" Barbara asked.

"Yes," Paz said. "Filipinos love to fish. Many Filipinos earn their livelihood from fishing. My father was once a commercial fisherman."

"Paz is all excited," Terri said. "She's becoming an American citizen on the Fourth of July."

"How nice," Barbara said.

"I came to the United States as a mail order bride, but the man dumped me before we could be married."

"I guess he didn't want to be married to some Filipino floozy," Terri joked.

"I only used him for money and a green card," Paz said.

"What part of the Philippines are you from?" Barbara asked.

"My home is a farm on the slopes of Mount Apo near Davao City. My parents still live there. I send money home to them. Davao City is a major seaport on the island of Mindanao."

"My home is a ranch on the slopes of the Santa Cruz Mountains in California," Barbara said. "That's where I was born and raised. I now live on a spread near Marion in Southern Illinois." As the three young ladies were talking, they were interrupted by a rebel yell from the bucolic gentleman who had been waiting in line with his family at the fishing clinic.

"Yeehaw!" the man cried. "There's Barbara Grogan." His wife and daughter were overjoyed.

"Oh no," Barbara cried.

The man and his family came rushing over. They looked like they had just fallen off a turnip truck, crawled out of a cracker barrel, gathered a mess of raspberries in yonder woods, and devoured a whole truckload of Moon Pies. They appeared to be the kind of people who flossed their teeth with straw.

"Can I have your autograph?" the little girl asked Barbara.

"Sure," Barbara replied.

Terri gave Barbara a piece of paper and a pen.

"What's your name?"

"Earline Early," the little girl replied. "I've watched your show ever since I was a girl."

"What are you now, a boy?" Barbara quipped.

"I'm Eb," her father said. "And this is my wife, Flo. It is a pleasure to meet you, Ms. Grogan."

"Eb and Flo, how cute," Barbara said. "Eb like the farmhand on *Green Acres*, and Flo like the waitress on *Alice*. I saw you waiting in line at the fishing clinic. Sorry I had to leave so abruptly. It's nice to meet you."

"My wife and I come from northern Arkansas," the hayseed said. "We have been fishing our entire lives. We moved to the St. Louis area five years ago. We now live in Festus, which is about thirty miles south of here."

"There's no Riviera in Festus, Missouri," Terri said, referring to the George Jones / Tammy Wynette song *We're Not the Jet Set*, which mentions Festus.

"There used to be a Riviera swimming pool in Festus," Eb said.

"Festus is a name from the Bible," Flo said.

Barbara said that she was very familiar with the twin towns of Festus and Crystal City.

"I'm a member of the Gateway Bassingals here in St. Louis," Flo said, "and my daughter is going to join as soon as she's old enough."

"We're both fishing moms," Barbara said. "I have a little boy about the same age as your daughter."

"During your bass fishing demonstration today, you mentioned that you're actively involved with Bassingals," Flo commented.

"Yes," Barbara said. "I'm sort of a Bassingal ambassador. I'm on the board of directors of many Bassingal chapters throughout the United States, including the Gateway Club here in St. Louis."

"I can't wait to join Bassingals," Earline squealed.

"Where do you guys like to go fishing?" Barbara asked.

"The Lake of the Ozarks," Eb replied. "We own a cabin on the lake. We go there every chance we get."

"Earline gave us quite a shock last week," Flo said. "She caught a piranha. She was with her father on the Niangua arm of the Lake of the Ozarks. As she pulled the piranha into the bass boat, she was bitten rather badly. Of course, she didn't realize it was a piranha until it was too late. Piranhas look just like crappie except for the big teeth. Earline caused quite a sensation at the lake. People were afraid there might be hundreds of piranhas swimming around just as the summer swimming season is beginning. But the authorities reassured everyone, saying that this was just an isolated incident. A novelty. The coves at the lake are not teeming with flesh-eating piranhas waiting to feed on unsuspecting victims. Piranhas are an exotic tropical fish from South America that cannot survive in cold water. Piranhas cannot tolerate cold winter weather, and therefore they can't survive in northern lakes such as the Lake of the Ozarks. They are not going to thrive or reproduce here. Piranhas are sometimes released into the Lake of the Ozarks after they become too large for home aquariums."

"I read something about that in the *Post-Dispatch*," Barbara said. "That was you?"

"Yes," Earline said proudly, showing off the bite marks on her fingers.

"You're quite a celebrity," Barbara congratulated. "Maybe I should be getting your autograph."

"Thank you," Earline said.

"I can think of just a few other instances where anglers caught piranhas at the Lake of the Ozarks."

Barbara patted Earline on the back. "You're lucky you weren't seriously injured."

"We took her to the emergency room," Flo said. "She needed stitches. That's how everyone learned about the piranha attack."

Terri waited for the conversation about piranhas to end, and then she introduced Paz to the Earlys.

"Paz is all excited," Terri said. "She's becoming a United States citizen on the Fourth of July."

"Were you on our side?" Eb asked.

"What do you mean?" Paz inquired.

"Are you South Vietnamese or North Vietnamese?"

"I'm from the Philippines," Paz said hotly.

"You look Vietnamese," Eb stated.

"Today, June twelfth, is Philippines Independence Day, and I intend to celebrate by building a fire and roasting meat over the hot coals." Paz tended to speak in a circumlocutory way, as was true of many people who are learning a new language. She could have just said that she was going to have a barbecue.

"Happy Philippines Independence Day!" Flo said. Eb also wished Paz a happy holiday.

"Early…that's an interesting name," Terri said.

"Yes," Eb said with rube-like laughter. We get a lot of jokes about our name. The Confederate General Jubal Early is one of our ancestors. He really whooped those Yankees at Bull Run, Fredericksburg, and Chancellorsville."

Flo had a camera, and she took numerous photos of her daughter and Barbara together. Then Terri took the camera and snapped photos of the Earlys and Barbara together. Finally, Flo took back the camera and clicked a few more snapshots of her family and Barbara.

"I almost forgot," Flo said, reaching into her purse for Barbara's book. "My husband purchased *The Mayfly Madam* as a birthday present for me. Can you autograph it?"

"Sure," Barbara said, taking the book and scribbling her name in it. Her handwriting wasn't very good.

"When is your birthday?"

"June twenty-first, the first day of summer."

"And the longest day of the year," Barbara added. "Happy birthday!"

"Thank you!"

"How did you happen to choose that title for your book about fishing?" Eb asked.

Barbara laughed as she handed the book back to Flo. "The mayfly is the best fishing bait there is, especially for trout. Unfortunately, the poor mayfly only has a lifespan of one day. Makes me think of some of my relationships with men." Barbara paused for a moment and then added, "The title is a humorous take-off on *The Mayflower Madam* by Sydney Biddle Barrows, a call girl whose ancestors came over on the *Mayflower*. After all, I am known as the Happy Hooker."

"That was Xaviera Hollander," Flo said.

"We have to go," Eb said. "Earline has a dental appointment. We don't want to be late."

"We're always early," Flo said.

"Here's your autograph, Earline," Barbara said.

"Thanks," the little girl said, grabbing the piece of paper.

After reading Barbara's personalized message, Earline piped enthusiastically, "She signed it BEST FISHES!"

Barbara waved goodbye to the Earlys and yelled, "Drop me a line, catch you later!"

Eb Early laughed and told Barbara that he would keep in touch.

"Big Hoosiers," Barbara chided, after the Earlys were out of earshot. "That's the trouble with my job. I'm always being accosted by Hoosiers. Hoosiers love to fish."

"Those people come from out in the boondocks," Paz said. "Boondocks is actually a Filipino word from the Tagalog language. Boondocks is derived from the Tagalog word *bundok*, which means 'mountain.'"

"I guess I better get going," Barbara said. "I was planning to go fishing today on Crab Orchard Lake near my home in Southern Illinois."

"Stick around," Terri said. "Since you're going to visit my friend Dinty, I've decided to give you a free makeover." Terri's makeup application skills were better than average, and she usually charged fifty dollars for a beauty session.

"Thank you," Barbara said. "That's very nice of you."

Terri took Barbara to the far end of the counter for privacy.

"I've never done a celebrity makeover before," Terri said, after she had seated Barbara in a comfortable chair.

"I think I need a complete image overhaul," Barbara said. "An extreme makeover."

"I think I'll begin by finding the right makeup for you," Barbara said, sorting through various Estée Lauder products. "Do you wear makeup when you film your television show?"

"Not really," Barbara replied.

"The wrong type of makeup can make you look several years older than you really are. I need to find a foundation that matches your skin tone. If your foundation is too light or too dark, it can look like you're wearing a mask. I'll also experiment with different shades of eye shadow, blush, and lip color to complement your skin tone and eye color."

"Thank you," Barbara said.

"Maybe I should get a job as a celebrity makeup artist," Terri said as she applied mascara to Barbara's eyelashes."

"People say I look like Kim Basinger," Barbara bragged. She pronounced the name BASS-inger, which is incorrect. The correct pronunciation is BAY-singer. Barbara had bass fishing on her mind. Terri laughed silently to herself. No amount of makeup could make Barbara as beautiful as the actress Kim Basinger. It was unfortunate but true that Barbara would always be more cowgirl than cover girl.

"Men are always telling me I have allure," Barbara said, fingering the fishing lure attached to her cowboy hat.

"Better take off your hat," Terri said. "I want to fix your hair."

Barbara removed her hat and set it on top of the cosmetics counter.

"Do you have a special man in your life?" Terri asked.

"I have a string of boyfriends," Barbara answered.

"You mentioned you have a young son."

"Yes. I'm a single working mother."

"Are you divorced?"

"No," Barbara intoned. "I'm a widow. My husband drowned five years ago on a Canadian fishing trip."

"I'm sorry," Terri lamented.

"Drowning is an occupational hazard in my business. I was with my husband when our boat capsized. He died saving my life."

Terri didn't know what to say, so she concentrated on her work. She had decided to go for a natural look, opting to enhance Barbara's beauty without bringing too much attention to the makeup. When Terri was finished, she handed Barbara a hand mirror made from a heavy resinous material that looked like real alligator skin. Barbara gazed into the antique faux alligator skin hand mirror. She complimented Terri on a job well done.

"You want your eyebrows a little darker?" Terri asked.

"They're fine," Barbara said, reaching for her creel. She carried a creel instead of a purse. "Let me pay you something."

"You don't owe me anything," Terri insisted. "Just make sure to visit my good friend Dinty. Seeing you will mean so much to him."

"Okay," Barbara said, "but I have to pay you for the White Linen."

"Your money is no good around here," Terri said. "It's a pleasure to meet you and have you as a friend."

"Thank you very much," Barbara said. "It's nice meeting you. I hope we will be good friends."

"You look drop-dead gorgeous," Terri exaggerated. "I want a photo of you for my portfolio." Terri kept a Polaroid camera behind the counter so she could take pictures of the women she worked on. She had a scrapbook of her makeovers. In case she ever had to look for a new job, she wanted to show a prospective employer what a talented cosmetician she was. Terri photographed Barbara and then handed the camera to Paz, who took a shot of the two young ladies together. Barbara autographed both photos with a personalized message.

"I want one more picture to put on display with the other celebrity photographs," Terri said, aiming the camera at Barbara. On display were photos of several St. Louis luminaries who had purchased Estée Lauder products at the Crestwood Famous-Barr store. Mary Frann, the *Newhart* actress, grew up in nearby Webster Groves and came back to St. Louis often to visit her family. Phyllis Diller lived in Webster Groves before she became famous, and still had a special fondness in her heart for the St. Louis area. Bob Costas began his broadcasting career at KMOX Radio in St. Louis and was a regular customer of the Crestwood Famous-Barr store before achieving national prominence as a sports announcer. He still visited the store occasionally when he was in town. He liked Terri and always made sure she waited on him when he bought perfume for his wife. Terri enjoyed talking to him, and they would engage in long conversations. Cardinal pitcher and broadcaster Al Hrabosky was a regular customer, and Terri had waited on him several times. She had also met his wife, who often accompanied him.

"Give Barbara her ten-gallon hat back," Terri said to Paz who had put on the cowboy hat. Paz doffed the hat and placed it on Barbara's head. "There you go, partner," Paz said, using the parlance of the Old West. She then straightened her earrings, which had become displaced by the movement of the hat. Paz wore her earrings across the helix at the top of the ear. Perhaps this was a custom in the Philippines.

"Please come again," Terri told Barbara, placing the White Linen in a small shopping bag.

"I will," Barbara replied, taking the bag with her left hand and waving goodbye with her right hand.

"Bye! Thank you!"

"Bye-bye!" Terri said. "Catch you later."

The Estée Lauder cosmetics counter was located near the main entrance of the Famous-Barr store, and Barbara was quickly out the door.

"I haven't given a free makeover since I was going to beauty school," Terri told Paz after Barbara had gone. "We would experiment on guinea pig customers who didn't care how they looked as long as they didn't have to spend any money."

A colored woman had been waiting for service while Terri and Paz talked with Barbara. After telling the black woman how beautiful she was, Terri grabbed a cut-glass bottle of White Linen perfume and raised it in the air. "Wanna catch some fish?" she asked, pointing at the bottle.

Chapter Seven

The weather finally cleared on the day that Terri and Glen visited Forest Park. After many days of cloudy skies and rain, the sun broke through at last. Sunday, June 13, was a day so peaceful and still that the meteorological report confined itself to the single sentence: "All quiet on the weather front!"

Terri and Glen agreed to meet at the Jefferson Memorial on the northern edge of Forest Park. Of course, the building was now called the Missouri History Museum, but Terri would always say Jefferson Memorial, which was the name when she was a little girl.

Forest Park is located in the central west end of St. Louis, just a few miles from downtown. Consisting of over 1,300 scenic acres, it is one of the largest urban parks in the nation. In 1904, the park was the scene of the Louisiana Purchase Exposition, more commonly known as the St. Louis World's Fair. Over 1,500 buildings were constructed for the Fair; some of which still stand in the park today.

Forest Park was officially dedicated on Saturday, June 24, 1876, the day before Custer's Last Stand.

The Jefferson Memorial is a museum of westward expansion. Completed in 1913, the building was constructed with funds from the Louisiana Purchase Exposition of 1904. The museum was built at the entrance to the 1904 World's Fair. The Jefferson Memorial is now the permanent home of the Missouri Historical Society. The society's museum collections, printed and manuscript sources, and pictorial holdings are especially important in the fields of the heritage of St. Louis and the westward expansion of the United States.

Terri arrived at the museum before Glen, and she studied the map of the Louisiana Purchase that was etched into the pavement in the courtyard. She climbed the steep stretch of steps on the north side of the building and entered the loggia between the two original wings of the museum. On the other side of the loggia was the museum addition. Terri still had trouble accepting all the changes that had been made to the museum. The original building, long and narrow, consists of two wings separated by a loggia which canopies Karl Bitter's statue of Thomas Jefferson. Terri told Glen she would meet him in front of the towering marble figure of the seated Thomas Jefferson. She stood by the statue and waited. When she was a little girl, her parents had taken numerous photos of her standing next to Tom Jefferson. The words FATHER OF THE LOUISIANA PURCHASE were still there on the base of Tom's statue.

The Signing of the Treaty, a bronze tablet in high relief, is placed on the east wall of the loggia. Terri walked over to the sculpture which is also by Karl Bitter and represents Monroe, Livingston, and Marbois putting their signatures to the Louisiana Purchase treaty on April 30, 1803. A many-branched candelabrum is on the table and four large books are piled beside it. Monroe stands at the left, behind the chair, while Livingston is seated, his face uplifted. At the right the treaty lies on the table in front of the books, and Marbois stands in the act of signing it. His posture has the lithe and exquisite precision that characterize what we read of the man. The expressions of the three men makes one feel that they are aware of the service they are rendering. The inscription, well balanced and well spaced, reads, "The instrument we have signed will cause no tears to flow. It will prepare centuries of happiness for innumerable generations of the human race. The Mississippi and the Missouri will see them prosper and increase in the might of equality under just laws, freed from the errors of superstition, from the scourges of bad government and truly worthy of the regard and care of Providence." The words are Livingston's, expressing the general satisfaction of the three after they had signed the treaty. The relief was unveiled on April 30, 1913, and was presented by the Louisiana Purchase Exposition Company.

The United States signed the Louisiana Purchase Treaty on May 2, 1803, paying four cents an acre and doubling the size of the country. The total cost was 15 million dollars.

St. Louis is home to the first Jefferson Memorial. The Jefferson Memorial in Washington, DC, wasn't built until 1937. Terri thought of the movie *Born Yesterday* and the scene where Judy Holiday stands in the rotunda of the Jefferson Memorial in Washington. The words of Thomas Jefferson have shaped American ideals. Many of these impressive, stirring words adorn the rotunda of his memorial in St. Louis. Terri reflected on some of the lines from the Declaration of Independence. Thomas Jefferson was sort of a phony, she thought. An elitist who pretended to be a man of the people. And he wasn't such a nice guy—a slave named Sally Hemmings was his mistress.

The statue of Thomas Jefferson weighed sixteen tons. Terri remembered that figure because of the song *16 Tons* by Tennessee Ernie Ford. She sat down on a lion-legged stone bench next to the statue of Old Tom. For about fifteen minutes, she watched people come and go, and then she walked back to the east wall of the loggia to look at the Signing of the Treaty once again. Terri had always liked this relief sculpture of the Louisiana Purchase.

Terri walked into the museum annex and stood underneath the *Spirit of St. Louis*, which was suspended from the ceiling. Looking like an aluminum sardine can, this plane had been used in the 1957 movie *The Spirit of St. Louis*, starring Jimmy Stewart. According to a signboard, this plane was built by Ryan Aircraft of San Diego shortly after that same company built the original *Spirit of St. Louis*, which now hangs in the Smithsonian Institution.

Another signboard said the following:

ST. LOUISANS HAVE ALWAYS HAD A SPECIAL ATTACHMENT TO LINDBERGH'S STORY. YET THE FAMOUS PILOT ONLY LIVED HERE FOR A SHORT TIME, AND HIS LIFE WAS NOT WITHOUT CONTROVERSY. WHILE AMERICANS WELCOMED LINDBERGH AS A HERO IN 1927, THEY WONDERED AT HIS REFUSAL TO SPEAK OUT AGAINST NAZI AGRESSION IN EUROPE A DECADE

LATER. SO WHAT IS IT ABOUT THIS MAN AND THIS PLANE THAT CONTINUES TO THRILL ST. LOUISANS? PERHAPS IT IS OUR FEELING THAT ANY OF US CAN SUCCEED AGAINST THE ODDS, IF WE DARE TO FLY HIGH.

Suddenly, Glen appeared from behind and surprised Terri. She quickly swung around and jumped up on Glen, wrapping her arms around him, holding him close, kissing him over every square inch of his face. A crowd of onlookers gathered to watch.

Glen had his arms around Terri, and he was holding her in the air. "Whoa," he said humorously, letting Terri down slowly so that her feet were now touching the floor. "There hasn't been a welcome like that since Lindbergh landed in Paris!"

Terri and Glen went straight to the River Room in the west wing of the museum. The River Room was the only exhibit that had been left the same during the recent modernization of the museum. It was the only area without audiovisual, interactive displays that made you feel like you were in the twenty-first century instead of the nineteenth. The River Room acknowledged the historic role that the port of St. Louis played in the opening of the West. The collection comprised a full sweep of river transportation, from dugout, keelboat, and the elaborate floating palaces of the nineteenth century, down to the modern diesel-powered towboats of today.

A large wooden signboard proclaimed, STEAMBOAT ROUND THE BEND.

Terri and Glen entered past a model of the famous riverboat *J. M. White*, a beautiful steamboat-Gothic structure with luxurious appointments. The boat was modeled in detail down to her cotton bales. Aboard, the food must have been sublime, the company elegant. Travel was then at the height of graciousness. Of course, there was always the possibility of the vessel grounding on a sandbar, running her bottom out on a snag, bursting a faulty boiler and blowing up, or of the leisurely traveler being conned by a professional riverboat gambler.

The focal point of the River Room was the original pilot house of the *Belle of Calhoun*, one of the last paddle wheelers on the Mississippi. The pilothouse had been salvaged after a 1947 accident.

In a glass-enclosed area, reminiscent of an old-fashioned department store window, was a simulated ladies' cabin of a typical western river steamboat of the 1870s.

A female mannequin was wearing an authentic period outfit complete with hoop skirt and petticoat. The furnishings in the cabin represented the peak of elaborate Victorian decor and had come from several well-known nineteenth-century steamboats, including the *J. M. White*, the most luxurious of all the boats.

In another glass-enclosed area was a male mannequin dressed like a riverboat sharper, wearing a beaver hat, puffy shirt, red vest, string-tie, and black suit coat. Sitting at a table in the saloon of a steamboat, he was playing poker with another mannequin who looked like an easy mark.

Throughout the River Room were display cases with boat models, steamboat silver and china, bells and whistles, as well as portraits of prominent rivermen. One section of the room told the story of the rivers during the Civil War, while a nearby case contained the victory bowl from the most famous of all Mississippi races in which the Robert E. Lee beat the Natchez. The modern-day river scene was represented by two carefully constructed scale models of towboats in a diorama setting and a model of a typical river lock and dam.

The first item that Terri and Glen noticed was a dugout canoe made from a hollowed-out tree trunk. It was approximately twenty feet long and was located to the right when you came in. A sign said that French fur trappers had used this canoe and had called it a pirogue.

"There's a hole in this pirogue," Glen said. Although it was indeed true that there was a small round hole in the pirogue, Glen had made the statement to test Terri's knowledge of country music. *There's a Hole in My Pirogue* was the name of a country song that Johnny Horton had recorded in the early 1960s. Since Terri did not mention the song, Glen assumed that her perception of country music was limited.

Realizing that *There's a Hole in My Pirogue* was a rather obscure song, Glen decided to run another test. "Goodbye, Joe," he sang. "Me gotta go, me-oh-my-oh. Me gotta pole my pirogue down the bayou." This was a line from the classic Hank Williams song *Jambolaya*, or as Glen liked to call it, *The Ballad of the Bouillabaisse*. Terri did not mention either Hank Williams or the song *Jambolaya*, and Glen became further convinced that she was not a country music enthusiast.

"I thought a pirogue was a type of pasta from Poland," Terri muttered. Terri was thinking of a pierogi, which is a pasta shell filled with mashed potatoes and diced onions. Pierogies are very popular in Poland.

Climbing a short flight of steps, Terri and Glen entered the original pilothouse of the *Belle of Calhoun*. A view of the Mississippi unfolded before them, painted on a screen that hung outside the pilothouse window. A young man, who looked like the actor James Fransiscus, was also in the pilothouse. In 1947, the *Belle of Calhoun* had run aground at Grand Tower Island, the historic graveyard of the Mississippi. The boat needed extensive repairs. The original wooden pilothouse, salvaged from the wreckage, now bore this inscription: HER SALVAGED TREASURE YET SHALL KEEP, HER GLORY FRESH IN MIND.

Terri caught the scent of weathered timber and tarred rope.

Eleven feet square, domed, and trimmed with gingerbread, it was a typical riverboat pilothouse. Inside was the captain's wheel, nine feet in circumference, made of oak and ash. A pot-bellied stove was also inside. On the wall were framed newspaper accounts of the boat's accident. The *Belle of Calhoun* had nosed into the island at two thirty in the morning. Rocks from the revetment on the island's bank cut a five-foot hole in a forward compartment. The hold began to fill with water. Watertight compartments that had just been installed kept the boat from sinking to the bottom. The newspaper stories had several photographs of the wrecked boat. There was also a photo of Captain William Hardin, master of the *Belle of Calhoun*. It was the general consensus that he was drunk when he steered his boat into the island. Captain Hardin was only thirty years old at the time of the accident. He was now seventy-six and was still the boat's captain. He would be in charge on June 23, when Casino Calhoun had its maiden voyage.

The original portrait of Anna, painted in 1913, was also hanging on the wall of the pilothouse. In her youth, Anna had looked like a Hapsburg princess, or the traditional idea of one. Her fine-boned face with its curiously shy serenity made one think of the Viennese beauty Hedy Lamarr. In the portrait, Anna appeared to be blushing, her long eyelashes coming down over her lowered eyes. The innocence of those big, deep violet eyes contrasted with the passionate promise of her wide mouth.

"There she is," Glen exclaimed when he saw Anna's portrait.

The young man, who looked like James Fransiscus, was admiring Anna's Lamarr-esque face and thick sweeping hair which came down to her shoulders. "That's a beautiful girl," he said as Terri and Glen approached. "I think I'm in love with her."

"That's my grandmother," Glen retorted. "Believe me, she's no great prize."

The young man was taken aback and left the pilothouse without saying another word.

From the windows of the pilothouse, the two young people looked out on the River Room. Beneath them, a woman was sitting on a bench with a notebook in her hand. She was making a sketch of a steamboat. An elderly museum guard was snoozing in his chair. The young man who looked like James Franciscus was now standing between two famous Currier and Ives lithographs, *High Water on the Mississippi* and *Low Water on the Mississippi*. He was staring back and forth at the two paintings.

Grasping a rope, which hung through an auger-hole bored in the ceiling of the pilothouse, Glen began ringing the old-time steamboat bell on the roof. Five deep, mellow notes floated through the room. Then he pulled down the speaking tube and shouted into it: "Ahoy, engine room!! Give me full speed ahead. Let her have it, every ounce you've got!" He grabbed the lever of the operating-control standard, better known as the boat's telegraph. Moving the lever to the ALL AHEAD FULL position, he spun the pilot wheel as though he were a contestant on the television program *Wheel of Fortune*.

In one corner of the pilothouse was a large brass cuspidor filled with sawdust. Apparently, the old-time riverboat captains had done a lot of spitting. Picking up the spittoon, Glen looked inside and then expectorated.

"Nhggggh."

"That's really gross!" Terri shouted.

Terri and Glen sat down on a wooden bench that was directly underneath Anna's portrait.

"I feel her eyes on me," Glen said.

"The painting has cracked with age," Terri observed.

"So has she," Glen wise-cracked.

Terri kissed Glen lightly, playfully, and suddenly he was kissing her with a passion he did not think himself capable of. She fitted her slimness to him, and they rolled in comic contortions, locking arms, bumping noses, banging against the wooden bench, trying to achieve a sensuous rhythm but winding up with an awkward but romantic wrestling hold.

"People get married in this pilothouse," Glen said, between kisses. "It's like getting married in a gazebo in the park."

"Let's get married right now, right here," Terri requested. "Go make the arrangements with the museum staff. Maybe we can find an old-time riverboat captain to perform the ceremony."

Terri and Glen made love in the pilothouse until they heard footsteps on the short flight of wooden stairs. It was the old museum guard, who looked sort of like Mark Twain. He had white bushy hair and a large white mustache. He looked nautical in his guard's uniform and hat.

"Here's the old-time riverboat captain I asked for," Terri whispered to Glen.

"Let me know if you have any questions," the old museum guard said, fingering a brass button on his loose-fitting blue uniform. "I'm an expert on the Mississippi."

Glen thought he looked more like Albert Einstein than Mark Twain.

The couple talked to the museum guard for a short time and then left the gingerbread-covered pilothouse. Since they were planning to wear period costumes on the maiden voyage of Casino Calhoun, they carefully studied the outfits that the male and female mannequins were wearing. Terri was an accomplished seamstress and said she knew how to make vintage clothes. She also knew the owner of a vintage clothing store. Glen said that his grandmother had saved period outfits that had belonged to his grandfather.

"I wonder what it was like to live back then," Terri said whimsically, studying a low slipper chair, which was useful to tightly corseted ladies who found it difficult to bend low to put on their shoes.

During their tour of the River Room, Terri and Glen learned all about gambling, steamboat racing, showboats, and whirlwind social activities that predominated during the era. There were rousing tales of river disasters, such as collisions, ice breakups, explosions, fires, and snaggings. The River Room also traced the story of the Mississippi River Valley from the time of the mound builders through the periods of exploration and colonization before the coming of the steamboat.

The River Room was still the same as it had been when Glen and Terri were children and used to come to the museum with their parents. The room still had the same glass cases filled with items found aboard the old riverboats. The items were still the same— hand tools, china, silverware, clothing, river charts, firearms, paintings. One glass case still contained a few links of the large iron chain that the Confederates had stretched across the Mississippi River between Columbus, Kentucky, and Belmont, Missouri. Links to the past. During the Civil War, the Confederates had used the chain to keep Union gunboats from coming down the river.

Nothing in the River Room had changed. Only Terri and Glen had changed. It was nice to have a place where things stayed the same. Certain things should stay the way they are. You ought to be able to stick them in one of those big glass display cases and just leave them alone.

Terri and Glen were looking at a nineteenth-century lithograph of *The Jolly Flatboatmen* by George Caleb Bingham, who painted the picture in 1857. The original oil painting hangs in the St. Louis Art Museum. Bingham, of Missouri, did a series of river pictures, several of which were lithographed and widely distributed in the 1840s and 1850s. Bingham took the central figures from sketches in his notebook, sketches that he had made from close personal observation. The central figure in *The Jolly Flatboatmen* is the dancer who pivots joyfully with his hat in one hand and a red bandanna in the other hand. The fiddler is swaying to his own rhythm, and a young boy is beating the time with his knuckles on a pan. Other rivermen are sprawled about the boat. They are looking on with lazy, amused indifference. Two men are smoking their pipes. Another man is taking a swig of liquor from a brown jug. The fun-loving Missouri flatboatmen are having a celebration at the end of a journey downriver.

"Those men are all overweight," Terri said after studying the painting carefully.

"I don't think they worried about being overweight in those days," Glen said. "They were too busy with other things. Men were supposed to be big so they could build log cabins and fight Indians."

Terri and Glen looked at another lithograph by George Caleb Bingham that hung next to the pirogue. The painting was called *Fur Traders Descending the Missouri* and showed a fur trader and his half-breed son seated at opposite ends of a pirogue. The long, narrow boat makes a single dark line on the misted river. In the stern is chained a bear cub, seen only as a black oval. One gets the impression that the scene takes place early in the morning.

"Missouri is an Osage Indian word meaning 'Land of the Big Canoe,'" Glen said.

An elderly couple paused before an exhibit called *The Civil War on the River*. They were particularly interested in an old tabloid, which had been printed on the back of a wallpaper during the siege of Vicksburg. Next to the yellowing newspaper were several rusty links of the iron chain the Confederates had used to blockade the Mississippi between Columbus, Kentucky, and Belmont, Missouri. There were quite a few old lithographs on display: *Union Admiral Porter Runs Rebel Blockade at Vicksburg*, *Bombardment and Capture of Island Number 10*, *Destruction of the Rebel Ram Arkansas*, and *The*

Ironclad Gunboat Osage in Action. Other items on display included the sword of a Confederate officer aboard the Arkansas, the uniform of a small boy who had served as an orderly aboard a Union frigate, and a rare photograph of the St. Louis boatyard where James Eads had built Union ironclads.

Taking one last look at the Civil War exhibit, the elderly gentleman whispered something in his wife's ear. She laughed, and they moved on, murmuring companionably to each other.

Near the door was a large wall-hung, metal-framed, glass scrapbook that contained mementos of the Mississippi. Before they left the River Room, Terri and Glen leafed through the numerous pages of old river photographs, steamboat schedules, advertisements, menus, types of cargo, tonnage, war, peace, work, play. There was an arresting page of sepia-toned photographs that was entitled STEAMBOAT KILLERS. This page was devoted to steamboat wrecks caused by boiler explosions, collisions, floods, ice, fires, etc. Steamboats were never known for their longevity. The average life of a steamboat on western waters was two years.

The elderly museum guard who looked like Mark Twain was sitting in his chair by the door. "The Mississippi is an interesting subject," he said. "It's a fact that more people work on the river today than in the nineteenth century. Today, barges carry more cargo than the old steamboats ever did."

Terri and Glen said goodbye to the old guard and then moved to a different section of the museum.

Terri wanted to see the 1904 World's Fair exhibit, which was in the west wing. There were glass display cases filled with World's Fair souvenir plates, souvenir goblets, souvenir beer steins, photographs, tickets, parking permits, maps, and stock certificates. A life-size mannequin wore the uniform of the Jefferson Guard (the official police force of the 1904 St. Louis World's Fair). A sword, worn by one of the original Jefferson Guards, was hanging from the mannequin's waist. On display was the shovel used by David R. Francis at the World's Fair ground-breaking ceremony in 1903. Next to the shovel was a photograph of Francis breaking ground. In the same display case was a sterling silver punchbowl that Francis had received as a congratulatory gift.

Terri was especially interested in the important role played by the Philippines at the 1904 St. Louis World's Fair. The United States had acquired the Philippine Islands six years earlier in 1898 at the end of the Spanish-American War. America's newest protectorate, the Philippines was a country rich in natural resources. It was desirable to promote a close relationship between America and the Philippines. Located on forty-seven acres at the southwest corner of the fairgrounds, the Philippine Reservation was set off from the rest of the fair by an artificial body of water known as Arrowhead Lake. Over one hundred buildings typical of Philippine architecture covered the grounds, each designed to serve as a residence for 1,100 Filipinos. Westerners were given a more intimate knowledge of the social, commercial, and industrial capabilities of different Filipino tribes.

There were many photos of the Philippine Reservation on display, but Terri concentrated on the pictures of Igorot tribesmen. The Igorots were indigenous people known for their cannibalistic practices. They were fierce-looking, scantily-clad savages who ate dog meat at the World's Fair, probably because human flesh was not readily available. These were the ancestors of Paz Militante, who was born an Igorot on the island of Luzon. When Paz was very small, she moved with her parents to the island of Mindanao.

"This girl looks a lot like Paz," Terri said, pointing at an Igorot girl in one of the photos.

Glen agreed after studying the image of the raven-haired, bare-breasted Igorot beauty.

Terri saw a movie poster for *Meet Me in St. Louis*, which is a nostalgic piece of Americana that continues to transcend the years. The poster showed Judy Garland singing on the trolley.

"Meet me in STL," Terri said as she studied the poster. The movie takes place during the 1904 St. Louis World's Fair.

There was a spot in the corner for watching movies. It looked like the kind of minitheater that rich people had in their homes. There were six rows of upholstered movie seats with five seats in each row.

Terri sat in the middle of the back row. She was all alone. The only movie ever shown in this theater was *Meet Me in St. Louis* with the forever young Judy Garland. The film ran continuously on an LCD screen that was six feet wide and three feet high. Terri arrived just in time to see her favorite scene in the movie. This scene always captured her heart. Judy was ready to sing about the boy next door. Judy comes down from the stairway and stands next to a ficus houseplant. She strokes a leaf of the houseplant and then begins singing. "The moment I saw him smile." She returns to the stairway and leans over the banister. "I knew he was just my style." She leaves the stairway and heads toward the open window. "My only regret is we've never met. Though I dream of him all the while." She is now framed in the large picture window. "But he doesn't know I exist," she sings as she sits down on the windowsill. "No matter how I may persist." She stares out the window with a wistful look on her face. "So it's clear to see…there's no hope for me." There is an untrimmed rosebush that is starting to creep in through the window. The rosebush rustles in the breeze. "Though I live at 5135 Kensington Avenue and he lives at 5133."

Terri called for Glen to come and join her.

Judy has on a white dress that extends almost to her ankles. People wore a lot of clothes in those days, even in the summertime, and Judy is also sporting a second outfit that resembles a seersucker suit with vertical blue-and-white stripes. She is wearing a large white bow tie and a large white belt. Her auburn hair is curled in front and hangs to her shoulders.

Terri stared strangely at the screen and lip-synced the words to the song. Glen came over and sat next to her.

"You used to be the boy next door," she said.

"I lived across the street," Glen remarked.

"That's close enough," Terri confided. "Anyway, in the book *Meet Me in St. Louis*, the boy does live across the street and not next door."

Judy was now into the main body of the song:

How can I ignore the boy next door?
I love him more than I can say

Doesn't try to please me, doesn't even tease me
And he never sees me glance his way
And though I'm heart-sore, the boy next door
Affection for me won't display
I just adore him so I can't ignore him
The boy next door.

Judy now gets up from the windowsill and walks over to the gilt-edged mirror at the bottom of the stairway. She primps and preens in front of the antique full-length mirror and then does a little dance before returning to the window. She sings very slowly: "I just adore him so I can't ignore him…the boy next door." She then pulls the lace curtain shut, covering her face. Terri snuggled against Glen and kissed him. "Love thy neighbor," she purred. "That's what it says in the Bible."

"I don't think the Bible is referring to romantic love," Glen expounded.

"Dating a neighbor can save you a lot of money on transportation charges," Terri said. "Would you like me if I were Judy Garland?"

"Judy Garland didn't have any talent," Glen said in a matter-of-fact voice.

"I can't believe you said that. Judy Garland is my favorite entertainer."

The two young people watched a little more of *Meet Me in St. Louis* and then walked down to the basement of the museum.

"This is where the West begins," Glen said, after studying an exhibit about mountain men, the fur trade, and pioneers. There were Indian artifacts, flintlock rifles, and several Lewis & Clark journals.

"What's past is prologue," Glen added. "I don't know what that means."

"That's a quote from Shakespeare," Terri interjected. "*The Tempest*. It means history sets the scene for what comes later."

Glen walked over to a painting called *The Buffalo Hunt* by Carl Wimar. The canvas depicted the death of a buffalo at the hands of a bloodthirsty redskin. The savage, riding a white horse, was about to shoot the poor bison at point-blank range with a bow and arrow.

Glen began reading aloud from the placard beneath the painting. "This painting shows something of the danger and adventure connected with this daring type of hunting. Many Indians participated in the buffalo hunts and traded the skins with the white men. In a single season, Manuel Lisa brought 15,000 buffalo skins to St. Louis. In 1840, the American Fur Company slaughtered 67,000 buffalo."

Next, Glen turned his attention to an exhibit called *The Trapper*. On display were two muzzle-loading Hawken rifles, beaver traps, beaver pelts, two buckskin suits, Indian blankets, and trinkets for the Indians. "I'd like to be a mountain man," Glen said. "Just like Robert Redford in the movie *Jeremiah Johnson*. I have all the qualifications. I'm independent, self-reliant, I love the outdoors, and I know how to use a gun. The next time a mountain man job opens up at the employment office, I'm going to apply."

Terri and Glen learned about the three founders of St. Louis: Pierre Laclede Liquest, Madame Rene Auguste Chouteau, and Auguste Chouteau. There were oil paintings of all three people. Glen began reading out loud from a large placard: "Laclede, the founder of St. Louis, came to New Orleans as a 'gentleman traveling for pleasure,' and there he met and married Madame Chouteau. In 1764, the couple traveled up the Mississippi River to found the city of St. Louis. A fur trader, Laclede was quiet in demeanor, hasty in temper, and was known to have remarkable skill and strength as a fencer. He was a man of education and culture."

A glass display case contained the flying suit Lucky Lindy wore to Paris. There was a life-size photograph of Lindbergh wearing the suit. Spread along the bottom of the case were a few of the items he took with him on the trip—sunglasses, maps, a flask, two very old sticks of chewing gum. In bold letters was a famous Lindbergh quote: "If I had to choose, I would rather have birds than airplanes." Next, Terri and Glen climbed a staircase to the library of the Missouri Historical Society. Glen's grandmother was a charter member of the society, and Glen was a member too. He often did research in the library for his book about the Grosse family. The two young people entered sideways through the library doorway. It was necessary to enter sideways, since books were stacked everywhere. After showing his membership card to a librarian, Glen led Terri down a narrow corridor. On one side were the offices of the Missouri Historical Society. On the other side was a reading room. The corridor was lined with file cabinets which contained copies of old MHS bulletins. On top of the cabinets were marble busts of famous St. Louisans. The marble heads were ivory white and looked like they belonged in a mausoleum.

At the end of the corridor was a large room filled with shelves and shelves of books. There were approximately one hundred thousand books there. Most had to do with the history of St. Louis, the history of Missouri, the westward expansion of the United States, and genealogy. The library also contained approximately two million documents, diaries, letters, papers, pamphlets, periodicals, and maps. Entering the book-filled room, the two young people looked around and then began making their way through the literary labyrinth. Everywhere books had run wild and taken possession of the environment, breeding and multiplying like tropical undergrowth. Glen said he needed a machete to cut his way through. The distance between bookshelves was so narrow that Terri and Glen were forced to travel at a snail's pace. "I read that James Michener did research in this library for his book *Centennial*," Glen said as he inched his way through the denseness. "Have you read *Centennial*?"

"Yes I have," Terri replied as she followed Glen through the maze. "It's really good."

"I think it's one of the best books ever written," Glen said. He paused for a moment. "Michener came here primarily to get information on the early fur trade. If you recall, the first section of *Centennial* deals with Pasquinel, a French Canadian trapper who brings furs to St. Louis. In St. Louis, Pasquinel meets his first wife, who is the daughter of his business partner. However, he deserts his wife for the freedom of the frontier and has an affair with an Indian girl while he's out in the wilderness. Eventually, his wife finds out about the affair and gets really mad." Reaching a clearing after their long trek across the room, Terri and Glen sat down at a writing table. The table was set back in an alcove.

"This is what I love about libraries," Terri said. "There are always so many little nooks and crannies where a man and a woman can be alone. Let's have a talk, Glen. This spot is nice and private. I guarantee you that no one will interrupt us." Terri and Glen talked about getting married and where they would live and if they would have enough money. Glen said he liked to take hunting and fishing trips, and Terri said that was fine with her, but she would stay home. She did agree to cook the wild game that Glen shot and the fish that he caught. The young couple made many plans for their new life together. "May God bless our marriage," Terri prayed, "and may it be happier than the marriage of Elly Zahm and Levi Zendt in *Centennial*. Elly, played by Stephanie Zimbalist, is killed by a rattlesnake not long after marrying Levi, portrayed by Gregory Harrison. Elly and Levi head west from Pennsylvania in 1845. Elly is pregnant when she is bitten by the snake. Levi is devastated by her death and withdraws from life, becoming a mountain man. I never knew a rattlesnake could kill someone that fast."

Sitting next to a large open window, Terri and Glen had a good view of the Forest Park golf course across the street. The course was lush and green because of all the rain St. Louis had received recently. The temperature was ninety-eight degrees, and there wasn't a breath of wind. The library did not have air conditioning, and Terri and Glen were beginning to sweat. Moving closer to the open window in a futile attempt to cool off, Terri glanced out at a group of golfers on the first tee. She watched one of the men slice his ball into the street. After leaving the library, Terri and Glen had a bison burger in the museum restaurant, and then they took a walk through Forest Park.

Terri picked up a free map of Forest Park before leaving the Jefferson Memorial. She studied the map and pointed in a southwesterly direction. "Let's go to Art Hill," she said. "That's my favorite spot in the park." She reached out and took Glen's hand. "Come on," she said, tugging him along. Terri and Glen took a shortcut through the golf course. This was where the Pike was located at the 1904 World's Fair. The Pike was a large carnival with many attractions. The original 1904 fire hydrants were still there in the middle of the golf course. Terri and Glen had to dodge golf balls and they heard men yelling the word *fore* over and over. The young couple crossed two bridges over rain-swollen canals and found themselves at the foot of Art Hill. The St. Louis Art Museum was at the top of the hill. In winter, this was a popular spot for St. Louisans to go sled-riding. Terri and Glen hiked to the top of Art Hill, where they had an excellent view of the Grand Basin. They gazed down at the wide expanse of clear blue water. A few canoes were out; one of them was stuck in shallow water, another rocked lazily in the sun, and from a third, Terri noticed the glint of a fishing line arcing through the air. The Grand Basin had changed only slightly in appearance since 1904. During the World's Fair, artificial waterfalls raced down Art Hill and splashed into the Grand Basin. These waterfalls were known as the Cascades. Capitalizing on and memorializing the fair's main attraction, Scott Joplin had composed a rag called "The Cascades" and caught in it the bubble and flow of the watercourse. Terri led Glen to a secluded grove of trees near the art museum, which was one of the few permanent buildings of the 1904 World's Fair.

She casually put her arm around Glen's shoulder. "My favorite spot," she said. "How do you like it?"

From here, they had a panoramic view of Forest Park. They could see the Grand Basin to the north and also the Post-Dispatch Lake to the east.

"This is where it was all at," Terri said, making a sweeping gesture with her hand. "The World's Fair, I mean. That beautiful Ivory City that flourished here eighty-nine years ago. All the buildings were called palaces. Over there alongside the Grand Basin were the palaces of mines and metallurgy, liberal arts, education and social economy, manufacturing, electricity and machinery, varied industries, and transportation."

Terri sat down in the tall grass at the top of Art Hill. "You'll find I'm an incurable romantic," she said, picking a blade of grass and wrapping it around her finger.

"I like that quality in a woman," Glen said, sitting down beside her. He gazed into her eyes for a moment and then buried his face in her neck.

They kissed seriously, not playfully like before. Their bodies merged. Terri moved her thigh between his legs. Her breasts were pressed firmly against his chest. Glen could feel their mouths growing hot as they dropped to a prone position in the cool grass. They attacked each other, tearing up the grass with their kicking heels, grunting, and moaning under the canopy of trees.

Their lovemaking was short but utterly releasing. Afterward, Terri lay in the grass and turned her face away. On his back, Glen stared up at the blue sky.

In front of the art museum was the famous equestrian statue of Louis IX (Saint Louis) of France. Terri and Glen passed by the Apotheosis of Saint Louis statue before heading down Art Hill. The statue represents Saint Louis, the crusader, clad in armor of the thirteenth century and holding aloft his inverted sword forming a cross. The pedestal is granite and the horse and rider bronze. The statue was once the top symbol representing the City of St. Louis before the Gateway Arch was built.

Terri and Glen were embracing as they sauntered down Art Hill. They had spent a wonderful day together, and they looked forward to the rest of the summer. The good old summertime. Summer was just beginning. They talked excitedly about the grand opening of the Belle of Calhoun Casino on June 23.

Chapter Eight

The *Belle of Calhoun* was all decked out in bunting and civic pride. The boat was having a ripple effect on the local economy of Cahokia. Many unemployed residents of Cahokia had obtained jobs on the floating casino. These employees were wearing pride on their sleeves. They were also wearing garters on their sleeves. They probably had aces up their sleeves. The boat was rigged and ready, as the old nautical saying goes. The slot machines were rigged. The video poker machines were rigged. The dice games were rigged. The roulette wheel was rigged. The Wheel of Fortune was rigged. And all the table games were rigged. The *Belle of Calhoun* was ready for the shakedown cruise, and the crew members were ready to shake down the passengers for money.

Because of high water, the plans for the christening ceremony had been changed. Originally, Anna was supposed to smash a bottle of champagne against the boat's bow. The new plans called for her to shatter a bottle of champagne over the two-ton brass bell, which was located on the Texas Deck at the very top of the boat. The Texas Deck, short and narrow, contained the pilothouse and the officers' quarters. This type of deck was added to many steamboats after 1845, the year Texas became a state. Steamboat cabins were named for states, and the officers' spacious quarters were named for the largest state. A shipboard bell is considered a significant part of the ship's equipment and history. Bells have played both a practical and a symbolic role in the life of ships and boats. One of the most memorable traditions for sailors and their families involves the use of ship's bells as baptismal fonts for shipboard christenings. Children of the ship's company baptized according to this custom can also have their names inscribed on the ship's bell. Likewise, it is also a common practice to christen a ship by breaking a bottle of champagne over the ship's bell.

Gracing the big roof bell of the *Belle of Calhoun* was a full-length carved figure of the young Anna, her right arm extended as though pointing the way up the river, her left hand holding an American flag which furled gracefully at her side. Carved of wood and painted, this five-foot statue of Anna was a beautiful figurehead. The raven-haired figurehead in her purple gown seemed confident and casual about her ability to calm the river. Battling the wind, she embodied the spirit of St. Louis as she looked down over the river. Soothing the river gods, she made sure the voyage would be safe.

Terri, Glen, Anna, and Dinty arrived in Glen's houseboat, and they went immediately to the Texas deck for a meet-and-greet. From the Texas deck, Terri could see Channel Five's live truck parked on the levee. The truck had just arrived, parked on the rugged cobble-stones, and raised its forty-five-foot antenna. A female reporter, with a microphone in her hand, was standing by the truck. She was talking about the festivities live on the air. A circle of floodlights illuminated her. The police kept onlookers back. Terri recognized the girl as Pam Keller, who had been with Channel Five for many years. Terri loved seeing celebrities in person, and she mentioned this to Dinty, who was leaning close beside her. The cameraman followed Pam as she interviewed several well-dressed people who were waiting in line to board the boat. She asked the people why they had come and if they thought they would win any money. She also talked with members of the St. Louis Ragtimers, who were playing jazz and blues music for the passengers. Pam followed the long purple carpet that led into the boat. The purple carpet was actually the train of a purple dress that a beautiful raven-haired girl was wearing. The girl was trying to look like Anna in the famous painting. People walked down the "carpet" and said hello to the girl before boarding the boat. The girl greeted everyone with a warm hug. After interviewing the raven-haired girl and hugging her, Pam boarded the boat and came up to the Texas deck. When Terri saw the blindingly bright floodlights attached to the television camera, she whispered, "We don't belong here, Dinty, we're from the wrong side of the tracks."

"That's okay," Dinty replied, "as long as there's no train coming."

Pam thrust her microphone into Anna's face and asked, "Are you Annabelle Calhoun?"

"I'm Anna, the Belle of Calhoun, you dipstick," Anna responded in an angry tone of voice.

"Sorry," Pam said. "You must be very excited about tonight."

"I'd rather be home watching myself on television," Anna said in a sarcastic tone. "No, seriously, I am very excited about tonight. This is a momentous time for the St. Louis area, a chance for us to return to our roots. Once again the Mississippi River is playing an important role in the workings of our region."

"I love your beautiful purple gown," Pam complimented. "Who are you wearing tonight?"

"This gown is a Vera Wang original," Anna said flippantly.

"How is it that you came to be known as the Lavender Lady?"

"It's because of Empress Alexandra of Russia, whose favorite color was lavender."

"Whatever happened to her?"

"She was executed by the Bolsheviks in 1918. Red was never her color."

"So that's why you were known as the Czardine."

"The Czarina," Anna corrected, aware that Pam was having some fun.

"Who is your date tonight?" Pam asked.

"This is Dinty, who lives across the street from me."

"Nice to meet you, Dinty," Pam said. "You must be very excited."

"Yes, I am," Dinty began, but he was interrupted.

"We make the perfect couple," Anna declared, putting her arm around Dinty. "Belle," she said, indicating herself. "And the Beast." She laughed, indicating Dinty. Dinty frowned. He didn't like being embarrassed in front of a large television audience. He felt like issuing a rebuttal but held his tongue.

"How can you let her talk to you that way?" Terri whispered to Dinty.

"I've had it up to here with that Senior Cinderella," Dinty mumbled.

"Why did they name a boat after you?" Pam asked Anna.

Anna was perturbed by the question. "I was friendly with the fleet," she replied sarcastically.

Next, Pam interviewed Paz, who was there with her new Filipino boyfriend. He was almost forty years older than Paz. He was a doctor from the Philippines who was now practicing in St. Louis. Young Filipinas liked older men, especially if they had a lot of money.

"You must hate this hot weather," Pam said to Paz.

"Why is that?" Paz asked.

"You're an Eskimo, right?"

"I'm from the Philippines," Paz retorted. "I'm used to hot weather."

"It's nice you brought your father," Pam stated.

"He's my boyfriend!" Paz announced boldly. "He's a doctor from the Philippines. I call him Dr. Phil."

Paz and the doctor wore traditional Philippine clothing, appropriate for a romantic couple. Paz looked beautiful in her Maria Clara dress and the doctor was very handsome in his Barong Tagalog shirt.

Pam directed her attention to the doctor whose name was Wong. He revealed that Paz was his patient, and that was how they met. "She's what I was looking for," the doctor said lovingly.

"A caring, sweet-natured Filipina."

Paz laughed. "What can I say? That is my nature. A girl must be true to her nature." She pretended to fan herself, but she was only showing off the enormous diamond engagement ring Dr. Wong had given her. "Mahal kita!" she told the doctor.

"Mahal na mahal rin kita!" Dr. Wong replied.

Terri felt sorry for the poor doctor if he thought he had found a stand-by-your-man, Stepford wife from the Philippines. Paz was no great prize.

Anna noticed a group of elderly women congregating together. They were attracting a lot of attention because they were all dressed alike.

"Who are they?" Anna asked Terri.

"That's the Red Hat Society," Terri responded. "They all dress in purple except for their red hats."

"Nice," Anna exclaimed jubilantly.

"Why don't you go over and join up. They'll probably make you exalted queen mother."

"That's a good idea!" Anna agreed. "I really should associate with women of my own age and vintage."

She went over to greet the Red Hatters. The leader of the group rushed forward and hugged Anna with outstretched arms as though welcoming back a long-lost friend. The purple-suited lady then placed her red hat on top of Anna's head. Anna was now one of the group. The Red Hat Society was formed because of a poem named "Warning" by Jenny Joseph. "When I am an old woman, I shall wear purple," the Red Hatters chanted to Anna. That was the first line of the poem. "With a red hat which doesn't go, and doesn't suit me," they added, quoting the second line.

The Texas deck was beginning to fill up with reporters and paparazzi. The mainstream media had boarded the boat. Some of the celebrities and distinguished guests came up to the Texas deck to be interviewed by the news media. "Look this way!" one of the photographers yelled to Anna. "And wipe that Southern Belle simper off your face."

"I do declare," Anna said. "Everyone thinks I'm a Southern Belle. Don't they know that Calhoun County is in Illinois?"

A disheveled reporter, with notebook in hand, approached Anna. Anna recognized the man because he wrote a daily column in the St. Louis *Post-Dispatch* and also appeared on a weekly television talk show. "Excuse me," the man said, "are you Bella Calhoun?"

"They're treating me like a rock star," Anna stated after speaking with numerous reporters and posing for hundreds of photos. With her purple hair and purple outfit, she was extremely photogenic.

"You look like a rock star," Terri insinuated.

Terri watched Captain Hardin walking among the reporters and paparazzi on the Texas deck, applying smiles and little witticisms and even a bit of elbow touching and back slapping where it seemed appropriate. For a gruff river man, the old captain was accomplished at public relations. The captain looked and sounded a lot like Clint Eastwood, squinting into the sun as he greeted the various dignitaries. The captain had on a uniform that made him look like a German U-Boat commander, which was sort of appropriate since he had taken numerous boats to the bottom. His black uniform had many shiny brass buttons. An anchor was pictured on his black hat along with the word CAPTAIN. Terri thought the captain looked liked Clint Eastwood in the movie *Magnum Force*, when he impersonates an airline captain in order to board a plane and kill some hijackers.

Terri struck a pose for the cameras. She looked like Scarlett O'Hara in her hoop skirt and bonnet. The paparazzi followed her, but she wasn't annoyed. She felt like a supermodel. Terri was enjoying her fifteen minutes of fame. She liked schmoozing with TV and newspaper people. This meet-and-greet was a good idea, she thought. The photographers had snapped many photos of her because she was dressed in period clothing and looked like she belonged to another age. The fact that she was a beautiful young girl also helped. Glen was dressed like an old-time riverboat gambler, and he was also receiving a great deal of media attention. Just like in the old days, it seemed as though the entire community had come out to greet the arrival of the steamboat. Passengers and visitors swarmed over the levee, and it was a wonder to Terri that they weren't walking all over each other. As it was, there was plenty of pushing and jostling. Terri couldn't help but notice that here on the Mississippi, the black folks were working, while the white folks were playing. Several African American men were carrying supplies onto the boat. Slaves, Terri thought to herself. One of the Negro deckhands was singing *Old Man River* as a rap song. He was singing loud enough that his voice carried up to Terri on the Texas deck. *Old Man River* has all the elements of a good rap song: misery, violence, substance abuse, prison, and the subjugation of blacks by the white man. Terri thoroughly enjoyed this hip-hop version of *Old Man River*, and she started applauding. She suddenly became aware that many other people on the boat had also been listening to the song. Hip-hop superstar Nelly, a St. Louis native, had been waiting in line with other distinguished guests, and he began applauding and yelling, "Bravo! Bravo!" Nelly was scheduled to perform later that evening aboard the *Belle of Calhoun*. Other well-known St. Louis entertainers were also slated to appear: Chuck Berry, Tina Turner, Fontella Bass, and Billy Davis Jr. of the *5th Dimension*.

Terri and Glen waltzed across the Texas deck to the podium by the forward railing. This spot was visible to spectators on the boat and on shore. Dinty followed Terri and Glen. Then came the captain. Anna hobbled behind the captain.

"Here comes the face that launched a thousand ships," Dinty muttered to Terri and Glen.

"I heard that!" Anna shouted. She held a champagne bottle in her hand. "I'll launch you," she threatened, waving the champagne bottle above her head.

"Okay, Ms. MilliHelen," Dinty razzed. "Make like Helen of Troy and christen this ship." Dinty explained that a MilliHelen is the amount of beauty it takes to launch a single ship.

Anna stood at the forward railing of the Texas deck and looked down at the crowd that had assembled below her on the large open-air observation deck, also known as the hurricane deck. She was standing next to the boat's bronze bell. "Do you know what they call this thing here inside the bell?" she asked Dinty.

"No," Dinty replied.

"The clapper," Anna responded, clapping her hands loudly. She grabbed the lanyard that was attached to the clapper, and she rang the bell. She turned to Dinty and said, "Ask not for whom the bell tolls, it tolls for thee." The moaning and groaning of the bell brought the crowd to attention. People continued to assemble on the open-air observation deck. A pleasant breeze swept across the river. Loudspeakers had been set up so people on the boat and on shore could hear the proceedings.

Several dignitaries arrived at the speakers' platform. The mayor of St. Louis greeted Anna, shaking her hand, whispering something in her ear. Freeman Bosley Jr. had been the mayor of St. Louis for just two months. He was the Gateway City's first black mayor. The mayor of Cahokia was also there. Congressman Dick Gephardt had stopped by to say hello and perhaps garner a few votes. Also in attendance was the county executive of Calhoun County, Illinois. The reigning Ms. Apple Blossom was there, a beautiful young woman named Candace

Miller, who was wearing a swimsuit and crown. She was the modern-day equivalent of the Belle of Calhoun. Calhoun County still had a beauty pageant except the winner was now called Ms. Apple Blossom and not the Belle of Calhoun. Actually, Anna was the only Belle of Calhoun there ever was. Candace Miller, who was wearing a sash that said Ms. Apple Blossom, put her arm around Anna for a photo op. There were no blacks living in Calhoun County. No blacks had ever lived in Calhoun County. To avoid a public relations nightmare, the Calhoun delegation included a token black man who was up on the speakers' platform. This man did not live in Calhoun County. He was the boyfriend of Candace Miller, who was as white as an apple blossom.

Anna had her photo taken with a ninety-eight-year-old lady who had come up to the speakers' platform. This was Estelle Rice, who, in 1913, had been runner-up for the title of Belle of Calhoun. She had lost the title by only 456 votes. She was still not ready to forgive Anna for winning the crown. Estelle could not believe that Anna, who was only thirteen years old at the time, had become the Belle of Calhoun. She had called Anna a whore and the Mistress of the Mississippi.

"It's a shame to waste good booze," Anna said, grasping the magnum of champagne with a firm hand. She peeled off the foil and carefully unraveled the muselet, which is the wire cage that holds the stopper in place. She then forcibly removed the plastic bottle stopper. There was a loud pop, and some champagne gushed out. She took several quick swigs of the sparkling, bubbly beverage and then put back the stopper and the muselet.

"Okay, Champagne Lady, do your stuff," the captain ordered, adjusting the microphone.

Anna raised the bottle of bubbly in her hand and prepared to christen the boat's bell. First she had to say a few words: "In the name of the state of Illinois, I christen thee *Belle of Calhoun*." She paused for a moment and then added: "God bless this ship and all who sail in her."

Terri covered her mouth with her hand to stifle a giggle as Anna intoned, "Let's man our ship and bring her to life."

Dinty sighed. He was growing impatient. "Be careful!" he yelled as Anna swung the bottle. "Don't crack the bell." The crowd roared with laughter.

"From one belle to another," Anna proclaimed as the bottle smashed against the boat's large bell.

From one ding dong to another, Terri thought to herself.

Champagne spouted out, and Anna tried to quickly drink some. She then threatened Dinty with the jagged edge of the bottle.

"I'm the Belle of Calhoun!" Anna yelled in exaltation. "God bless me and all who sail in me." Anna looked above her at the boat's tall smokestacks, raising her hands upward. She then brought her hands down to her large breasts. "This belle is pretty well stacked," Anna confided to the crowd.

Now, in accordance with maritime tradition, the crew members boarded the boat in single file as a brass band played *Anchors Away.*

It was now time for the boat to depart on the inaugural cruise. The captain headed toward the pilothouse. "Would you like to see the captain's bridge?" he asked, taking out his false teeth.

"Sure," Terri responded eagerly. She groaned when she saw the captain holding his false teeth in the air. Terri gave Glen a funny look.

"No, seriously," the captain said after putting his bridge back in his mouth, "come with me and I'll show you how I pilot the boat."

Terri, Glen, Anna, and Dinty entered the pilothouse along with Captain Hardin. Glen grabbed a lanyard hanging from the ceiling and blew the steam whistle.

"Don't mess with my toot-toot!" the captain yelled.

"Is it okay if I smoke in here?" Terri asked.

"Sure," the captain replied. "I'm a smoker myself. They asked me if I wanted the *Belle of Calhoun* to be a smoke-free casino, and I said no way. I don't respond to any politically correct bells or whistles."

The pilot house offered a 360-degree view and was equipped for all navigational duties, with three wing stations to assist in docking. The engine room housed three Cummins KTA-50M engines each supplying 1,250 horsepower. To aid in maneuverability, the boat was also equipped with two 300 horsepower Caterpillar 3208 Thrusters. Electrical power was supplied by three main Cummins/Onan KTA-

38 G2 generators with a capacity of 800 kilowatts each. And there was also a backup generator for emergencies.

Captain Hardin put his headset on and stood in front of the large pilot wheel. Speaking through the headset's microphone, he barked orders to crew members below deck. He blew whistles for friends to go ashore. Then, the gangways were withdrawn. He checked gauges and flipped switches. He truly believed what Mark Twain had said about riverboat captains being like gods.

"I'm King of the River," the captain proclaimed as he started the boat's engine and prepared to get under way.

"Half-horse and half-alligator."

"Bet I know which half is the horse," Terri whispered to Glen.

The boat was equipped with all the modern conveniences—hydraulic steering, echo sounders, pneumatic hoists, television, radar, and a state-of-the-art communications system. But in spite of all this modern technology, the captain remained an old-time riverman, faithful to the ways of the past.

Captain Hardin took off his captain's hat and put on a black cowboy hat. "You know a dream is like a river," he sang into the headset's microphone. "Ever changing as it flows. And a dreamer's just a vessel. That must follow where it goes. Trying to learn from what's behind you. And never knowing what's in store. Makes each day a constant battle. Just to stay between the shores. And I will sail my vessel till the river runs dry…"

Terri and Glen looked at each other and laughed. They continued to listen to the captain's wailing.

"There's bound to be rough waters," the captain intoned as he spun the pilot wheel. He suddenly switched songs.

"What goes up must come down, spinnin' wheel got to go 'round."

"I'm afraid the captain, like his steamboat, is around the bend," Terri told Glen.

Suddenly, the captain stopped singing. "I heard that!" he shouted. "Get your sterns out of my pilothouse!"

Terri, Glen, and Dinty quickly left the pilothouse, but Anna stayed behind.

"Maybe you didn't hear me," the captain bellowed. "Get your purple butt out of my pilothouse."

Anna still didn't move.

"Get your purple curple out of my pilothouse!" Captain Hardin blasted.

Anna left the pilothouse and joined the others to wave farewell to people on shore. The *Belle of Calhoun* moved slowly down the dock to the accompaniment of last messages and shouted farewells of those on the levee. As he was waving farewell, Glen noticed a group of religious protesters on the shore. An eccentric minister was firing verbal broadsides at the *Belle of Calhoun*. "777, sign of the devil!" he yelled. There were around twenty protesters who were carrying cardboard signs with anti-gambling messages like, "You are a child of God, do not board Satan's steamship" and "Wake up and smell the brimstone." Glen pointed out the protesters to Terri. "What are they doing here?" he asked. "This is a place for high rollers, not holy rollers."

"You can bet that's a Protestant group," Terri said. "No Catholic would ever protest gambling."

Several of the protesters ran after the boat, their signboards slung over their shoulders. The fanatical Protestant protesters shouted and gesticulated in an effort to get the boat to stop. Captain Hardin paid no attention to these religious zealots. Terri, Glen, Anna, and Dinty took a tour of the *Belle of Calhoun*. They examined the 50-foot high neon paddle wheel. The Belle of Calhoun was 447 feet long with a 70-foot beam. She stood 58 feet tall with an 11-foot draft. The boat was designed to comfortably hold 3,000 people, including patrons and employees alike. There was a state-of-the-art surveillance system, an American Dynamics 2050 Video Matrix System with dual camera bays. The system had 272 video inputs and 16 outputs. Cameras were strategically placed in 260 positions to monitor all areas of the boat. Terri, Glen, Anna, and Dinty traversed all three decks of the boat to see where the best gambling was. Each deck had about 11,000 square feet of gaming space. When they finished their tour, they ran into Captain Hardin, who had left the helm in order to mingle with the customers. His first officer was now steering the boat.

"I'm shocked," the captain said, looking out at the sea of slot machines, dice tables, and roulette wheels. "Shocked...to find that gambling is going on in here...on my boat!"

Terri didn't know if the captain was trying to be funny or if he was being serious.

"This is my final voyage," Captain Hardin said. "I'm retiring after this trip."

"That's what the captain of the *Titanic* said," Terri asserted. "We took a tour and noticed there aren't enough lifeboats on board for all these passengers."

"The *Belle of Calhoun* is unsinkable," Captain Hardin proclaimed.

"The *Titanic* was supposed to be unsinkable," Terri informed the captain. "Are you prepared to go down with your ship?"

"This is a boat, not a ship," the captain grumbled, sidestepping the question.

Chapter Nine

Most casinos offered stage shows, and the Belle of Calhoun was no exception. Captain Hardin was the master of ceremonies. Hunched over like Ed Sullivan, he introduced the performers and waved for them to come onstage. The casino had a large auditorium, which was now packed with people. The first act was an Elvis tribute artist who was considered to be the best Elvis impersonator in St. Louis. He had on a 1950s Elvis-style gold lame suit, made by Presley's costumer Nudie Cohn. Despite the 1950s outfit, the impersonator was representing the old Elvis and not the young Elvis. He was overweight and had a puffy face just like the old Elvis. He was disappointed that the new Elvis postage stamp, released earlier that year, bore the image of the young Elvis and not the old Elvis. People had been given a chance to vote, and the young Elvis won. The stamp was issued on January 8, 1993, which would have been the fifty-eighth birthday of the King.

The orchestra played a few bars of *2001 A Space Odyssey* and then switched to the drum and trumpet fanfare that was part of every Elvis introduction. There was wild applause from the audience as the Elvis entrance music was being played.

The ersatz Elvis stumbled his way through a pair of swinging doors that had been set up onstage just like in the movie *Viva Las Vegas* during the title number.

"Bright light boat," the pseudo Elvis sang. "Gonna set my soul, gonna set my soul on fire." He was joined by some showgirls who were dressed like Folies Bergère dancers. There were also three girl backup singers. The ten-piece orchestra was providing accompaniment.

Got a whole lot of money that's ready to burn so
    get those stakes up higher.
There's a thousand pretty women on the deck
    out there.
They're all livin' the devil may care.
And I'm just the devil with love to spare.
Viva Cal-houn. Viva Cal-houn.
How I wish that there were more than twen-
    ty-four hours in the day.
Even if there were forty more I wouldn't sleep a
    minute away.
Oh, there's blackjack and poker and the roulette
    wheel.
A fortune won and lost on every deal.
All you need's a strong heart and a nerve of steel.
Viva Cal-houn. Viva Cal-houn.
Viva Cal-houn with your neon flashin' and your
    one arm bandits crashin'
All those hopes down the drain.
Viva Cal-houn turnin' day into nighttime.
Turnin' night into daytime.
If you see once you'll never be the same again.
I'm gonna keep on the run.
I'm gonna have me some fun.
If it costs me my very last dime.
If I wind up broke, well, I'll always remember
    that I had a swingin' time.
I'm gonna give it everything I've got.
Lady Luck please let the dice stay hot.
Let me shoot a seven with every shot.
Viva Cal-houn. Viva Cal-houn.
Viva, Viva Cal-houn.

The Presley pretender cavorted with the showgirls and then
sang one last time: "Viva Cal-houn. Viva Cal-houn. Viva, Viva
Cal-houn…"

All this action was being shown on a giant Samsung LED video screen above the stage. The screen was thirty-three feet wide and seventeen feet high with nearly nine million pixels.

The real Elvis actually did perform on a riverboat in the 1966 movie *Frankie and Johnny*, with Elvis as Johnny and the beautiful Donna Douglas as Frankie. At the time, Donna Douglas was playing Elly May Clampett on the Beverly Hillbillies.

The opening credits of the movie *Frankie and Johnny* appeared on the giant video screen. A showboat, which also offered gambling, was cruising on the Mississippi River. The wannabe Elvis sang along:

> Come along, come along, there's a full moon
>   shining bright.
> Come along, come along, we're gonna hit St.
>   Louis tonight.
> Spend your money looking at the chorus line.
> Spend your money, win it on the number 9.
> Take your sweetheart even though she's never
>   been.
> If she's worried tell her that you always win.
> Come along, come along, there's a full moon
>   shining bright.
> Come along, come along, you're gonna win a for-
>   tune tonight.
> Hear the whistle, lady luck's about to go.
> Is she smiling, maybe yes or maybe no.
> Now's the time when nights are filled with sweet
>   romance.
> Don't be bashful step on up and take a chance.
> Come along, come along, there's a full moon
>   shining bright.
> Come along, come along, we're gonna hit St.
>   Louis tonight.

The audience loved this performance and reacted with thunderous applause. Elvis was once again King of the Mississippi as he was billed in the movie. Terri, Glen, Anna, and Dinty were sitting in the front row, and they were thoroughly enjoying the show.

The acronym ETA can stand for estimated time of arrival, expected time of arrival, or Elvis tribute artist. Reno Clinton was the stage name of the ETA who was performing for the large *Belle of Calhoun* crowd. The name Reno Clinton was a takeoff on Clint Reno, the character Elvis played in his first movie *Love Me Tender*. Clint Reno gets killed at the end of the picture.

Reno Clinton sang the title song *Frankie and Johnny*, which was based on an actual event that happened in St. Louis in 1899. Frankie Baker shot and killed her two-timing boyfriend, but she was acquitted. She claimed self-defense. The shooting had occurred in a rooming house in Downtown St. Louis. In the movie, Elvis sings the song as part of his act, and he is then shot by Donna Douglas, who has a gun loaded with blanks, except in the final scene when there is a real bullet in the chamber. Elvis manages to survive because the bullet hits a lucky piece in the pocket of his suitcoat.

Reno Clinton had sung the opening song from *Frankie and Johnny*, and now he sang the closing song:

> Everybody come aboard The Showboat tonight.
> We're gonna dance 'till the morning light.
> We'll have fun the whole night long.
> There'll be jokes and songs.
> Forget your troubles, forget your strife.
> You'll have the best time of your life.
> Hey everyone let's go, on with the show.
> Everybody's gonna gamble on The Showboat
>   tonight.
> The big casino's lit up bright.
> How can you lose just wear a grin you'll be sure
>   to win.
> Lady Luck's waiting there inside.
> The wheel of fortune's about to ride.
> Hey everyone let's go on with the show.
> Way down by the lobby, the boat's at the bank.

Bring money to spend you're welcome my friend.
Just walk up the plank.
Everybody come aboard The Showboat tonight.
Look around at the happy sight.
We'll guarantee that you'll have a ball.
Come on one and all.
Well what a great night you've got in store.
You'll want to keep coming back for more.
Hey everyone let's go on with the show.

The pseudo Presley, Reno Clinton, now moved out into the audience and began singing a medley of Elvis hits that had some kind of connection to gambling and good fortune. He surveyed the crowd for the prettiest girl he could find, and he chose Terri, who was in the front row.

"Come on and be my little good luck charm, uh-huh, huh, you sweet delight," he crooned to Terri, who was embarrassed. Glen was jealous and thought about punching Elvis.

I want a good luck charm hanging on my arm to
    have and to hold tonight.
Don't want a four leaf clover.
Don't want an old horse shoe.
Want your kiss 'cause I just can't miss.
With a good luck charm like you.

Glen gave Elvis a dirty look.

Don't want a silver dollar.
Rabbit's foot on a string.
The happiness in your warm caress.
No rabbit's foot can bring.

The spurious Elvis Presley grabbed Terri by the hand and pulled her to her feet, kissing her cheek lightly. He then finished his song:

"Come on and be my little good luck charm, uh-huh, huh, you sweet delight. I want a good luck charm hanging on my arm to have and to hold tonight."

Sensing Glen's anger, Reno Clinton released his hold on Terri, who quickly dropped back into her seat. "Thank you…thank you very much," Reno said sincerely and contritely in a faux Elvis Memphis Southern drawl.

Reno then began his next song *Shake, Rattle, and Roll* in his resonant and convincing Elvis voice. He pretended to shoot craps, clenching and shaking his right fist, opening his palm to release the imaginary pair of dice. *Shake, Rattle, and Roll* was originally a ragtime tune about shooting dice in New Orleans in the early 1900s.

Reno found another girl to flirt with and sang *Beginner's Luck* and *Hard Luck*, which are both songs from the movie *Frankie and Johnny.* Both songs deal with the correlation between being lucky in love and being lucky at gambling.

The real Elvis performed many songs that had some kind of connection to gambling and good fortune. Reno Clinton rendered a few more, devoting only a few seconds to each song. There was *Easy Come Easy Go, Fame and Fortune, Follow That Dream, From a Jack to a King, Golden Coins, Got My Mojo Working, How Can You Lose What You Never Had, I Got Lucky, I Got Stung*, and *Playing for Keeps.*

Reno Clinton sauntered back to the stage for his grand finale. He was aware of the dangerous high water conditions on the Mississippi River, so he sang *Down by the Riverside*, followed by that greatest of all flood songs, *Bridge Over Troubled Water.*

> When you're weary, feeling small.
> When tears are in your eyes, I will dry them all.
> I'm on your side, when times get rough.
> And friends just can't be found.
> Like a bridge over troubled water
> I will lay me down.
> Like a bridge over troubled water.
> I will lay me down.
> When you're down and out.

When you're on the street.
When evening falls so hard.
I will comfort you.
I'll take your part.
Oh, when darkness comes.
And pain is all around.
Like a bridge over troubled water.
I will lay me down.
Like a bridge over troubled water.
I will lay me down.
Ooh, I'll be your bridge.
Yes, I will.

Unbeknownst to anyone on the *Belle of Calhoun*, the Mississippi had been rising rapidly that night. It was originally thought the smokestacks would clear all the bridges, but suddenly there was a jolt as the tallest smokestack scraped gently against the Jefferson Barracks Bridge. There was no damage, but the crowd reacted as though the boat had just struck an iceberg. All the gamblers aboard the *Belle of Calhoun* thought they were about ready to cash in their chips Titanic style.

"Don't be alarmed!" Captain Hardin announced to the frantic, panicking crowd in the auditorium. He had to shout in order to be heard over all the yelling and screaming. "A smokestack grazed a bridge. That's all. We're not sinking. Get back in your seats and enjoy the rest of the show."

Gradually, the crowd simmered down when they realized there was no danger.

"It looks like we hit the bridge over troubled water," the simulated Elvis quipped, making a joke in order to relax the people, calm their fear, and put them at ease. "Like a river flows surely to the sea," he sang. "Darling so it goes. Some things are meant to be. Take my hand, take my whole life too. For I can't help falling in love with you." He turned to one of the girl backup singers and gave her a come-hither look with his bedroom eyes. "For I can't help falling in love with you." He had chosen the sexiest and boldest of the three girls. She played along with his advances.

It was now time for Elvis to perform his biggest showstoppers, which he always saved for last. *Suspicious Minds*, from 1969, was his seventeenth and final number one hit. The real Elvis made his last movie in 1969 and then returned to the concert stage in the 1970s. *Suspicious Minds* was the song his audiences most wanted to hear.

"We're caught in a trap," the makeshift Elvis sang as he continued his flirtation with the beautiful, blond-haired, blue-eyed backup singer. The other two girls had black hair.

Elvis and the blonde were serenading each other. The chemistry between them was off the charts. They were looking into each other's eyes as they sang a seductive duet.

"We're caught in a trap," they both sang, making sensual mouth movements.

> I can't walk out.
> Because I love you too much, baby.
> Why can't you see.
> What you're doing to me.
> When you don't believe a word I say?
> We can't go on together.
> With suspicious minds.
> And we can't build our dreams.
> On suspicious minds.
> So if an old friend I know.
> Drops by to say hello.
> Would I still see suspicion in your eyes?
> Here we go again.
> Asking where I've been.
> You can't see the tears are real.
> I'm crying. Yes, I'm crying.
> We can't go on together.
> With suspicious minds.
> And we can't build our dreams.
> On suspicious minds.

Oh, let our love survive.
I'll dry the tears from your eyes.
Let's don't let a good thing die.
When honey, you know I've never lied to you.
Mmm, yeah, yeah.

Now, Reno moved away from the blond backup singer and returned to the center of the stage, where he repeated the song in a martial arts manner, jabbing the air with his hands in a series of karate moves. He jackhammered his right leg and swung the microphone stand around while emphasizing, "I'm caught in a trap. I can't walk out." He did this several times. He resembled a whirling dervish. For the song's final line, he dropped to one knee and raised his arms to heaven like Al Jolson. The audience applauded enthusiastically amid some whistles and hoots. Reno stood up and bowed at the crowd, flashing his pearly capped teeth.

For his final number, Reno always did *An American Trilogy*, which the real Elvis performed for the first time at a Madison Square Garden concert in 1972. *An American Trilogy* consists of three nineteenth-century songs: *Dixie* to represent the Confederacy, the *Battle Hymn of the Republic* to include the Union side, and finally the African American spiritual *All My Trials* for the slaves.

"Oh, I wish I was in the land of cotton," Reno sang.

Old times there are not forgotten.
Look away. Look away. Look away Dixie Land.
In Dixie Land where I was born.
Early on one frosty morn.
Look away. Look away. Look away. Dixie Land.

The real Elvis was born in Tupelo, Mississippi, at four thirty-five in the morning on January 8, 1935. Tupelo is in the heart of Dixie. In January, the average low temperature in Tupelo is thirty-two degrees, so Elvis was not lying when he sang he was born in Dixie early on one frosty morning.

The three girl backup singers performed the chorus of *Dixie* as Reno listened.

> I wish I was in Dixie! Hooray! Hooray!
> In Dixie Land I'll take my stand, to live and die
>   in Dixie!
> Away! Away! Away down south in Dixie!
> Away! Away! Away down south in Dixie!

Then, Reno sang the first verse and chorus of *Dixie* before moving to the 1861 Julia Ward Howe classic *Battle Hymn of the Republic*. There was a crescendo drum roll during the transition from *Dixie* to the *Battle Hymn of the Republic*. The trumpets were blaring.

> Mine eyes have seen the glory of the coming of
>   the Lord.
> He is trampling out the vintage where the grapes
>   of wrath are stored.
> He hath loosed the fateful lightning of His terrible swift sword.
> His truth is marching on.
> Glory, glory, hallelujah!
> Glory, glory, hallelujah!
> Glory, glory, hallelujah!
> His truth is marching on.

Finally, there was the Negro spiritual *All My Trials*.

> So hush, little baby.
> Don't you cry.
> You know your daddy's bound to die.
> But all my trials, Lord, will soon be over.

The trilogy was not over yet. Reno stared at the orchestra as he waited for a flautist to finish playing Dixie. Then, like the real Elvis used to do, Reno psyched himself up before the dramatic conclusion.

He shouted something to the orchestra, pumped his right arm, and triumphantly sang, "Glory, glory, hallelujah! His truth is marching on."

As he walked off the stage, Reno made the Hawaiian shaka symbol, folding in his middle fingers to reveal only his little finger and thumb. The real Elvis had learned that in Hawaii, where the gesture originated, It means to hang loose, chill out, and be cool. "Thank you," Reno said. "Thank you very much! You're a fantastic audience."

The orchestra played some Elvis departure music, and Captain Hardin returned to the microphone. "Ladies and gentlemen," he began slowly after the Elvis exit music was over. "Elvis has left the boat."

There was laughter from the audience, and then Captain Hardin introduced the next act.

"Ladies and gentlemen, please welcome that international singing sensation who is loved by millions of people around the world. A St. Louis native and a very good friend of mine: Tanya Tucker."

Instead of applause, there was stone-cold silence. The orchestra leader walked up to the captain and whispered something in his ear.

"Tina Turner!" the captain shouted apologetically.

The real Tina Turner, not an imposter, appeared on the stage. She was greeted warmly by the audience. She knew everyone was anxious to hear *Proud Mary* because they were on a riverboat casino on the Mississippi, but she stalled around as she always did before singing the song. She promised she was going to sing *Proud Mary* and then started talking about her life and about growing up in St. Louis. She was joined by her retinue of scantily clad backup dancers who also provided vocal accompaniment. Tina had on a revealing dress that resembled a negligee. Her enormous wig looked like a lion's mane. "Is there something you want?" she asked enticingly. "Something you need, something maybe you've been waiting for? And if so, then I'll give it to you." She pretended like she was going to start singing *Proud Mary* and then asked, "How about something nice and easy? I'd like to do that for you. But there's just one thing. You see, we never ever do nothing nice and easy. We always do it nice and rough. So we're gonna take the beginning of this song and do it easy. Then, we're gonna do the finish rough. This is the way we do *Proud Mary*. And we're rolling, rolling, rolling on the river. Listen to the story." Tina and the backup dancers swayed gently to the music. They sang softly in a casual and relaxed manner.

> I left a good job in the city.
> Working for the man every night and day.
> And I never lost one minute of sleeping.
> Worrying about the way things might have been.
> Big wheel keep on turning.
> Proud Mary keep on burning.
> Rolling, rolling, rolling on the river.
> Cleaned a lot of plates in Memphis.
> Pumped a lot of pane down in New Orleans.
> But I never saw the good side of the city.
> Until I hitched a ride on a riverboat queen.
> Big wheel keep on turning.
> Proud Mary keep on burning.
> Rolling, rolling, rolling on the river.
> If you come down to the river.
> Bet you gonna find some people who live.
> You don't have to worry if you have no money.
> People on the river are happy to give.
> Big wheel keep on turning.
> Proud Mary keep on burning.
> Rolling, rolling, rolling on the river.

Then, suddenly, Tina and her group took it up a notch, changing the tone from slow, sultry, and soulful to fast, funky, and frisky. The orchestra rapidly increased the tempo. Tina and the girls picked up the beat and stepped up the pace. They began spinning around like twirling ballerina toys. To indicate the rolling movement of the paddlewheel, the backup dancers moved their hands in a circular fashion, like a referee does to indicate traveling in basketball and a false start in football.

The audience was enthralled by the swirling, hand-rolling dance moves. Terri was thoroughly enjoying this slow-to-fast electrifying performance.

Tina and the girls kept up this dizzying rendition of *Proud Mary* until they were exhausted and had to take a break.

Tina got in a plug for the new movie *What's Love Got to Do with It*, which was based on her life. The movie was opening in theaters around the United States in just two days on June 25, 1993. Tina had attended the premiere in Los Angeles on June 6. She liked the movie and was happy with Angela Bassett's lip-synched performance. However, the critics thought Angela lacked Tina's charisma. Phil Spector thought the movie demonized and vilified Ike Turner, which wasn't fair. Terri planned to see the movie at the theater in Crestwood Plaza.

Next, Tina sang *What's Love Got to Do with It*, which was about the unimportance of love.

> What's love got to do, got to do with it.
> What's love but a secondhand emotion.
> What's love got to do, got to do with it
> Who needs a heart when a heart can be broken.
> What's love got to do, got to do with it.
> What's love but a sweet old-fashioned notion.
> What's love got to do, got to do with it.
> Who needs a heart when a heart can be broken.

The song *River Deep, Mountain High* is not about pioneers traveling west from St. Louis in the 1800s but rather about the highs and lows of love. Tina now performed the song, which was one of her biggest hits. Released in 1966, the song was an immediate success in England but at first didn't do well in the United States because it was too pop for rhythm and blues fans, and too rhythm and blues for fans of pop music. But eventually, the song caught on in the United States and became one of Tina's signature songs.

> Do I love you, my oh my oh baby.
> River deep, mountain high.

If I lost you would I cry.
Oh, how I love you, baby, baby, baby, baby.
And I love you, baby, river deep, mountain high.

Next, Tina performed her first hit song *A Fool in Love*, written by her husband Ike Turner. Tina recorded the song in St. Louis in 1960, and it became an immediate success.

There's something on my mind.
Won't somebody please, please tell me what's
    wrong.
You're just a fool, you know you're in love.
You've got to face it to live in this world.
You take the good along with the bad.
Sometimes you're happy and sometimes you're
    sad.
You know you love him, you can't understand.
Why he treats you like he do when he's such a
    good man.
He's got me smiling when I should be ashamed.
Got me laughing when my heart is in pain.
Oh no, I must be a fool.
'Cause I do anything you ask me to.
Without my man I don't want to live.
You think I'm lying but I'm telling you like it is.
He's got my nose open and that's no lie.
And I, I'm gonna keep him satisfied.
A wave of action speaks louder than words.
The truest thing that I ever heard.
I trust my man and all that he do.
And I, and I do anything you ask me to.

Tina sang a few more of her greatest hits, and then she relinquished the stage so another St. Louisan, Fontella Bass, could perform. Fontella was wearing a checkerboard suit and cap just like on the classic November 6, 1965, edition of *Shindig*, which also featured the Rolling Stones. Fontella performed her signature song, *Rescue Me*.

Rescue me.
Or take me in your arms.
Rescue me.
I want your tender charms.
'Cause I'm lonely and I'm blue.
I need you and your love too.
C'mon and rescue me.
C'mon, baby, and rescue me.
C'mon, baby, and rescue me.
'Cause I need you by my side.
Can't you see that I'm lonely?
Rescue me.
C'mon and take my heart.
Take your love and conquer every part.
'Cause I'm lonely and I'm blue.
I need you.
And your love too.
C'mon and rescue me.
C'mon, baby.
Take me, baby.
Hold me, baby.
Love me, baby.
Need me, baby.
Can't you see that I need you, baby?
Can't you see that I'm lonely?
Rescue me.
C'mon and take my hand.
C'mon, baby, and be my man.
Rescue me.
Rescue me.
Mmm-hmm, mmm-hmm.

Captain Hardin did not know who Fontella Bass was, and he mumbled her introduction. Glen could not decipher what the captain said.

"Who's that?" Glen asked Terri, as he listened to Fontella sing.

"Fontella Bass," Terri replied. "She had a big hit with that song back in 1965." Terri paused for a second and then added, "After all these years, she still hasn't been rescued."

In 1993, Nelly was just beginning his career as a hip-hop artist, and he was there with his group of fellow St. Louisans, known as the St. Lunatics. Nelly congratulated Fontella Bass as he took the stage. *Rescue Me* was the only song in Fontella's repertoire.

Inspired by the Negro deckhand he heard earlier, Nelly performed a hip-hop, rap version of *Old Man River*. The St. Lunatics provided musical accompaniment. Rap differs from spoken-word poetry in that rap is usually performed in time to an instrumental track. Stylistically, rap occupies a gray area between speech, prose, poetry, and singing. Nelly incorporated rhyme, rhythmic speech, and street vernacular into his hip-hop version of *Old Man River*.

"There's an Old Man called the Mississippi," Nelly chanted over the backbeat of his band the St. Lunatics. His tone grew more hostile as is typical with rap singers. "That's the Old Man that I wants to be," he demanded. "What does he care if the world's got trouble?" he insinuated. "What does he care if the land ain't free?" he admonished.

Nelly now employed a measured, rhythmic cadence like a protester at a political rally.

> Old Man River.
> That Old Man River.
> The smartass must know something.
> But don't say nothing.
> He just keeps on rolling.
> He just keeps on rolling the shit along.
> He don't plant taters.
> He don't plant cotton.
> But them that plants 'em are soon fucking
>   forgotten.

But Old Man River.
He just keeps on rolling the shit along.
You and me. We sweat and strain.
Our balls are busted and racked with pain.
Tote that barge and lift that bale.
You get a little drunk and you land in jail.
My ass gets weary and sick of trying.
I'm tired of living, but sacred of dying.
But Old Man River.
He just keeps on rolling the shit along.

Many people in the audience were shocked by this hip-hop, rap version of *Old Man River*, but there were others who thoroughly enjoyed the song. Nelly had improvised the song, and he now performed another improvisation based on *Louie Louie* by the Kingsmen. The song was about Saint Louie Louie.

Saint Louie Louie, oh no, me gotta go.
Yeah, yeah, yeah, yeah, yeah, oh baby.
A fine little girl she waits for me in that city on
     the Mississippi.
Me catch the ship across the sea.
Me sailed the ship all alone.
Me never think I'll make it home.
Three nights and days I sailed the sea.
Me think of girl constantly.
On the ship, I dream she there.
I smell the rose in her hair.
Me see the Mississippi, the moon above.
It won't be long me see my love.
Me take her in my arms and then.
I tell her I'll never leave again.
Saint Louie Louie, oh no, me gotta go.
Yeah, yeah, yeah, yeah, yeah, oh baby.
Meet me in Saint Louie Louie, oh no, me gotta go.
Yeah, yeah, yeah, yeah, yeah, oh baby.

Louie Louie by the Kingsmen was fair game for parodies since nobody actually knew what the song was about.

Nelly wrapped up his act, and then it was time for the Father of Rock-and-Roll to perform. Chuck Berry was born in St. Louis in 1926. He did a medley of his greatest hits, including *Maybellene, Nadine, Roll over Beethoven, School Days, Rock & Roll Music, Sweet Little Sixteen, Johnny B. Goode, No Particular Place to Go*, and *Back in the USA*.

Jazz trumpeter Miles Davis was born in nearby Alton, Illinois, in 1926. He died at the age of sixty-five in September of 1991. The casino orchestra paid tribute to Miles Davis by playing *Seven Steps to Heaven*, which was one of his greatest hits. *Seven Steps to Heaven* was written by Miles Davis and the English jazz pianist Victor Feldman. The song was introduced by the Miles Davis Quintet in 1963.

The tribute to Miles Davis was the last act of the evening. Captain Hardin said a few parting words, and then the audience filed out of the auditorium.

Chapter Ten

Poker was not yet part of the gambling regimen on Illinois riverboat casinos, so Captain Hardin got together his own private game. He invited Glen and Dinty to participate. He found a few other men who wanted to play in the high-stakes game. A casino employee named Mississippi Eddy would be the dealer. He was an elderly black man with white hair. He would not be a participant in the game. He was the kind of friendly, fatherly figure that casinos employed to lull patrons into a false sense of security. Who would ever believe this benevolent, avuncular gentleman was out to cheat them? The captain established a limit of five thousand dollars. A high roller named Wendell "Fats" Weinstein decided that limit wasn't high enough and angrily declared he would not play in the game if the stakes weren't raised. When Captain Hardin refused to raise the limit, Wendell got up from the table, uttering a string of profanities. He stormed out of the room. "I'm sorry about that," the captain told the others. "A man's got to know his limitations." The captain looked like Clint Eastwood and also tried to sound like him.

"Now, we need another player in the game," the captain stated. "You," he said, pointing at Dr. Wong. "Come and join us. Whenever I watch poker on TV, there's always a Chink in the game." He was thinking of Johnny Chan, the Orient Express, who was one of poker's first superstars. He won the World Series of Poker in 1987 and 1988.

Anna whined and pouted. "Why can't I get in the game? My money's the same color as his."

"Are you sure about that?" the captain asked skeptically.

Dr. Wong took out his wallet and produced a purple one hundred Philippine Peso note. Manuel Roxas was on the front. The

Mayon Volcano was on the reverse side along with the picture of a whale shark.

"Here's some purple money from the Philippines," Dr. Wong said, handing the currency to Anna. "You can have it. I can't spend it here in America."

"This game is for men only," the chauvinistic captain said.

Dr. Wong sat next to Captain Hardin. Paz came over to wish her boyfriend good luck. He gave her a hundred-dollar bill to go and play the slots. Slot machines were invented so women would have something to do while their men were playing poker.

"She's only after your money," Captain Hardin told Dr. Wong after Paz had walked away.

"I know she's only after my money," the good doctor admitted. "But as Canada Bill replied when asked why he continued to play in a poker game he knew was crooked, 'I know the game is crooked, but it's the only game in town.' She's the only girl who wants me."

Terri came over to the table to wish Glen good luck. "I hope to be the last man standing," Glen told her hopefully. "I mean sitting."

"We're going to play stud poker," the captain announced. "Is that okay with everyone?"

"It's fine with me," Glen said. "I'm one of the biggest studs around."

The others all agreed that seven-card stud poker was acceptable.

"Let's get acquainted over a drink," the captain said, signaling to a sexy, miniskirted cocktail waitress who was wearing a riverboat captain's uniform and hat. "She looks like a stripper in that outfit," Hardin told the others.

"Aye-aye, Captain," the girl said. Her name tag read, HEATHER.

Seven-card stud is played with a starting hand of two down cards and one up card dealt before the first betting round. There are then three more up cards and a final down card known as the river, with a betting round after each, for a total of five betting rounds on a deal played to the showdown. The best five-card poker hand wins the pot.

Seven-card stud was the game of choice aboard riverboats in the 1800s and also in Wild West saloons. The card game was popularized by American GIs during World War II. Seven-card stud is the purest form of poker.

There were seven men in the game. Clockwise around the table were Mississippi Eddy, Captain Hardin, Dr. Wong, Dinty, Glen, Grant "Doc" Richmond, Donald "Boots" McDermott, and Harold "Red" Holtz. Apparently, Captain Hardin was not familiar with the works of Nelson Algren, who listed "Never play poker with a man named Doc" as one of his rules to live by. Grant "Doc" Richmond was a former pitcher for the Cardinals who had a brief stint in the Majors before being relegated to the minor leagues. "I had a cup of coffee with the Cardinals," he told Glen, who had never heard of him, "before being sent down to Memphis." Donald "Boots" McDermott was a St. Louis fire captain who was an expert poker player because he had a lot of time to practice, sitting around the firehouse all day, playing poker with his firemen buddies. Harold "Red" Holtz was a former professional football player turned football coach turned sports announcer. He was currently the sports director of KMOX Radio. He was a high roller who made frequent trips to Las Vegas.

"I want you to know that I trust you all implicitly," the captain stated unequivocally, "but just in case…" He pulled out a pistol and placed it on the table. He was just joking. It was only a squirt gun. He had seen something like this in a movie once. "If I catch you cheating, you'll be thrown in the river just like in the old days."

"Come on, let's play some cards," Mississippi Eddy said. Each player purchased chips from the miniskirted waitress who had wheeled in a cart with a large tray of chips. There were piles of cash on the table and stacks of chips.

Glen took out his gambler's roll of hundreds, fifties, and twenties bound up with a rubber band. He purchased a thousand dollars' worth of chips from the sexy cocktail waitress in the old-time riverboat captain's outfit. "Good luck!" she whispered flirtatiously into Glen's ear. Terri gave the waitress a dirty look. Glen handed the waitress a red five-dollar chip as a tip and to bring good luck.

Anna decided to buy some chips to give to Dinty. In return, he would share his winnings with her. "Give me a stack of purple chips," she told the cocktail waitress.

"Purple chips are five hundred dollars each," the girl replied.

"What's your cheapest color?" Anna quickly asked.

"White. One dollar."

"Give me a stack of white chips," Anna instructed. She purchased the chips and handed them to Dinty.

"A good poker player never wears his heart on his sleeve," the captain theorized. "He wears it up his sleeve." Captain Hardin approached the game with the deliberateness of a chess player. He leaned far back from the table with his arms folded on his chest. Glen thought he noticed a furtive glance between the Captain and Mississippi Eddy, indicating they were in cahoots together. It may have been just his imagination, but Glen decided to keep an eye on these two men.

All the players had to ante up, and then Mississippi Eddy dealt three cards to everyone, two down and one showing. The cards had gold edges and were imprinted with Anna's old portrait along with the name Belle of Calhoun. Glen had the lowest card, the two of clubs, and he began the betting. He had taken off his black frock suitcoat, which he placed on the back of his chair, but he was still wearing his puffy shirt, string tie, red riverboat gambler's vest, and black felt Stetson Revenger Gambler's hat. "I'm just a no-account river gambler," he said. "I bet one hundred dollars." He pulled a derringer from his pocket and pointed it in the general direction of Mississippi Eddy in case the elderly black man had any ideas about dealing cards off the bottom of the deck. The derringer was only a cigarette lighter which Glen used to kindle a cigar. Dr. Wong pulled out a stogie which he asked Glen to light. Dr. Wong was no stranger to smoke-filled card rooms. He was an expert at Chinese Pai gow poker.

The men ogled the cocktail waitress as she delivered drinks and sandwiches. Glen had ordered a beer and a Reuben sandwich. John Montagu, fourth earl of Sandwich, was a profligate and gambler who invented sandwiches so he would not have to leave his card game to take supper.

Glen slipped a twenty-dollar bill into the cleavage of the wait-ress. "I've always wanted to do that," Glen said sheepishly to Terri, who was scowling.

The game was taking place in a large room reserved for private parties. People could come in and watch the action if they remained behind a rail. Soon, some railbirds began to gather.

Captain Hardin liked to talk and tell jokes during a poker game. While other players were quietly contemplating big-money decisions, the captain would gab away nonstop, acting for all the world like he was in a nickel-and-dime garden party game. His cease-less chatter unnerved many opponents and sometimes got them to play recklessly and lose large sums of money.

Glen decided he was going to play aggressively, using a go-for-broke strategy. He had the savvy and instincts of a riverboat gambler in the 1800s, a man who doesn't cower, who doesn't hesitate to reach for his holster and draw, always trusting his trigger finger.

Glen doubled through quickly, turning his $1,000 in chips into $2,000. Players who were able to get an early chip lead were at a decided advantage. The extra chips allowed them to make aggres-sive bets and buy pots with raises and bluffs without fear of being eliminated.

There's an old saying that if you can't spot the sucker at a poker table, then you're the sucker. Luckily, Glen noticed many suckers at this poker table. Their fear of elimination played right into his hands. Glen's cutthroat style definitely served him well. He immediately sized up those players who were content to wait patiently for a good hand and who wouldn't make a heavy bet even if they had a good hand. When Glen sensed a sign of weakness, he put that player to the test. Never give a sucker an even break is the first rule of gambling.

Grant "Doc" Richmond was afraid of losing money, and he was playing way too cautiously. It was easy to beat someone like that. Grant was folding every hand.

Gradually, players began to fall by the wayside, and Grant Richmond was the first to go. After Glen won a pot with a pair of jacks, Grant threw down his cards and exclaimed, "My limit has been reached, gentlemen." He pushed back his chair, bowed to the group, and departed without another word.

"This is a gentlemen's game just like on the old-time riverboats," the captain said after expressing his condolences to Grant Richmond. "There will be no hard feelings about losing. If there is a dispute, we will settle the matter like gentlemen…with a duel. Pistols at twenty paces. We will go to an island in the Mississippi for the duel just like in the old days."

The remaining players were not amused by the captain's humor.

Harold "Red" Holtz was originally from Texas, where many professional poker players come from. He was an expert at Texas Hold'em Poker, but had played a lot of seven-card stud before Texas Hold'em became the rage of the land. He had on a cowboy hat, a western shirt, and a pair of worn Wrangler jeans. His enormous belt buckle showed a royal spade flush engraved over a map of Texas with the words Never Fold. On his right wrist was a fake World Series of Poker bracelet. He had purchased the bracelet in a jewelry store after failing to make the cut at the World Series of Poker in Las Vegas.

Fortunately for the others, Red was a little rusty at seven-card stud, and he made some crucial mistakes. Perhaps more than in any other poker variation, bluffing is the keystone of successful stud play. Red, who was used to playing Texas Hold'em, was not a good bluffer, and Glen could tell right away when he was bluffing.

"I think you're trying to buy it, pal," Glen told Red, who had placed a thousand-dollar bet with only a pair of sevens in his hand. "I call," Glen announced confidently. Glen won the pot with a pair of eights.

There was no doubt about Red's disappointment. It was obvious. He frowned for a minute, glanced at his shrinking pile of chips, and then remembered that a gentleman never displayed his feelings in a poker game. He forced a smile. He loved the game of poker as much as he loved football and the state of Texas.

Mississippi Eddy ripped the cellophane from a new deck of cards and put the jokers in his shirt pocket. He shuffled six times, once each for the number of men remaining at the table. He slammed the deck down in front of Harold "Red" Holtz, who was on the right.

Red removed a contiguous range of cards off the top of the deck. "Cut 'em thin and win," he said. Mississippi Eddy then placed those cards at the bottom of the deck. Cutting cards is important so the bottom card cannot be seen.

Red Holtz hoped to make a comeback, but his situation rapidly deteriorated. He won the occasional hand, but those victories were never large enough to shore up his eroding funds. He continued to bet heavily on weak hands and ended up squandering his resources. Finally, Red slammed down his cards and pushed back his chair. He slowly stood up. He was unsteady from the liquor he had drunk and enraged by his losses. Liquor and anger are not a good combination. Red was all set to start a fight when a security guard grabbed him from behind and escorted him out of the room.

"I hate poor losers," the captain said.

Donald "Boots" McDermott was wearing his fire captain's uniform. Glen was reminded of the novel *Fahrenheit 451*, where the firemen sit around playing poker all day and only leave the firehouse at night to burn books. The firemen in the novel don't put out fires. They only start fires. The temperature must be 451 degrees Fahrenheit in order for a book to burn. Fires look nicer at night and attract more attention.

McDermott's uniform looked similar to a riverboat captain's uniform. "We're equally ranked," he told Captain Hardin. "We're both captains."

Everyone laughed. "But don't forget I'm the captain of this table," Captain Hardin proclaimed. "What I say goes. I make the rules at this table. I will tell you what you can and cannot do."

In poker, a table captain is someone who believes they are God's gift to poker, having the right to criticize the other players and comment about the course of the game. This incessant chatter often drives other participants away from the table.

McDermott was used to winning money in poker games with rookie firefighters, but he was no match for more experienced players. He was wearing a Maltese Cross lapel pin, the emblem of the fire department. The Maltese Cross is the symbol of the fire service because many years ago, the Ottoman Turks failed in their attempt to burn out the people of Malta. The Maltese Cross and the Maltese Falcon both come from the Templars of Malta, who were knights representing the Order of St. John of Jerusalem.

"I think it's interesting," McDermott said, "that a Missouri steamboat captain named Willie Massie was playing poker with Bill Hickok when Wild Bill was shot in the back of the head by Jack McCall. Right before he was shot, Bill Hickok had accused Captain Massie of being a card cheat. It's a true story."

"Is that your way of subtly suggesting that I'm a card cheat?" Captain Hardin bellowed.

"Not at all," McDermott said defensively. "The bullet that killed Wild Bill ended up in Massie's wrist. Massie did not have the bullet removed and showed it off to people who wanted to see the bullet that killed Wild Bill Hickok. People were impressed by Massie's wrist jewelry. At first, Massie thought Wild Bill had shot him for being a card cheat but then realized Jack McCall was the shooter. Massie died thirty-four years later in 1910. He was buried in St. Louis with the bullet still in his wrist."

"I'm not a card cheat," Captain Hardin affirmed.

"Nobody said you were," McDermott replied.

The sounds of the game took over for Glen, as if everything else had been erased: the clinking of the chips, the noise of the stiff cards being shuffled before each hand, the dry announcements of bets and raises, the plunges into total silence.

Glen studied the facial expressions, body language, and betting style of the other players. He realized they were also studying him. Poker is a game of odds, simple math, and being able to read people.

At midnight, the game began to wind down with the captain and Glen the big winners. The captain was taking most of the conservative pots. The captain was playing a steady game of conservative poker that was hard to figure out. Glen was positive the captain was getting help from Mississippi Eddy. Glen and the captain had to come to grips with each other. Mississippi Eddy was a good mechanic who gunned cards out with the precision of a machine, and it was impossible to tell if he was dealing an occasional helpful card to the captain.

McDermott watched his pile of chips shrink from a mountain to a molehill. Confident that he had a winning hand, he reached into the pocket of his fireman's uniform and pulled out a manila envelope stuffed with cash. He pushed the money into the center of the table along with his remaining chips. "You are called Captain Hardin," McDermott announced as he displayed his cards.

Captain Hardin laid out his cards with a flourish. "A small straight flush, sir! Only six high, sir!"

"You lousy cheat!" McDermott hissed. "Your straight flush beats my full house!" McDermott felt a sickening sensation in the pit of his stomach. His face blanched. He gasped. Then, with tremendous effort, he stood up and walked out of the room.

"That's the luck of poker, sir!" the captain yelled as McDermott was walking away.

The captain chased Dinty and Dr. Wong from the game by making big wagers.

"Well, gentlemen," Dr. Wong said, getting up from the table. "Im through. It has been a pleasure."

Dinty yawned and followed suit. "It's past my bedtime," he said.

"It all boils down to this," the captain said to Glen. "A young Turk versus a seasoned veteran."

"I'm not Turkish!" Glen stated, moving to the chair vacated by Dr. Wong. Glen and the Captain were now sitting side by side for a two-handed game of seven-card stud.

"Eddy, you're outta here!" Glen yelled when he saw Mississippi Eddy getting a fresh deck of cards.

"What the hell are you talking about?" Eddy asked in a defiant manner.

"We'll deal for ourselves," Glen said authoritatively. He did not like this uppity African American.

Eddy and the captain seemed alarmed, but there was nothing they could do about it.

"Okay," the captain said, spreading a deck of cards out on the green felt table. "We'll draw to see who deals. High card wins."

"You go first," Glen ordered.

The captain drew the king of hearts.

"Great," Glen lamented. "Now, I have to draw an ace in order to win."

Glen waved his right hand over the cards as though performing a magic trick. He made a hocus-pocus gesture like a magician does. He blew on the cards for luck. He took out his lucky Eisenhower silver dollar and grasped it tightly. He turned his chair around and dangled his legs on both sides. Sitting astride on a chair is supposed to bring good luck. He crossed his legs, arms, and fingers.

The captain was growing impatient. "Are you going to draw or whistle Dixie?" he barked.

"I want to get this just right," Glen said tentatively. He deliberated a little longer and then suddenly blurted out: "This is stupid! How do I know you didn't plant that king of hearts in the deck in a spot where you could find it?"

"Since you don't trust me," the captain said, "we'll do this a different way. We'll spin a buck knife like they used to do on the old-time riverboats. Whoever the knife points to is the dealer. That's how the expression 'The buck stops here' originated. President Truman had a sign on his desk that said 'THE BUCK STOPS HERE.'"

"I never liked Truman," Dinty said. "He wasn't as honest as people thought."

A buck knife has a deer antler as the handle. The captain produced a large buck knife which he carefully removed from the sheath. He laid the sharp knife on the table. He spun the knife around with such force that it sailed off the table and nearly cut Terri, who was standing alongside Glen.

"This is stupid," Glen cried, after making sure that Terri was okay. "Let's just get someone else to deal. Someone that I trust."

Glen selected Dr. Wong to be the dealer. The venerable old gentleman was someone everybody trusted. The captain agreed that Dr. Wong should be the dealer.

"Okay," Dr. Wong said, grabbing a fresh deck of cards. "Here we go down the river playing seven-card stud."

This was a classic poker showdown. Glen and the captain were evenly matched. They were the only participants at the table, and everyone else had to step back. Nobody was allowed to wander around the room and perhaps communicate with one of the players by using hand signals, coughs, eye blinks, or scratches of the head.

The first few hands were undramatic. The two men played cautiously, eyeing each other like a pitcher and batter in a baseball game. Glen lit another cigar. The captain smoked a cigarette.

Glen was hoping for a quick kill. He wanted to gut the captain as fast as possible. But in the first hour, Glen barely managed to stay even, winning about half of the pots and not making any progress. Dr. Wong was a straightforward dealer, and the cards were not coming Glen's way. Glen's patience would pull him through.

The captain refrained from his usual freewheeling banter. He was all business. He was lost in concentration. Glen was surprised by the captain's silence. There should be amusing repartee at a poker game. Players should be telling vulgar jokes and trading friendly insults. Conversation is an important part of any seven-card stud game. It helps to create the necessary illusion and confusion. But it should be confined to the game itself. The silence of the captain was suspicious.

The hour was growing late, and the captain was getting impatient. He wanted to end the game with a dramatic victory. The next hand began well for him. On third street, the captain's two down cards were the king of hearts and the king of clubs. His up card was the ace of clubs. Glen's up card was the two of diamonds. His down cards were the six of spades and the ace of spades. On fourth street, the Captain received the eighth of clubs faceup, and Glen was dealt the two of hearts. Glen had a double deuce, which was the name of the sleazy nightclub in the 1989 movie *Roadhouse* starring Patrick Swayze. The fictional Double Deuce was located in Jasper, Missouri, which is part of the Joplin metropolitan area. In the movie, the owner of the Double Deuce says his nightclub is outside of Kansas City, which is 157 miles north of Joplin. On fifth street, the captain received the ace of hearts, and Glen was handed the seven of hearts. The captain kept increasing his wager as his hand improved, and Glen played along, matching the pot. The captain was an experienced poker player, and he knew Glen was bluffing. On sixth street, the captain received his third ace, the ace of diamonds. Glen was dealt his third deuce, the two of clubs. The captain had a full house, aces up. He knew Glen could not beat that.

"The river!" Dr. Wong yelled as he dealt the seventh and final card facedown to Glen and the captain. "Down and dirty."

The captain was so sure he was going to win that he didn't bother to look at his final card.

Glen was so sure he was going to lose that he didn't bother to look at his final card either.

This was further evidence that Glen had been bluffing, and the captain moved all his remaining chips into the center of the table. The pot was now approximately five thousand dollars.

Before folding, Glen decided he would have a look at his final card, and he was met by the most beautiful surprise of his life. There staring back at him was the two of spades. He didn't know if Dr. Wong had deliberately fed him the card or whether this was all on the up-and-up, but he didn't care.

"Aren't you going to fold?" the captain asked in an angry undertone. "Aren't you going to fold?" The captain was perturbed. "I know what you're thinking, punk. Does he have four aces or only three? Well, to tell you the truth, in all this excitement, I don't know myself. But being that I have a five-thousand-dollar bet on the table which will wipe you clean out, just ask yourself one question. 'Do I feel lucky?' Well, do you, punk?"

Glen looked at the ace of spades in his hand and the two of spades and then said confidently, "Umm, yeah, I feel lucky. I call. Four deuces." He spread the four winning cards on the table.

The captain slowly reached for his final card and threw it off the table when he saw it was not the ace of spades.

Overjoyed, Glen raked in the pot. Terri congratulated him, and so did the crowd that had gathered to watch the action. The captain walked away dejected.

Glen would never forget how four deuces had saved his bacon. The Four Deuces was the name of the sleazy nightclub in the 1976 movie of the same name starring Jack Palance and Carol Lynley. Al Capone had been a patron of the Four Deuces nightclub at 2222 South Wabash Avenue in Chicago.

Captain Hardin returned to the pilothouse to dock the boat. The inaugural cruise of the *Belle of Calhoun* was coming to an end.

"Glen and I are going up to the top deck for a while," Terri announced to the others.

"What for?" Dinty asked.

"We're going to play shuffleboard," Terri replied facetiously.

"Okay." Dinty laughed. "But don't take too long. The boat will be landing soon."

Terri and Glen went up to the Texas deck for a quick tête-à-tête in the moonlight. When they returned, they decided to try their luck at the slot machines.

"They're supposed to have the loosest slots in town," Glen said, sitting down at one of the machines.

"And also the loosest sluts in town," Terri informed Glen as she watched Heather approaching.

Terri glared at the sexy cocktail waitress in the old-time riverboat captain's uniform.

Heather congratulated Glen on winning big, and Glen slipped another twenty-dollar bill into her cleavage as a way of thanking her for bringing him good luck in the poker game. Glen liked the botanical name Heather. Just the way the name rolls off the tongue sounds sensual. The name Heather has its origins in England and Scotland, where the purple-flowering plant of the same name is very common.

Terri selected an Elvis the King slot machine. She loved listening to the siren song of the slot machines: the jangly music, the whir of spinning reels accompanied by loud beeps and chimes, and the metallic clanging of coins after a payout.

Terri thought it would be wise to gamble along with the King, and she was right. She won two hundred dollars right off the bat. She decided to stop. She cashed in her coins, keeping just one as a souvenir. All the casino coins had an etching of Anna's old portrait.

Terri went in the gift shop and purchased a *Belle of Calhoun* souvenir—an actual bell in the shape of a woman wearing a wide hoop skirt. The clapper was underneath the skirt. Presumably, the woman was Anna, and the words Belle of Calhoun appeared on the small hand bell.

Now, Terri wanted to find Paz because the boat was approaching the shore. There were big crowds around the gaming tables and the slot machines. Terri thought it would be hard to locate Paz. One craps table had a huge crowd around it, people packed at least three deep. Shouts and hollers roared up from the center. The men and women were well dressed, and they wore expensive jewelry. Terri wedged herself through the outer ranks of the crowd. Peering over a man's shoulder, she caught a glimpse of the craps shooter in the process of making a pass. It was Paz. The rail in front of Paz was filled with chips, not just black chips, but purple chips, and lots of them.

Terri was happy that Paz had won thousands of dollars. She congratulated Paz and then said good night. The boat had docked, and people were heading for the exits. Paz might have lost all her winnings if she had continued to gamble, so it was good the cruise had ended.

Terri, Glen, Anna, and Dinty left the floating casino together and walked along the wharf until they reached Glen's houseboat. The trip across the river only took ten minutes. Glen moored his houseboat at the Grosse family pier. He helped Anna ascend the Osage Steps, which were illuminated by one-hundred-watt light bulbs. Terri and Dinty went on ahead. Soon, everyone was back at the Grosse Mansion, where they decided to have a nightcap before calling it a night. It had been a very enjoyable evening.

Chapter Eleven

On July 3, Barbara Grogan came to visit Dinty at the Stag Club. She was driving way too fast, going down South Broadway, and patrolman Mike Dolan pursued her. She did not stop when she noticed a police car in back of her. Instead, she increased her speed. Barbara was a wild girl. She tried to lose the police car by turning into a side street. There was a chase through the streets of South St. Louis. When Mike finally caught up with Barbara's red Ford Bronco pickup truck, he raced up to her and yelled, "I'm going to throw the book at you. Let's see your license."

Barbara produced her license.

"This is a fishing license!" Mike screamed.

"You didn't specify driver's license." Barbara snickered.

Mike examined the license and then said apologetically, "Hey, wait a minute, you're Barbara Grogan, aren't you? I watch your show every week on TV."

"So you're the one. Sorry, no autographs." Barbara pushed away the ticket book that Mike held in his hand.

"Hey, look, I could never give a ticket to you. I saw the words Happy Hooker on the side of your truck, and I thought this must be a tow truck."

"My show is coming on soon. How are you going to watch it?"

"I tape your show every week," Mike said. "Hey, look, I'm really sorry about this. Where were you going in such a hurry?"

"I'm going to visit Dinty Smith at the Stag Club. He's one of my biggest fans."

Mike told Barbara that he worked as a bouncer at the Stag Club. "Say hello to Dinty for me," Mike said in parting. "I'm taking my vacation in a few weeks, and I'm going fishing at the Lake of the Ozarks. Where is the best spot on the lake to catch bass?"

"Try the Niangua arm of the lake, but watch out for piranha." Barbara did not mention the piranha attack on Earline Early.

"Good luck with your fishing!" Barbara called loudly as Mike Dolan was walking away. Then, under her breath, she added the word: "Flatfoot."

Barbara parked across the street from the Stag Club in front of the Grosse Mansion.

Brent and Wade tried to hit on her as soon as she walked through the door of the Stag Club. They were avid outdoorsmen and recognized her immediately.

"Follow me and find contentment," Wade sang, following Barbara to the bar.

"Follow me to rippling streams," he continued. "Find a world that embraces free open spaces. Come on and follow me." Wade paused for a second and then added, "*The American Sportsman*, starring Curt Gowdy and Grits Gresham. That used to be my favorite show. Now, your show is my favorite show."

Barbara made a quick appraisal of the situation and then gave Wade the cold shoulder.

"Whattaya say you and me go out in the woods and explore nature together?" the fat-faced fireman suggested.

"You're an outdoor enthusiast, huh?" Barbara inquired with a laugh. "Then take a hike!"

Wade departed voluntarily, mumbling something under his breath. Barbara greeted Dinty, who was overjoyed to see her. Dinty gave Barbara a hug. He had waited for this moment for many years. He quickly served her one of his famous margaritas. Then, he threw one of his nationally known brain burgers on the grill.

Dinty congratulated Barbara on being a trailblazing woman in the male-dominated sport of fishing. "Fishing is a sport that has never shown much gender equity," Dinty said.

"Yes," Barbara replied. "I'm proud that I can compete toe-to-toe with the men."

Barbara and Dinty discussed how the 1972 law Title IX applied to fishing. Title IX is a federal law stating that women cannot be prohibited from participating in a sport.

The old man and the young woman talked about the fundamentals of fishing.

Barbara autographed a photo of herself with the personalized message: TO MY FISHING BUDDY DINTY. She also gave Dinty a copy of *The Mayfly Madam*, which she autographed.

Dinty told her he owned her other books: *The Efficient Fisherman* and *The Proficient Fisherman*.

"I have a new book coming out at Christmastime," Barbara plugged. It's called *The Young Woman and the Sea*. I hope you'll buy it."

Dinty switched stations on the TV in back of the bar. The Happy Hooker Show would be on soon at three o'clock. During a periodic news update, it was announced that Don Drysdale had died that day at the age of fifty-six. A broadcaster for the Los Angeles Dodgers, he was in Montreal for a game between the Dodgers and Expos. He died of a heart attack in his room at a Montreal hotel. It was also announced that the last of the Three Stooges, Joe DeRita, had died that day at the age of eighty-three.

"Celebrities often die in pairs," Dinty said solemnly.

Don Drysdale had once been a guest fisherman on *The Happy Hooker Show*, and that was the broadcast that aired on this day as a memorial tribute to Don.

Barbara was surprised to see the Don Drysdale broadcast for she thought today's show would be her fishing excursion with former Cardinal manager Whitey Herzog, who was an avid outdoorsman.

"Don Drysdale and I were friends in California," Barbara said. "We filmed this show at Lake Mirage near Don's home in Rancho Mirage, California. Despite the name Lake Mirage, there really is a lake there. It is no mirage."

Brent and Wade sat at the other end of the bar in order to watch their favorite show.

Barbara had a change of heart and gave autographs to the two sleaze ball firemen.

Sydney Melbourne came over to watch *The Happy Hooker Show*, and Dinty introduced her to Barbara.

"How's tricks, honey?" Sydney asked with her annoying Aussie accent. "Hey, everybody!" she yelled. "There's a hooker at the bar."

Some of the men got excited until they realized it was only Barbara Grogan. One man came over to get her autograph.

"You'll have to excuse her," Dinty told Barbara consolingly. "She's from Down Under."

"Down under what? A rock?"

"She's from Australia."

A commercial came on with Barbara advertising a revolutionary new fish scaler called Fish-O-Matic. Then, she did a commercial for a new Internet service called Fish Online, which provided all sorts of fishing information to people who were tired of searching the net and coming up empty.

Barbara did another anti-drug promo where she lectured about her blistered butt and pier pressure.

Don Drysdale talked about playing baseball with Robert Redford on the Van Nuys High School team. Drysdale and Redford both graduated from Van Nuys High School in 1954.

Let Me Go, Lover! by Joan Weber was at the top of the charts in 1954, and Barbara now sang that song as she released a trophy bass back into the water. "Oh, let me go, let me go, let me go, lover. Let me be, set me free from your spell."

Barbara introduced a new fishing video in which she performed with a group of Chippendale dancers who were dressed in tight rubber fishing waders and skimpy fishing vests that revealed their bare chests. The men also wore bucket hats with fishing lures attached.

The show passed by quickly, and soon it was time for Barbara to make her closing comments. "Make sure to join me next week," she began slowly. "When I'll be fishing for tarpon with Dolly Parton. Until next time, this is the old Happy Hooker wishing you good luck with your fishing and reminding you that you don't have to be outdoors to be an outdoorsman. So long, everybody. Tight lines!"

Dinty sadly said farewell to Barbara as the closing credits rolled by on the TV screen, and Barbara's theme song played in the background. But his greatest dream in life had now been realized. He had met Barbara Grogan in person, and they had watched her show together.

Barbara assured Dinty she would keep in touch. She kissed Dinty and also gave him an enormous hug. She then left the Stag Club and headed for her truck. She encountered a great deal of traffic on Lavender Street and walked down to the corner to cross at the stoplight. After crossing the street, she walked past the Grosse Mansion and entered her truck on the passenger side. Suddenly, she heard someone yelling at her. It was Glen. He had just watched *The Happy Hooker Show*, and now he had come out to his truck to run an errand. Barbara examined the interior of the truck she was in. This was not her truck. Glen owned an identical red Ford Bronco pickup truck. She was in Glen's truck. In the rearview mirror, she saw her truck parked one space down. A red Volkswagen was in between the two pickup trucks.

Glen approached his truck with caution, thinking a burglar was inside. He considered running back to the Grosse Mansion to call the police. "Come out with your hands up," he cried. Barbara sheepishly stepped out of the truck and profusely apologized to Glen.

"I'm extremely sorry about this!" Barbara atoned. "I thought this was my truck. My truck is the same model as yours. It's parked right over there."

"Hey, wait a minute, you're Barbara Grogan, aren't you? I just watched your show on TV."

"So you're the one. Thanks for watching." Barbara explained she had been visiting with Dinty Smith, who was one of her biggest fans.

"You're even prettier in person than you are on television," Glen complimented.

"Well, you got that part right," Barbara responded arrogantly.

"Can I have your autograph?" Glen asked.

"Sure," Barbara said, scribbling her name in a notebook. She ripped out the page and handed it to Glen. "I've always been fascinated by these old riverfront homes. Can you give me a quick tour?"

"I'll be glad to," Glen said provisionally. "But first I have to batten down the hatches on my houseboat. Extreme weather is predicted for this afternoon with the possibility of a tornado. I was just going out to buy some rope to tie canvas covers over my houseboat."

"I have rope in my truck," Barbara chimed in eagerly. "I'll help you. I'm an expert when it comes to houseboats."

Barbara fetched long anchor ropes from her truck and accompanied Glen onto the grounds of the Grosse Mansion. They passed by Harriet Winslow, who was standing in front of the house. Glen introduced Harriet to Barbara. "This is our caregiver," he told Barbara, wrapping his arm around Harriet. "She gives REALLY good care."

Harriet quickly disentangled herself from Glen's grasp. "You better watch out for him," she told Barbara.

Barbara and Glen heard tornado sirens as they climbed down Lavender Hill on the Osage Steps.

"I hear air raid sirens," Glen said, engaging in another one of his military fantasies.

"Those are tornado sirens," Barbara corrected.

"A tornado comes down from the sky just like a bomb from an enemy aircraft," Glen reasoned.

The homeless people had all gone Downtown for the Veiled Prophet Fair under the Arch. It was a good place to panhandle. The homeless camp was deserted.

Barbara and Glen climbed aboard the houseboat and began tying heavy-duty canvas tarps around the windows.

They tied the tarps together to create one giant cover. Barbara didn't need all the rope she had brought along. She left two large ropes on the shore.

The sky suddenly became very dark. At this moment, a tornado was cutting a swath through South St. Louis, uprooting trees, overturning cars, and damaging buildings.

As the sky turned blacker than night, Barbara turned to Glen and asked what they should do. Glen told her they were safer on the boat because tornadoes tend to avoid water.

Barbara and Glen heard and saw the tornado coming, but there was nothing they could do. They braced for impact. The tornado came down like a bomb from a Japanese airplane on December 7, 1941.

The wooden dock was destroyed. Timbers flew everywhere, and Glen's houseboat was set adrift with a gaping hole in the hull. Barbara was knocked overboard, but she managed to grab the bow line, and Glen pulled her from the water and onto the boat.

"You saved my life," she said worshipfully.

"We're rudderless," Glen announced, realizing that the rudder of his houseboat had been destroyed. The mangled propeller was also inoperable. "I have no way to steer the boat, and on top of that, the electrical system was knocked out."

Glen's houseboat, rapidly taking on water, became engulfed in the swift current.

"We'll just go with flow," he said calmly. "That's all we can do."

"We can only stay afloat for a short time before the boat sinks," Barbara said. "Let's put on life jackets and start bailing water out of the boat."

"I don't have any life jackets," Glen said remorsefully.

Barbara chastised him for violating the first rule of boating safety.

Waves crashed across the bow as the houseboat was pummeled with high winds and rain. Barbara and Glen clung to the railings as the boat careened like a bucking bronco. It was clear they wouldn't be able to steer the boat to either shore. They yelled for help to a group of workers on a barge that was tied up because of the high water, but the rivermen only shouted profanities.

"The vulgar boatmen," Glen lamented.

Barbara and Glen were both experienced boat people, and they knew enough not to panic. They began bailing water to buy extra time afloat. Glen had a water pump but couldn't use it because the boat's electrical system had been knocked out of commission.

The rain thickened and stung Barbara's face and skin. She pushed matted hair off her forehead and sheltered her eyes with her hand.

A tubular wave swept over the boat, forcing Barbara and Glen to literally hit the deck. They crawled along the deck so they were not blown overboard by the powerful wind.

The boat drifted into the middle of the river, which was not where they wanted to be.

"We've got to head towards shore," Barbara implored.

"I'm afraid the only shore we're going to reach is the heavenly shore," Glen confided.

"Don't say that!" Barbara lambasted.

"You're right," Glen uttered, as his life flashed before him. "I don't think either one of us is going to reach the heavenly shore. The only river we're going to cross is the River Styx."

"I'm going to heaven when I die, and that won't be for a very long time!" Barbara shouted caustically.

Glen had a battery-powered boom box and he inserted an Elvis CD with the song *Just a Closer Walk with Thee*.

"Since we're going to die," he said mournfully, "I thought I'd put on some appropriate music."

"Will you get that thought out of your head!" Barbara hollered. "Make up your mind that you're going to live!"

Barbara and Glen buckled down and began bailing water as fast as they could, using large plastic buckets.

The houseboat moved swiftly downstream, and soon Barbara and Glen found themselves many miles below St. Louis.

There were no signs of civilization. Nobody was around to help them. The situation looked dire. The two young people prepared to abandon ship.

"So now the end is near, and so I face the final curtain," Glen sang. He had named his houseboat *My Way* and now he intoned the song as he looked back at his life, which was about to end way too soon.

Suddenly, Barbara had an idea. She grabbed a wooden chair, which she intended to use as a personal flotation device.

She found another chair for Glen.

"What are you doing?" Glen inquired after singing the last line of *My Way*.

"I'm rearranging the deck chairs," Barbara said flippantly. "We can use these wooden deck chairs to keep us afloat after we jump overboard."

"Do you think that will work?"

"All we can do is pray with all our might."

The bow of the houseboat was beginning to sink beneath the surface of the river.

"Hold on tight to your chair," Barbara cautioned, "and we'll jump when I count three. Head towards the Missouri shore. It looks closer."

"Are you a good swimmer?" Glen asked.

"I grew up on the water," Barbara replied.

"Me too. We have a lot in common."

"See you on the Missouri shore." Barbara slowly began her countdown.

"Wait!" Glen shouted suddenly. Through the rain and mist, he spotted something in the middle of the river. It was an island.

The same island where Grandfather Grosse had come for his lion-hunting expedition in 1916. This was Lovers Island.

Barbara and Glen were relieved and remained on the houseboat, which was headed straight for the island. Lovers Island was 1,078 acres of bottomland forest. The island was three miles long and a half mile wide. With consummate seamanship, Barbara and Glen kept the houseboat afloat and on course for the island. The current was very strong, and it was with great difficulty that the houseboat maneuvered towards the island.

Chapter Twelve

Birds rose in raucous protest as the houseboat slammed stern-first into the island, skidding across the riprap and revetments that lined the bank. The large rocks tore a hole in the boat's hull. Glen quickly jumped ashore with his Danforth anchor, which he planted in some soft earth behind a cottonwood tree, after first wrapping the rope around the tree. Barbara helped him tie the stern line and the bow line to large trees on the island. After securely tying up the house-boat, Barbara and Glen began to bail water out of the boat, using mops and buckets. After mopping up, they climbed the ladder and trimmed willow boughs that hung over the top deck.

Cottonwood trees were shedding seed fluffs that looked like snow. The top deck was now covered with cottony white seed fluffs, which Barbara and Glen swept away. It was like shoveling snow.

Next, they gathered driftwood for a barbecue in the hibachi on the foredeck. The air was fetid with the rank smell of wet earth and wet vegetation. Barbara squirmed as mosquitoes began biting her. Glen moved fretfully as he felt stings on his hands and arms.

Barbara and Glen gradually adjusted to their environment and situation. In the houseboat's galley, there was sufficient food for several days. The pantry shelves were loaded with canned vegetables and canned meats. There were baking mixes for making biscuits and cornbread. In the refrigerator was a cabbage for making coleslaw. Barbara and Glen intended to catch their dinner from the river. Catfish, coleslaw, and cornbread are an excellent combination.

Glen opened the refrigerator door to reveal many bottles of Grosse beer. Some of the bottles had tipped over during the wild ride on the river. Glen straightened out the bottles.

"I always keep my refrigerator fully stocked with Grosse beer," he said, picking up the glass shards of a bottle that had broken.

"Well, that's the most important thing," Barbara proclaimed. "What are those bottles without any labels?"

"Oh, that's my new light beer. I haven't come up with a name for it yet."

"Can I try your new Bilgewater Beer?" Barbara asked. "That would be a good name for it."

"Sure," Glen answered, taking out a bottle and opening it. He handed the bottle to Barbara. "It has half the carbs of Bud Light. Only ninety-nine calories."

Suddenly, they heard a small plane passing overhead. They ran to the foredeck and tried to signal for help, but the pilot didn't see them beneath the canopy of trees.

Glen rushed back inside the boat to get a flare gun, which he quickly loaded. He returned to the foredeck and fired a star shell into the air. "Happy Fourth of July!" he cried, watching the star shell's bright explosion in the gathering darkness. "A lot of good it does shooting off a flare gun on July third. Even if someone does see it, they'll just think we're celebrating the Fourth of July."

"You're right," Barbara said. "All we can do is just sit back, relax, and wait to be rescued."

"We're cut off from civilization," Glen said. "It's sort of fun being marooned on a deserted island. I'm glad the power was knocked out so we can't use the radio to signal for help."

There was a sofa on the foredeck of Glen's houseboat. Like Beavis and Butthead, Barbara and Glen sat down on the couch and began fishing for their dinner.

"This is my casting couch," Glen elaborated, casting his fishing line out on the water.

"Be careful what you fish for," Barbara warned. "You just might catch it."

"I've weighted down my line to go after bottom-feeding catfish. I'm a bottom-line type of guy."

It is not uncommon for romance to blossom between a man and woman who share a life-threatening experience.

Although they had known each other for only a few hours, Barbara and Glen soon began making love on the couch. They snuggled together while continuing to fish. Glen held his fishing pole in his left hand, and his right arm was wrapped around Barbara.

"Fishing is a great sport," he said after kissing Barbara deep and hard on the lips. "Fishing is the only sport that allows for multitasking." He returned to his lovemaking, hoping the catfish wouldn't bite and interrupt his sensual pleasure.

A tugging on his line forced Glen to quell his passion and reel in an enormous hawg catfish. Barbara also caught a trophy-size catfish. Flies began swarming around the catfish, which were quickly placed in a live well.

Barbara and Glen returned to their fishing. They caught several more good-size catfish using chicken livers for bait.

Glen was using a net to haul in his catfish. "I'm caught in a net," he sang, mimicking Elvis. "I can't swim out. Because I love you too much, baby."

Barbara and Glen resumed their lovemaking. "I've waited my entire life for someone like you," Glen revealed.

"An outdoor girl who loves to hunt and fish. I'm so glad we found each other. It was fate. It was the storm that brought us together."

It was raining again, but Barbara and Glen were snug and dry on the covered foredeck of the houseboat.

Barbara paused from kissing Glen in order to speak. "I guess that makes this…the perfect storm!" She quickly continued her coupling and smooching.

"This fish is a throwback," Glen decided after catching a catfish that was too small. He released the fish.

"We're both throwbacks," Barbara stated. "Throwbacks to an earlier time. We should have lived a long, long time ago, when all the woods were full of game and all the lakes and rivers were full of fish."

Glen had filled a Styrofoam cooler with all the ice from his refrigerator. He then wedged bottles of Grosse beer into the cooler. He retrieved two bottles of Grosse beer and handed one to Barbara.

"This beer is way past its expiration date, but it's still good," he informed her.

"We're both way past our expiration dates," Barbara philosophized.

Glen carefully examined the next catfish he caught and announced, "This fish is a keeper!" He threw the fish into the live well.

"You're a keeper," Barbara theorized. "I've been waiting all my life for a man like you. Now that I've found you, I don't want to lose you."

Barbara was an expert at preparing fish. She selected two nice catfish from the live well and gutted them. She threw the heads in the river. After removing the skin, she cut the fish into fillets, which she carefully deboned. She cleaned the fillets and rolled them in cornmeal.

Glen built a wood fire in the hibachi and placed a frying pan on the grill. He poured Crisco Pure Canola Oil into the frying pan, and then dropped in the catfish fillets.

Barbara went into the galley and whipped up some coleslaw. She combined shredded cabbage and carrots in a large bowl. She then whisked in mayonnaise, sour cream, onion, sugar, vinegar, mustard, celery salt, salt, and pepper.

She couldn't use the electric stove because there was no power so she baked some cornbread on the hibachi grill.

Barbara and Glen set up a folding table on the foredeck in preparation for their dinner. They set the table with Chinet paper plates and plastic utensils. When dinner was ready, they sat down on folding chairs and said grace.

"Bon appétit," Glen announced, taking a large helping of catfish. "And watch out for the bones!"

The ice chest was next to the table, and Glen reached in for another round of Grosse beer.

This is great," he said after pulling out two bottles of Grosse. "An al fresco meal of freshly caught fish, a romantic setting, a pleasant companion, topped off with an ice-cold Grosse beer. You know…it doesn't get any better than this."

"Being outside makes you feel good inside," Barbara added.

Barbara and Glen thoroughly enjoyed their catfish dinner. As they ate, they threw bones in the river. Although Barbara had deboned the catfish, it was impossible to remove all the bones. Fish were jumping alongside the boat.

The river was deserted. Barbara and Glen were all alone. The only signs of life were the jumping fish and the birds that inhabited the island.

Darkness arrived quickly, and the romantic couple used battery-powered lanterns and flashlights. They went up to the top deck, where they danced underneath the light of the moon, which had appeared from behind a cloud. Glen had a country music CD in his battery-operated boom box. He selected *Hell and High Water* by T. Graham Brown, which he thought was a fitting song for this occasion.

> Now, baby, don't worry, if he troubles your mind,
> 'Cause it'll all wash away, girl, in the river of time,
> If you need a shoulder, I'll be around,
> I'll be your rock to hold onto, till the river goes
>   down.
> It's hell and high water, that you're goin' through,
> But come hell and high water, I'll be here waiting
>   for you.

"What a great song," Barbara said, clinging to Glen. "That'll be our song. It will always remind us of how we met."

The next selection on Glen's CD of greatest country hits was *You're the Reason God Made Oklahoma* by Shelly West and David Frizzell. As they slow-danced to the sensuous rhythm of this song, Barbara and Glen tried to interpret what the song meant and finally came to the conclusion that Oklahoma was a place for people who loved country living. Oklahoma was still a place where outdoorsmen could feel at home. Barbara mentioned that she had filmed many episodes of her television show in Oklahoma.

> You're the reason God made Oklahoma.

You're the reason God made Oklahoma.
You're the reason God made Oklahoma.
And I'm sure missing you.

"You're the reason God made Missouri," Barbara softly whispered into Glen's ear as they danced.

"And you're the reason God made Illinois," Glen replied matter-of-factly.

"There's nothing more romantic than country music," Barbara theorized. "The moon, the stars, and the strumming of guitars."

When it was after midnight, they went to Glen's bed to make love.

"I apologize that my bed isn't bigger," Glen remarked, getting a pillow for Barbara.

"That's okay," she said. "We're not going to need a lot of room."

Barbara and Glen removed their clothes and fell down together on the bed. They were hungry and began feeding on each other. Their naked flesh was a prime target for mosquitoes and biting flies.

Glen explored every inch of Barbara's body before mounting her. "Do you think it's wise to have unprotected sex?" he asked after entering Barbara.

"This is so good it's worth the risk," Barbara moaned as she rocked her body in cadence with Glen's rhythms. She convulsed as spasms of pleasure swept over her.

Barbara and Glen heard the patter of rain above them on the top deck roof of the houseboat. A torrential rain had started again causing the river to rise even higher.

"I felt the earth move," Barbara wailed as she experienced an orgasm.

"That was just the boat rocking back and forth in the water," Glen assured her.

When they took a break from making love, Barbara told Glen about her horses and about her spread in southern Illinois near the town of Marion.

"Why do girls like to ride horses so much?" Glen inquired.

"I know, but I'm not going to tell you," Barbara replied naughtily. "I've had horses in my life ever since I was a little girl growing up on a ranch in California. I still own the ranch in the Santa Cruz Mountains, and I return there every chance I get. I've filmed episodes of my TV show there on my ranch."

Glen lit a cigar and then retrieved another bottle of Grosse beer. "There's nothing I like better," he said, "than to settle back with a good smoke and a good pour." He slowly deposited the contents of the bottle into a glass.

Barbara lay back in bed and stared at the ceiling, where she noticed a water stain in the shape of a fleur-de-lis, the symbol of St. Louis. Old copies of *The Waterways Journal* were strewn on the floor. She reached down and picked up a copy with a full-page advertisement on the front cover. She had never seen a publication with a full-page advertisement on the front cover. The ad was for the Bison Marine Products Company, whose motto was "A Stampede of Savings." *The Waterways Journal* was known as The Riverman's bible. Published in St. Louis since 1887, the journal was the leading authority on the inland waterways of the United States.

"After we're married," Barbara began, "you can take care of my horses when I'm away filming my television show. Would you like that?"

"Yes," Glen said. "I love horses. Grandfather Grosse owned a small ranch in House Springs, Missouri. The ranch remained in our family for many years, but we finally had to sell it. I learned to ride horses there. I had my own horse that I took care of."

"Wonderful," Barbara said. "We have so much in common."

Chapter Thirteen

Terri had been invited to the Grosse Mansion for a Fourth of July barbecue. As she drove down South Broadway, she saw hundreds of volunteers filling and stacking sandbags in preparation for the onslaught of the Mississippi River. She encountered a military checkpoint consisting of a large sandbag bunker to protect against the flood. National Guard soldiers were standing behind the bunker with rifles, and there was a .50-caliber machine gun mounted on top of the sandbags. *This looks like a war zone,* Terri thought. The military grade acrylic sandbags were just like the kind used in Operation Desert Storm to protect American soldiers from Iraqi bullets. There were several armored personnel carriers parked nearby. This looks like a scene from *The Longest Day*, Terri contemplated, where the American troops are establishing the Normandy beachhead. She started to hum Paul Anka's theme song from *The Longest Day*, and in her mind she heard Mitch Miller and his gang singing the song. She had once seen Mitch Miller in person, at a concert in St. Louis, and he had performed *The Longest Day*, which was one of his greatest hits.

As she drove up to the checkpoint, Terri was stopped by an overzealous National Guard captain named John Ash.

"Who won the World Series in 1940?" he demanded.

"You've been watching too many war movies." Terri laughed, realizing that he was thinking about Operation Greif during World War II, when German soldiers pretended to be Americans. Greif was the German word for Griffin.

"Who won the World Series in 1940?" Ash reiterated hostilely.

"The New York Yankees, I guess."

"Wrong! It was the Cincinnati Reds! Step out of the car! Let's see some identification!"

"You like playing war, don't you," Terri said, irritated that she was being forced to leave her car.

She showed her driver's license to the captain. "You're fighting a flood here, not the Germans."

"We're going to hold out here until the last man."

"Why do the men have rifles, and why is there a machine gun?"

"In case there are looters or people who cause trouble. We're also going to test out a new method of flood control."

"What's that?

"We're going to shoot at the flood."

Terri realized this man was a total right wing nutjob.

"This is now a restricted area because of the flood," the captain said. "The only people who can pass through this checkpoint are residents of the neighborhood."

"I'm going to a barbecue at the Grosse Mansion," Terri said. "Can't you let me through?"

"Sorry!"

Terri saw patrolman Mike Dolan talking with some National Guardsmen who were filling sandbags. "That policeman knows me," she told the captain. "He can vouch for me. Please let me talk to him."

"Okay. Go ahead."

As Terri was walking over to speak with Mike Dolan, she heard someone yell "Hey, baby," and she turned to see Brent and Wade standing there. It was Brent who had spoken. "Hey, baby," he said again. "We're volunteer firemen. We volunteered to help out."

"Oh, it's you too," Terri managed to say.

"We're not just firefighters," Wade said. "We're also waterfighters." They were working with a group of shady-looking characters who were stacking sandbags. Mike Dolan was there to supervise these guys who were prisoners from the City Workhouse. Apparently, Brent and Wade knew some of these convicts. Barbara quickly edged away from the two scumbag firemen and their slimebucket friends.

Terri said hello to some National Guardsmen who were taking a break after many hours of strenuous work. "Thank you for your service guys!" she said encouragingly. She was greeted with grunts and funny looks.

Mike Dolan accompanied Terri back to the checkpoint, and he explained to Captain Ash that it was okay to let Terri pass through.

When Terri arrived at the Grosse Mansion, she noticed the lawn was strewn with branches, and a small tree had fallen over. "This place looks like a cyclone hit it," she told Anna, who was surveying the damage.

"A cyclone did hit it," Anna lamented. "Glen was on his houseboat when the tornado struck. The boat is missing, and we haven't heard from Glen. We're afraid that he drowned."

Terri was visibly shaken by this news. "Have you contacted the police?" she asked.

"It's too early to file a missing person's report," Anna said. "We did contact the Coast Guard, but they don't know anything yet." Anna was wearing a purple T-shirt from the Alzheimer's Association that said, "Go Purple for Alzheimer's."

Dinty, Paz, and Dr. Wong were there already, and they consoled Terri, who was facing the grim possibility that her boyfriend was dead. Terri tried to picture what life would be like without Glen. She was in a state of shock. Glen's parents were also there, and they were both crying.

Terri remembered Glen's parents from years ago, but she had forgotten their first names.

"This is my daughter…Violet," Anna told Terri.

It figures, Terri thought to herself.

"Hi, Violet," Terri said, offering her hand, but Glen's mother was very upset and didn't acknowledge Terri's greeting.

"Let's get something straight right from the start," Violet exclaimed. "My mother and I are not cut from the same cloth. We have exactly no common threads. I hate the color purple. I despise it. I even get sick when I eat eggplant."

After pausing for a moment, Violet continued her tirade. "Some people leave their mark in this world," she huffed. "Others just leave a stain. A grape stain."

Everyone went out on the terrace overlooking the river. Harriet Winslow was instructed to stay inside by the telephone for any word about Glen. Harriet had broken the news that Glen was on his houseboat when the tornado struck, but she had not mentioned his female companion.

The barbecue took place as planned. Dinty threw some hamburgers on the grill. Anna provided party favors for everyone. The men had to wear Uncle Sam hats, and the women put on Statue of Liberty crowns.

"Where's your hat?" Violet reprimanded, noticing that her mother had remained bare-headed.

"Right here," Anna said, picking up a tricorn hat like the kind favored by American patriots during the Revolutionary War.

"My hat it has three corners," Anna sang, after putting on the hat. "Three corners has my hat. And if it doesn't have three corners, then it is not my hat." Anna paused for a second and then added, "That's an old girl scout song."

"She was never in the girl scouts," Violet informed everyone.

After he donned his Uncle Sam hat, Dinty stroked an imaginary beard with his left hand while pointing at Terri with his right hand. "I want you!" he affirmed in a resonant voice.

"I want you too, Dinty!" Terri responded quickly.

Violet looked at her mother and then said slowly, "Mom…I've got something I want to tell you. I hope you won't be too disappointed or too shocked or too angry." Violet's long-suffering husband groaned. His name was Ray Wunsch. For many years, he had remained patient with his wife's chronic bickering.

"I've decided to go green!" Violet Wunsch began, straightening the cuffs of her lime-green blouse. "I've always been an environmentalist. Green is the color of life, of growth. Green, for lack of a better word, is good. Green is right. Green works. Green clarifies, cuts through, and captures the essence of the environmental spirit. Green, in all its forms, has marked the upward surge of mankind. And green, you mark my words, will not only save us but also the entire world."

Ray Wunsch rolled his eyes and smiled at Terri. It was clear that Violet Wunsch was showing signs of early Alzheimer's disease.

"It ain't easy being green," Anna admonished. "You better think it over."

Earlier that day, Paz and Dr. Wong went to the naturalization ceremony at the Old Courthouse. Paz was now a citizen of the United States. She told Terri about the ceremony. There were several Filipinos in the group along with many Mexicans and people from India. A few Eastern Europeans were also included. Paz and Dr. Wong wanted to be alone to celebrate. They began making out on a bench, underneath an oak tree, in a secluded section of the terrace. They were both wearing red Cardinal T-shirts with the birds on the bat. Asians love the color red.

When dinner was ready, Terri went over to the amorous Filipino couple. "Break it up, you lovebirds," she instructed humorously. "It's time to eat."

Paz and Dr. Wong had brought along a picnic basket filled with Filipino street food, which they tried to share, but they didn't get any takers. The basket contained *balut*, which are duck eggs with embryos inside. There were dark gelatinous chunks of coagulated chicken blood called *betamax*. There were *adidas*, which are grilled chicken feet and helmets which are grilled chicken heads. The picnic basket also contained chicken intestines known as *isaw*. You can't make a silk purse out of a sow's ear, but you can make a Filipino delicacy known as walkman. There were walkman pig ears in the basket. A one day is a baby chick that is killed immediately and then seasoned, deep-fried, and skewered on a stick. There were many one days inside the picnic basket.

Paz and Dr. Wong were left alone to enjoy their Donner-like dinner party.

Terri enjoyed the meal of barbecued hamburgers, french fries, coleslaw, and baked beans. She tried to picture the fabulous Gatsbyesque garden parties that had been held on this terrace during the glory days of the Grosse Brewery and then later during the

Roaring Twenties, when St. Louians flocked here for illegal booze. She could only imagine all the famous people who had been here. Perhaps Babe Ruth had eaten a hotdog on this very terrace while quaffing a Grosse beer. Terri told Dinty to throw a hotdog on the grill for her. What was a barbecue without hotdogs?

Terri poured herself another Grosse beer.

Anna served a red, white, and blue dessert consisting of strawberries, blueberries, and Cool Whip.

After dinner, Terri decided to go for a swim in the subterranean lake beneath the Grosse Mansion. Because drowning can occur in less than two minutes, swimming alone is never a good idea, but Terri was too upset to care. The others wanted to go with her, but she insisted on being alone because she wanted to swim in the nude. She waited a half hour because she had always been told not to swim immediately after eating. She also wanted to call the Coast Guard to learn more about Glen's disappearance.

There was something ominous about a woman swimming alone as depicted at the beginning of movies like *Jaws*, *Dirty Harry*, and *Piranha*. Who will ever forget Chrissie's last swim?

Terri went down into the cave, took off all her clothes, and jumped into the subterranean lake. The cool water felt good on such a hot day. Before air-conditioning was invented, members of the Grosse family had come to the cave to cool off during the long, hot St. Louis summers.

Terri swam through the clean, clear water. She felt a troglobite cavefish nibble at her toes. She dove beneath the surface and was surprised to discover how deep the lake was. On occasion, Glen allowed scuba divers to come here to practice their craft.

Terri dived to the bottom of the lake and picked up two stones which she brought to the surface. She intended to keep the stones as souvenirs. She was probably the first person to ever touch these stones in thousands of years.

The Grosse Cave, like many along the Mississippi River, was a classic karst cave that gets all the drainage during a rainstorm. The cave was like a sinkhole that rainwater is funneled into.

Terri had no way of knowing that the sunny sky had suddenly turned dark, and rain was now falling in torrents. The ground was already saturated from continuous rainfall over the past month. The cave began to fill with excess stormwater. To make matters worse, this additional rainfall was the straw that broke the camel's back, and the Mississippi River crested at 49.6 feet. The Mississippi swept through all the sandbag barricades, inundating the streets of South St. Louis. The soldiers stationed at the sandbag fortification on South Broadway found their position overrun. "This holding action is over!" John Ash yelled to his men. "Fall back to Lavender Hill." The soldiers fired a few shots at the floodwater, as if that would do any good, and then ran away as fast as they could.

The St. Louis area was under a barrage. Radio stations carried reports from the north, the south, the west, and the east of more levees breaking, more sandbags failing, and more people fleeing. The river flooded homes, businesses, and streets once considered untouchable.

The flood washed over the sandbag barriers beneath Lavender Hill, and water rushed into the cave through the secret entrance by the river.

Chapter Fourteen

"Oh no!" Terri screamed when she saw the cave begin to fill with water. "Oh my god!" The water poured into the cave like a tidal wave. There was nobody around to hear Terri's pleas for help.

Suddenly water was streaming around her feet. Terri felt the ground slip away. Then her head was under the surface, and she was fighting and gasping for air. The depth had risen sharply, and she kicked out frantically, trying to touch the bottom. The water shorted out the electric lights in the cave, and Terri was plunged into darkness. Her mouth was full of grit and dirt from the water. Once more her head went under, and this time, when she rose for air, she conked into the roof of the cave. Terri was terrified. Seized with panic, she again screamed out for help, but there was no response. She screamed once more, and water entered her mouth, leaving her choking. The cave roof was now barely inches from the surface of the water. Totally lost in the dark, she pulled herself along with her fingers on the cave roof without any idea of the direction she was taking. Her one aim was to preserve the tiny space of air that now meant life to her. She scraped her face on the cave roof to draw breath. Then, just when she had virtually lost the strength and will to go any farther, she heard Dinty calling to her. He had become concerned about her when the rain began. He knew how dangerous this cave could be during a rainstorm. He had not anticipated river water pouring into the cave. Dinty was an experienced scuba diver who belonged to a group named St. Louis Scuba, and he occasionally came here to this cave to dive in the subterranean lake. He was familiar with the cave and he knew how to lead Terri to safety.

Dinty had a waterproof flashlight, and he swam through the floodwater to join Terri.

"You risked your life to save me," Terri said gratefully. "Am I glad to see you!"

"Do everything I say," Dinty cautioned. "We're about one hundred yards from the cave entrance by the river. That's where we have to go."

Terri and Dinty were clinging to a ledge in an air pocket. It was too dangerous to stay there. They had to swim underwater and pray there were enough air pockets.

"Hail Mary full of.... grace!" Terri intoned. "The Lord is with thee. Blessed art thou amongst women, and blessed is the fruit of thy womb, Jesus. Holy Mary, Mother of God, pray for us sinners now and at the hour of our death. Amen!" Terri felt like adding that this was the hour of her death, but she held her tongue.

"What is it like...to die?" Terri asked slowly, her voice shaking, her lips trembling.

Dinty was scared. He knew they were in a great deal of danger. "People who have had near-death experiences," he began, "describe a tunnel with a bright light at the end of it." His voice was quivering. "And the light starts coming towards you. And you hear a mysterious sound like a raging wind...WOO-OOO, WOO-OOO, WOO-OOO, WOO-OOO...and you step into the tunnel." Dinty's face was contorted with fear. "And you're knocked down by a train!"

"How can you joke around at a time like this?" Terri scolded.

"I've always wanted to die laughing," Dinty remarked.

"They say a drowning man sees his entire life flash before him," Terri pondered. "I guess the same is true for a drowning woman."

"I just saw a life pass before my eyes," Dinty said, "except it wasn't my life, it was somebody else's life."

Terri was struggling in the water, splashing with arms and legs. She didn't know how much longer she could continue to tread water. Like a small animal, she clung to Dinty's shoulder to keep afloat.

"Hold on tight to me," Dinty instructed, "and we'll be one unit. We'll swim from one air pocket to another."

Terri thought about Belle Rosen played by native St. Louisan Shelley Winters in the 1972 movie *The Poseidon Adventure*. Belle Rosen was once the underwater swimming champion of New York

City for three years in a row. In the movie, she swims underwater and saves lives and then drops dead of a heart attack. *I hope Dinty has a strong heart,* Terri prayed.

"Take a deep breath," Dinty told Terri. She pictured a scene from the 1975 movie *The Drowning Pool,* where Paul Newman and Gail Strickland are being held prisoner in a large shower room, and they turn on all the water after plugging up all the drains and then float to the ceiling where they hope to escape through the skylight, except they can't break the glass. They are trapped in a small air pocket beneath the skylight and are seconds away from drowning when the bad guys open the door to the shower room, and all the water pours out. One bad guy is killed, and the other is injured. Paul and Gail are okay.

Terri prayed for a miracle like that to happen. She didn't want to be entombed in this cave.

"Take my hand, Dinty," Terri pleaded. "If we're going to die, I want to die holding your hand."

Dinty took her hand and began singing *The Ballad of Floyd Collins,* about a Kentucky man trapped in a cave in 1925. Floyd didn't make it. "Oh, come all ye young people and listen while I tell the fate of Floyd Collins, the lad we all knew well. His face was fair and handsome, his heart was true and brave. His body now lies sleeping in a lonely sandstone cave."

Terri and Dinty made one last desperate effort, worming their way through the flooded passageway, pressing their noses against the limestone ceiling to breathe from precious air pockets. Dinty's training as a scuba diver served him well, and he was able to keep Terri from panicking. He guided her to the air pockets and helped her respire. Dinty had carried out underwater rescues before by using the Buddy System, in which two people operate together as a single unit so that they are able to monitor and help each other.

Miraculously, Terri and Dinty made it safely out of the cave, but now they faced another danger. They were caught in the swift current of the Mississippi River and were being pulled rapidly downstream. They paddled towards shore, but it was a hopeless battle. Terri once again resigned herself to her fate.

Then, after they had lost all hope, they saw Zack and Sherry on the shore. The homeless couple held the ropes that Barbara Grogan had left behind the previous day. Zack threw his rope out to Dinty, and Sherry threw her rope to Terri.

The tornado had destroyed the homeless camp, and now the site was underwater. Zack and Sherry were alone. The other homeless people had gone elsewhere, but Zack and Sherry had remained because they wanted to rebuild the camp. They had been sitting on a log when Terri and Dinty washed out of the cave and into the river.

Zack and Sherry were strong, and they were able to pull Terri and Dinty from the raging water.

Terri and Dinty collapsed on the shore, thankful to be alive. Zack performed mouth-to-mouth resuscitation, while Sherry brought blankets for warmth. Even in summertime, hypothermia can affect people who have been in the water too long. Sherry gave some of her clothes to Terri, who was still naked.

"You're no longer homeless," Dinty managed to say after coughing up water. "I'm going to buy you a house."

Zack and Sherry didn't know what to say. This was the greatest act of kindness they had ever experienced.

Zack ran up the Osage Steps to get help. Soon, Ray Wunsch and Dr. Wong were there to offer assistance.

Dr. Wong checked the physical condition of Terri and Dinty and decided they were okay.

"What kind of doctor are you, anyway?" Terri inquired casually.

"I'm an obstetrician," Dr. Wong responded in a stilted Filipino dialect.

"An obstetrician?" Terri gasped, doing a spit-take with water that was still inside her lungs. "Isn't Paz your patient?"

"Yes."

"You mean Paz is…?"

"Yes. Paz is pregnant," the Filipino physician confirmed.

Great, Terri thought. *Now, Paz and I have yet another thing in common. We're both pregnant.*

"I'm also pregnant," Terri said. "Would you like to be my doctor?"

"Okay," Dr. Wong replied. "Stop by my office sometime. I'll give you a discount since you're a friend of Paz."

Ray Wunsch and Dr. Wong helped Dinty climb the Osage Steps. Zack and Sherry held Terri's arms on the way up the steep stairway.

Terri invited the homeless couple to join the party, and they accepted. They knew Harriet Winslow, who had once been a member of their indigent group.

Everyone went into the Purple Parlor to watch television and wait for news about Glen. Later, they would go out on the terrace to watch the Downtown fireworks. A fifty-two-foot floodwall had saved the Downtown area from the deluge. The fireworks display would take place as planned by the Gateway Arch. From the terrace, there was a good view of the Downtown area and the Gateway Arch.

Terri and Dinty told everyone about their ordeal as they rested in comfortable chairs. Anna brought them hot soup. "You're lucky to be alive," Violet Wunsch observed. "I hope my poor Glen was that lucky."

The local TV news programs were devoted to flood coverage. There were TV helicopters roaming the skies to broadcast all the devastation. A girl named Laurie Waters was telling viewers about the flood. She was a reporter for Channel 4 News. "Get out of here!" Dinty yelled at the TV screen. "We don't need more waters around here!"

Then, a TV weatherman came on to tell viewers that the Doppler radar predicted continuous rain.

"Dope-ler radar," Dinty said. "That weatherman is a dope. The TV station may pretend that they're interested in the news or in sports or whatever, but all they really care about is the weather. And it's true."

"Christian Doppler was an Austrian physicist," Anna said proudly. She liked to tell people about famous Austrians. "He described his Doppler effect phenomenon in 1842."

Dinty cut in. "Did you ever notice how a train whistle seems to change pitch when the train passes by?" he asked. "That's the

Doppler effect. The whistle is high-pitched as the train approaches and low-pitched as the train moves away."

"I'm sick of this flood coverage!" Violet Wunsch pouted, grabbing the remote control device. She switched channels to the 1989 movie *Miss Firecracker*, which was being shown because of the Fourth of July holiday.

"This is a good movie," Violet said. "It's about a country girl played by Mary Steenburgen who won a small-town beauty pageant many years ago, and she's still lording it over everybody. Sound familiar?"

Terri was growing impatient, and she phoned the Coast Guard again for news about Glen's whereabouts. "Semper Par," she said sarcastically after failing to get any information. She slammed the phone down. *Semper Paratus*, Latin for "always ready," is the motto of the Coast Guard.

When the call finally came, it was not from the Coast Guard but from the Missouri Air National Guard. Barbara and Glen had been rescued from the island by a National Guard helicopter. Violet Wunsch took the call, and she was overjoyed to learn her son had not perished in the ravaging flood. She whooped and howled with happiness. She was able to speak with Glen, who was resting at the squadron headquarters of the Missouri Air National Guard. He told his mother all about his perilous brush with death. She was too excited to scold him. She did not get angry when he mentioned he was with a young woman. He said he would be coming over to the Grosse Mansion very soon. Violet expressed her love before hanging up the phone.

"There's good news and bad news," Violet told Terri, who was standing right there. "The good news is he's alive. The bad news is he was with another girl."

Terri's happiness was dampened by the news about the other woman in Glen's life.

Glen told his mother to watch Channel 5 because a KSDK cameraman was aboard the helicopter. Everyone gathered around the television. Sure enough, in about fifteen minutes, there was a periodic news update about a dramatic helicopter rescue on the Mississippi River. A young couple had been airlifted off an island.

"There's Glen!" Violet shouted, watching her son dangling precariously in a harness in midair. After Glen was lifted into the helicopter, it was Barbara's turn to be rescued.

"That's a cute girl," Terri remarked jealously as Barbara was hoisted into the helicopter. Horrified, Terri realized that it was Barbara Grogan.

"Why weren't they rescued by boat?" Dinty asked.

"This is more dramatic," Terri responded.

The whole group was watching fireworks when Barbara and Glen arrived at the Grosse Mansion. A cadet with the Missouri Air National Guard drove them home. After thanking the cadet, they walked around to the terrace and greeted everyone. Glen and Barbara were embracing.

Violet Wunsch was in tears, and she hugged her son. "We have some wonderful news," Glen said, wrapping his arm around Barbara. "She's consented to be my bride."

"And he's consented to be my groom," Barbara said with a smug expression on her face. "As I take my trip down the bridal path."

"Will you knock it off with the horse analogies," Glen rebuked.

"I can't wait to get hitched," Barbara added enthusiastically.

Well, I see this is going to be a stable relationship, Terri thought to herself. She was shocked to see that Glen was now involved with another girl.

"Nice fireworks!" Glen said. "Barbara and I were making some fireworks of our own, if you get my drift."

"We were worried sick about you," Mr. Wunsch admonished. "We thought you were dead. We thought you had been swept away by the flood. And here all the while you were making love to a gorgeous chick."

"Thank you," Barbara said. "Everybody thinks so."

Terri snarled at Barbara. "Well, if it isn't that ravishing blond bombshell…Kim Bassingal."

"I never thought I'd see you again," Dinty said privately to Barbara. "The femme fatale of fishing."

"I want to thank you from the bottom of my heart," Barbara said joyfully. "If I hadn't come to visit you, I would never have met Glen."

"Hey," Mr. Wunsch yelled. "I know you. You're the Happy Hooker!"

"Oh my god!" Violet Wunsch exclaimed, throwing her arms in the air.

"Wait a minute," Mr. Wunsch said quickly in order to calm his wife. "She does a television program about fishing. That's why she's called the Happy Hooker."

"I'm relieved to hear that." Violet Wunsch sighed.

"She's the girl I've been waiting for my entire life," Glen revealed. "A girl who loves to hunt and fish. We also share the same political ideologies. I've finally found my soul mate."

"Soul mate?" Barbara inquired. "You make us sound like a pair of shoes."

"Seriously," Glen said "We were both in a great deal of danger. It's a good thing we're both experienced boat people or we would have been goners."

"We had a whirlwind romance," Barbara said. "In more ways than one. We fell overboard for each other, in more ways than one. It was sort of like that David Hasselhoff song from Baywatch. We were caught in the current of love."

"I've watched your show a few times," Mr. Wunsch said. "Don't you live in Illinois?"

"Yes," Barbara replied. "I have a spread near Marion in southern Illinois."

"My son lives in Missouri, and you live in Illinois," Violet declared. "Won't that create problems?"

"I don't think so," Barbara clarified. "There ain't no river wide enough to keep us apart. You know, this flood has torn a lot of people's lives asunder, but it brought Glen and me together, and for that I will be eternally grateful."

"She lives in Little Egypt," Terri remarked. "That's a section of southern Illinois named for a famous belly dancer."

"I'm sorry, Terri," Glen apologized. "It's over between us."

"It ain't over till it's over," Terri countered.

"Well, it's over," Glen confirmed.

"It ain't over till the fat lady sings," Terri said affirmatively. "Shut up, you old bag," Terri hollered when she noticed Anna was limbering up for a song. Glen encouraged Anna to sing.

"Barney Google," she began. "With the goo-goo-goo-ga-ly eyes. Barney Google had a wife three times his size. She sued Barney for divorce, now he's sleeping with his horse."

"That's enough of that," Glen cautioned.

Anna switched to "I Heard It Through The Grapevine" but Glen quickly squelched her.

"Backwoods bimbo…fishing floozy…whoring horsewoman." These were just a few of the insults that Terri hurled at Barbara. Terri finished drinking her Grosse beer and then smashed the bottle against a table. She threatened Barbara with the jagged edge.

"Put the bottle down, Terri," Glen warned.

Terri threw the bottle at Barbara, and Glen deflected it with a chair.

Terri then charged at Barbara, tackling her and dragging her over the railing of the terrace. The two girls fell a short distance onto the lawn, where they had a wrestling match. This was another classic catfight between a dark-haired girl and a blond-haired girl. Terri had dark hair, and Barbara was a blonde.

"Women are always fighting over me," Glen told his grandmother.

Terri and Barbara engaged in kicking, slapping, scratching, hair-pulling, and the ripping of clothes. Barbara threw a small flower pot at Terri but missed. Terri picked up a garden gnome figurine which she hurled at Barbara, but the projectile went wide of its mark.

Terri and Barbara were evenly matched, and there was no clear winner of the fight, but Terri now realized that her relationship with Glen was officially over.

"I'm glad we broke up," she yelled at Glen. "Now, I won't have to wear that stupid purple wedding gown!"

"What's this about a purple wedding gown?" Barbara asked.

"It's the purple dress my grandmother wore at her wedding. You'll get to wear it when we're married. I hope you weren't expecting a traditional white wedding?"

There was something in the way Glen asked this question that made Terri blurt out, "Don't you know she was married before? She has a young son."

Glen was dumbfounded. Barbara made it a point to keep her personal life secret and never mentioned her son on her television show.

"I was going to tell you," Barbara said diffidently. "I was just waiting for the right time."

Violet Wunsch pictured Glen and Barbara getting married. She saw them coming out of the church, and many people were there to wish them well. Barbara had on the purple wedding gown and was holding a bunch of purple grapes instead of a bouquet. She lifted the grapes above her head, nibbled on a few, and then tossed them over her shoulder to an unmarried girl in the crowd. The well-wishers showered the happy couple with raisins instead of rice. Then, Glen and Barbara had to run a gauntlet of fishermen with their poles raised like the military tradition of arches and crossed sabers except this was arches and crossed fishing rods. With a violent shake of her head, Violet Wunsch awoke from this nightmare.

Terri unwittingly became involved in an argument between Glen and his parents. "Terri's a wonderful girl," Violet Wunsch said. "We were going to compliment you on your good taste. And here you drop her in favor of this…cowgirl."

"We're going to give you a hard time over this," Mr. Wunsch said.

Glen and Barbara objected, which angered Mr. Wunsch, and he shouted, "It was that famous Missourian Harry Truman who said, 'If you can't stand the heat, stay out of the kitchen.'"

"I never liked Truman," Dinty said. "He was the guy who fired my good friend Doug MacArthur."

"Well," Barbara countered, "it was Dolly Parton who said, 'If you can't stand the heat, stay out of my bedroom.'"

"Do you really know Dolly Parton?" Dinty asked.

"I've said hello to her a few times," Barbara responded.

"You won't have to worry about us much longer," Glen said. "After we're married, we're going to live in the Idaho wilderness for a while. That's something both of us have always wanted to do."

"You jerk!" Terri yelled at Glen. "You bastard! You Nazi beast! I hope you two will be very happy together...living in the Idaho wilderness...with some white supremacist group."

Hell hath no fury like a woman scorned, Glen thought.

"My tax dollars paid to rescue you," Terri hollered. "I resent that."

Ray and Violet Wunsch realized there was no easy solution to this problem. They had to accept the inevitable. Glen and Barbara were going to get married.

"There's nothing we can do about it," Ray Wunsch said. "I guess they'll ride off into the sunset together. Him and his cowgirl."

"Come on, Dinty, let's go," Terri summoned. "These people are all whacko!"

Dinty was glad to get away from this bickering family with all their peculiarities. He quickly joined Terri, and they decided to go over and have a drink at the Stag Club.

"Bye, Paz," Terri called out. "Talk to you soon. Congratulations!"

Paz said goodbye, not sure why Terri was congratulating her.

Terri went into the house to get her purse, and Glen followed her. He cornered her in the kitchen. He gently grabbed her arm as she tried to get past him.

"I'm sorry, Terri!" Glen said compassionately and with great sincerity. "I'm going to miss you!" Terri struggled to free herself. Glen tried to calm her. "You'll be glad to know that I finally came up with a name for my new light beer."

"I don't really care," Terri scoffed, breaking free from Glen's grasp.

Glen paused and then said, "I've decided to call it Flood... Light."

Terri did not give her opinion about what she thought of the name.

"On the label I'll have a picture of a flood," Glen continued. "Bertha the Beer Girl will be running away from it in her long flowing dress. Of course, she'll have to be a little thinner if she's going to represent a light beer."

The others came into the house to say goodbye. The fireworks were over, and the party was coming to an end.

"A young girl and an old goat," Anna criticized as she watched Terri and Dinty leave together. "That's not going to last."

Paz and Dr. Wong looked at each other and laughed. Now, Paz and Terri had yet another thing in common. They both had older boyfriends.

Anna was upset, and Glen helped her sit down in her favorite chair. "Thank you," she said. "I've always depended upon the kindness of strangers."

"I'm your grandson!" Glen roared.

Chapter Fifteen

As they crossed the street, Terri and Dinty saw flood refugees entering St. Boniface Catholic Church, which had been turned into an emergency shelter for people displaced by the flood. The Red Cross and Salvation Army were providing food and lodging to those in need.

Some of the flood refugees were hoping to find shelter at the Stag Club, but Dinty yelled for them to stay away. The people then headed over to the Grosse Mansion.

The Stag Club was closed because of the Fourth of July holiday. Dinty took out his key and opened the front door. Terri entered the club ahead of Dinty. The odor of stale beer filled the air. The acrid aroma of cigarette smoke still lingered from the previous day when the club had been packed with people.

Terri was glad they were alone in the Stag Club. She asked Dinty to give her a tour of this building where she had lived when she was growing up. Dinty was happy to give her a tour of her childhood home. Her old bedroom was now Dinty's bedroom. She lay down on the bed and looked up at the ceiling where she had once taped a poster of Elvis Presley. The tape marks were still there. The room had not been painted in all those years.

"This is wonderful, Dinty!" Terri said. "I am overwhelmed with memories." She pointed to the spot where her tropical fish aquarium was located. "That's where my record player was over in the corner. I still have all the records." She walked to the window and pulled the drapes open. "I always loved looking out of this twelve-pane window," she said. "The wavy glass transformed my view of the neighborhood into a surrealistic work of art." She looked through the window at the dark sky and was reminded of *Starry Night* by Vincent

Van Gogh. A large antique desk that Terri had used as a child was still in the same spot. Her parents had left the desk behind when they moved away. The same shag carpeting was still on the floor. When she was a little girl, Terri had loved rolling around like a puppy on the deep pile shag carpet.

This room had been Terri's private space, her secret sanctuary away from her parents. She remembered boys coming to visit her when she was a teenager. Her first sexual experience had been here in this room. She had lost her virginity on the shag carpet, which was a comfortable and appropriate place to make love. In England, the word *shag* is a slang term for sexual intercourse. The boy had been in her graduation class at McKinley High School. Terri's parents had gone to the Ozarks for the weekend. Thankfully, she did not get pregnant, for the young man was like all her other worthless boyfriends and had no intention of marrying her.

"Let's go down to the piano," Terri suggested to Dinty. "I've lost two boyfriends in the last month. Play some music that will cheer me up."

Terri and Dinty walked down the rickety staircase which led to the kitchen of the Stag Club. They grabbed beers from the refrigerator as they passed through the kitchen. They came out onto the floor of the Stag Club and went over to the piano.

"What's that song that Judy Garland sings?" Terri asked, hopping up on the piano like Lauren Bacall in the famous photo with Harry Truman at the keyboard. "You know…in *A Star Is Born*?" Terri started to hum the melody, and Dinty began playing the introduction to the song.

"Take it, honey," Dinty urged. "Come on! Take it from the top!"

"From the top?"

"Yeah!"

"The night is bitter," Terri warbled. "The stars have lost their glitter. The winds grow colder. Suddenly you're older. And all because of the man that got away." Terri stopped singing. "The man that got away. That's the story of my life. Here I find the man of my dreams, and I lose him to a lady fisherman. I guess she has more skill when it comes to reeling in men. You know, men are like fish. They take the bait. Run with it for a little while and then break free. I just don't have any luck."

"He wasn't such a great catch," Dinty said as he continued to play the hauntingly beautiful *The Man That Got Away.*

"She really had it, didn't she," Terri said as she sat on the piano. "Judy Garland, I mean. I guess she was the greatest singer who ever lived."

"What are you talking about?" Dinty asked. "Judy Garland didn't have any talent."

"I can't believe you said that! I think you're shitting me. I have a feeling you're a big Judy Garland fan."

"You're right," Dinty confessed. "I have just about every record she ever made. She's my favorite entertainer. But how did you know that?"

"It's just something you said on the first day we met," Terri began. "You called Glen a stout fella. At first he was insulted. He thought you had called him fat. I had to explain to him that 'stout fella' is just an antiquated expression. In the 1941 movie *Babes on Broadway*, Judy Garland sings a World War II song called *Chin Up! Cheerio! Carry On*, which is about England's fight against the Nazis. That is a very obscure song, and the only person I ever heard sing it is Judy Garland. In that song is the line 'Don't give up, Tommy Atkins, be a stout fella,' and right after Glen asked for a Tommy Atkins mango tonic, you called him a stout fella. You were playing a simple game of word association."

"You're a pretty sharp girl," Dinty said. "Nothing much gets past you."

"I'm glad we have something in common," Terri said. "We're both big Judy Garland fans."

"You don't think that's strange, do you?" Dinty asked.

Terri paused for a second and then replied, "Everyone likes Judy Garland, not just gays." She paused again and then said reflectively, "I guess people in St. Louis are especially fond of her because she's in the movie *Meet Me in St. Louis.*"

Dinty played a medley of songs from *Meet Me in St. Louis.* Suddenly, there was a knock at the door. It was Mike Dolan, who was there in his official capacity as a St. Louis policeman. "The flood has caused some propane tanks to break lose on the river," he said. "The tanks are unstable and might explode. We're evacuating the entire area. You have fifteen minutes to leave."

Dinty thanked Mike, who left quickly because he had to warn everyone in the neighborhood.

"You can come out to my apartment and stay with me," Terri told Dinty.

"I have a better idea," Dinty said. "Let's leave St. Louis and head west."

"What do you mean?" Terri asked.

"Let's hop on a plane for Las Vegas."

"Who will take care of the Stag Club?"

"Sydney Melbourne can run things here for a while."

"That's sounds like a wonderful idea, Dinty. I'd love to go to Las Vegas with you. Paz can look after my apartment."

"I have an additional idea," Dinty said slowly. "I've never asked a girl to marry me before, but I'm asking you. Will you marry me?"

"You saved my life, Dinty. I belong to you. That's the best offer I've had all year. Of course I'll marry you."

"You're not shitting me, are you?"

"I could never shit you about something like that. This is the most wonderful thing that has ever happened to me."

Dinty was overwhelmed with happiness. "A Little White Wedding Chapel in Las Vegas is where Judy Garland married Mark Herron in 1965. That's where we'll get married. That chapel specializes in fast weddings. It is very easy to get married there."

"Nice," Terri said.

"I'm an extremely wealthy man. You'll be a very rich widow someday."

"That won't be for a very long time."

"After we're married, we'll live here in the Stag Club. I'll let you have your old room back."

"We'll be sharing that room, Dinty," Terri hinted subtly.

"And when you have your baby, we'll name him Dinty Junior."

"What if my baby is a girl?"

"Then, we'll name her Teresa, after you." Dinty had seen Terri's driver's license on the first day they met.

"So you found out my real name is Teresa. That's something I try to keep secret. Teresa sounds too angelic."

"But you are angelic! Mother Teresa. That's you."

Terri and Dinty heard sirens outside and decided it was time for them to leave.

"We'll take my car," Terri said. "We'll head straight for the airport."

Dinty went out the door first. "Age before beauty," he said. "If only I were fifty years younger."

"You got it wrong, Dinty," Terri confided. "If only I were fifty years older. Come on, let's go."

After locking the door of the Stag Club, Dinty joined Terri, and arm in arm they walked off into the night to begin their new life together.

About the Author

 Clint Hofer has lived in St. Louis his entire life. He attended the University of Missouri at Columbia, where he received a bachelor's degree in journalism. He loves the rich history of St. Louis, and his writing reflects that. He also loves the outdoors, and he has incorporated his love of nature into his novel. For many years, Clint has written about amateur baseball in the St. Louis area. St. Louis is one of the best baseball cities in America. Clint played baseball for the Stag Athletic Club, and he uses the name Stag Club in his novel. The fictional Stag Club is a tavern and not an athletic club. *The One That Got Away* is Clint's first book, and he worked on it for many years. The idea for the book first came to him while driving by a deserted brewery in South St. Louis. Because of Anheuser-Busch, St. Louis is the beer capital of the United States. Clint lives down the road from Grant's Farm, the ancestral home of the Busch family. He grew up hearing about the rich brewing heritage of St. Louis, and he has made use of that information in his novel. Although *The One That Got Away* is a comedy, Clint is actually a very serious person. Comedy writing is something that comes naturally to him. Comedy is a serious business.

CPSIA information can be obtained
at www.ICGtesting.com
Printed in the USA
BVHW041650171022
649641BV00016B/86